BREAKING THE TRANQUILLITY OF SOLITUDE

First Edition

First printed in the United Kingdom

Published by EDJ Publishing
www.edjpublishing.com

This is a work of fiction. Names, characters, businesses, places, events, locales, and incidents are either the product of the author's imagination or used in a completely fictitious manner. Any mention of or resemblance to actual persons, living or dead, or actual events is purely coincidental or contextual within the story.

Cover design and layout by www.spiffingcovers.com

Other books by Edward Johnson:

Breaking the Tranquillity of Solitude. Part 2

Breaking the Tranquillity of Solitude. Part 3

A Short Story to Keep You Guessing Over Tea – Unpublished

Memories of Sharks (A work in progress)

BREAKING THE TRANQUILLITY OF SOLITUDE

EDDIE JOHNSON

This book is for D.T

1966 – 2014

I know exactly what he would have said if he had read it.

I love those who can smile in trouble, who can gather strength from distress, and grow brave by reflection. 'Tis the business of little minds to shrink, but they whose heart is firm, and whose conscience approves their conduct, will pursue their principles unto death.

Leonardo da Vinci

CONTENTS

FOREWORD

Edward (Eddie) Johnson is not a man you just meet and slowly get to know – he is a man that arrives in your life fully established in whatever guise he is inhabiting at that very particular moment. Charity fundraiser, goalkeeper coach, film maker or domestic appliance shaman – Eddie is each and every one of them and a few others to boot – fully formed and ready to go.

Much like Mr Benn's trusty shopkeeper, Eddie will suddenly appear when you least expect him and, before you know it, you are involved in one of his amazing and often hair-brained schemes. A phone call from Eddie can be as unpredictable as a 1960s hippy acid trip and often twice as exhausting.

When Eddie asked me to write a foreword for his three-book series, I wasn't even sure what genre they would be – technical manuals on washing machine parts, perhaps; an exposé of Joe Hart's set positioning, or a Jeffrey Archer-style, money-obsessed, charity whodunnit saga?

Well, it was none of these and, now having read all three parts of *Breaking the Tranquillity of Solitude*, I know it all but defies genre, as indeed, does Eddie himself. It is a futuristic, Viking, space and time travelling, mind-reading, existential Pilgrim's Progress, twisted love story of a book that draws heavily on the weird nature of dreams, the impossibility of omnipresence, growing up in Wolverhampton, hero worship, Scooby Doo and games like cribbage. The books are a strange uncanny mirror of the author – the indefinable Mr. Johnson himself.

I exhort you to give this trilogy a go and for more than just one reason. Not least because it actually takes great courage to put pen to paper and open up your creative world to others (and I really admire Eddie for having done just that) – something that so many people only talk about doing – but that's the joy of the man – he is an eternal trier; never giving up on anything until the task, whatever it might be, is done.

My second reason is slightly more prosaic and personal – our washing machine has broken and if enough of you read his books he might just come and fix it for me for free!

With all sincerity though, in my opinion the books are not pretentious or grandiose, they are more onion-like, with multiple layers that repeatedly reveal hidden depths and different sides to the various characters as well as the author's own inner psyche. All in all, the whole thing was intriguing, a fun read with many surprises that hit you from all angles. I believe it will appeal and captivate a very broad range of readers on many different levels. Thrilling and amusing in equal measures; a very imaginative and thought-provoking series of books which kept my interest from beginning to end. I thoroughly enjoyed the read and genuinely think that you will too.

Well done, Eddie, and good luck with it all. You should be very proud of this achievement.

Nick Hancock – Stoke-on-Trent, 06/06/2019

PREFACE

As a first-time author, even the writing of this very preface has been a complex and interesting journey for me. Right up until the time I made the final decision to commit the basic ideas of the story to paper, I still had no idea what was fully involved in the process. I naïvely thought that you write a story, spell-check it and give it to lots of people to read. Well, over two years from initially picking up my pen and over twelve years from having the first inspirational ideas that developed into what you will read here today, I now know this is not the case. However, I am now tentatively ready to release those complex, eccentric and mysterious thoughts to the world.

Most importantly, I sincerely hope that you enjoy it as, realistically, that is the main point of any fictional book, but I also feel you may soon more sympathetically appreciate the unusual efforts I have had to go to in getting this far. After much research, I know that a preface such as this traditionally tells of either the purpose, scope or content of the work for non-fiction, or for works of fiction, it should be all about the whys.

Well, this story is what I like to call a 'fact-inspired fiction', which is slightly different from the current popular trend of fictionalising historic facts in so-called 'faction'. With this trilogy, there are many, one hundred percent accurate facts and many one hundred percent complete fictions. It will be your task, if you choose to accept it, to discern the two. The mix of both created the story but the story doesn't change the facts that inspired it. You may, if ever you find out the truth, be surprised at which are which.

Why? The reason I decided to write the book is quite simple but at the same time also extremely convoluted to explain. I will do my best to be brief as my research also taught me that the Preface and Prologue are not overly popular with certain types of readers and sometimes aren't read at all. Ironically, if you are that type of person you may not have read this point and are probably well into chapter one.

For many years I have been having, and still have, recurrent dreams. These dreams are so vivid in their minutiae that just over six years ago I slowly began to remember incidental details of some of them in my waking hours. A lot of the episodes were obviously related to things in my past such as music I liked, people I admired, things I had done and general experiences, etc, but some were much more capricious, mercurial and horrific. Weird and wonderfully diverse, they often had very confusing, frightening and sometimes violent subject matter. Some were more romantic or even of an erotic nature and others seemed to mix all these facets together in a sudden waking, sweat-inducing, nightmare type of effect.

After years of experiencing these apparently random images flying around my head, when waking, I had got into the habit of immediately grabbing a pencil and paper and writing down a few words of description about what had occurred in that specific dream. Before, as is the way with these things, it faded to irrelevance. After a year or more of doing this I decided it would be best that the writing equipment was left on the bedside table rather than the office table. Stubbed toes and rudely awoken partners do not good bed fellows make. Slowly over time, I was beginning to capture the essence of these irregular but repetitive paramnesia events.

Strangely, as the years progressed, I started to notice a pattern. I had quite often scribbled down the same things, almost word for word, time and again. There was some considerable consternation along the way and, getting all the information collated before even starting to write in earnest, was a major task for me. I was an untrained, inexperienced nobody who had no clue at this time that this was anything more than indigestion.

I did not have any great issue with the unusual content, although some of the mental images were quite scary and graphic. The problem I *did* have was that collation was only possible randomly; it wasn't as if these dreams were occurring or re-occurring every night. Patience was sometimes stretched when I was awoken by a particularly graphic episode and, with pen in hand at four in the morning, my mind would go blank, leaving me completely insomniated.

It would have been so much easier if I could have had a real-life working dream catcher to use, but no such luck, legends and customs did not help me. I do, however, think in some part that they strangely have inspired me on odd occasions.

Usefully though, whenever I had any one of these thirty or more individual episodic-type sleep experiences, it was always very much the same from beginning to end (and still is). Faces, names, details and outcomes all identical every single time.

Frustratingly, the differing stories rarely arrived in the same order and sometimes were months apart. Quite often I ended up, tending, as most people do, to desperately want to know what would have happened next. As the years rolled by it became more and more obvious, based on the nature of the actual content of these dreams, (music, work, friends, etc) that their individual and grouped relationships to me, were no longer coincidental. So much so, I decided to try to examine them in greater detail.

The possibility of creating a story linking the completely unrelated issues that the various episodes were comprised of, grabbed me and wouldn't let go.

The 'why then?' is just like a mountaineer saying the reason for risking life and limb on Everest or K2. It is because it is there! And because I can!

It was there – and nothing was going to change that, but I wanted to see if I could do something constructive with it. Also, the question of whether or not anyone else would find the result in the slightest bit interesting did occur and intrigue me.

In my life I have seen well above my fair share of movies and read many books that have obviously heavily influenced the content of the strange things regularly occurring in my head. I therefore decided to try to create something from it all and this is the story you will find here…

I have changed some of the names to protect the innocent, as the tongue in cheek line goes; however, I have left some true to their real life inspirational sources. As mentioned, much of the story is fact-based but many of the details are twisted to suit the desired outcomes and my own ego. I don't think anyone will be offended but I am happy to apologise if they feel I have not done them true justice or portrayed them well enough. As I said, it is my first attempt at formal writing.

It would probably have been a lot easier for me to have just written thirty-odd short stories using many different genres or even thirty short odd-stories. Finding a common thread that pulled all the fiction and truth together into a coherent story, was a massive undertaking of memory and imagination for me…BUT…

If you enjoy the results as much as I have enjoyed and hated in equal measures in collating it all, it will have been worth every moment.

ACKNOWLEDGEMENTS

Nobody has really helped me 'write' this book, but some have certainly steered me back towards centre when I have occasionally strayed from the beaten track. However, quite often the incidences of straying have gleaned some of the most interesting details. I feel I must particularly acknowledge two people: firstly, my niece's husband, Mark Parry, who very early in the process helped channel and re-direct my thought process on how to better structure the piece. It was his depth of knowledge that started me laying a path rather than digging a hole. Secondly, there is Paul Bullock, a friend and heavy rock music sympathiser who has been a constant sounding board for many of my diverse and basically weird ideas.

I could have sat and written more pages of famous influential acknowledgements than chapters of the book itself. Thanks has to go to those who, over the years, have had an impact on my life in one way or another and have indirectly inspired me to get this far. However, it is highly unlikely that you or even more so, they, would ever read such a list. Thus, I have decided to be as minimalist as possible in the representation of them and wanted to place them in no particular order.

My borderline OCD tendencies will not accept that 'random' truly exists for such a task as list making, so alphabetical order seemed a fair compromise – no importance of one over another is implied. I have listed a few that represent the many, so anyone who seems as if they might be missing may be covered by the mention of another. That is my excuse for having, no doubt, missed many and not having to type 20 pages or more. It is quite a good get-out for any mistakes and I'm sticking by it.

Before any of those mentioned or even not mentioned had influenced me in any way, there was far more crucially my dad, Harry Johnson Snr, and my mom, Marjorie, whom without I would not even exist let alone be in my current situation in life. I realistically owe them everything. The others include…

Dan Aykroyd, Meat Loaf Aday, Christina Applegate, Gordon Banks, Peter Benchley, Helena Bonham Carter, Richard Burton, Jim Carrey, Michael Clarke Duncan, Lewis Collins, Michael Conrad, Scatman Crothers, Robert De Niro, Johnny Depp, Bruce Dickinson, Aretha Franklin, Roger Federer, Morgan Freeman, Whoopi Goldberg, Bruce Grobbelaar, Nick Hancock, Tom Hanks, Oliver Hardy, Noddy Holder, Steve Harris, Michael Jackson, Samuel L Jackson, Stephen King, Stan Laurel and Bruce Lee.

Janet Leigh, James Mason, Freddie Mercury, Nichelle Nichols, Jack Nicholson, Jack Nicklaus, Edward Norton, Dolly Parton, Anthony Perkins, Brad Pitt, Elvis Presley, Keanu Reeves, Michael Rennie, Derek Riggs, Gene Roddenberry, Will Sampson, William Shatner, Robert Shaw, David Soul, Steven Spielberg, Patrick Stewart, Arnold Schwarzenegger, Quentin Tarantino, Christopher Walken, Bruce Weitz and definitely not forgetting the direct inspiration for the title of the work itself, Paul Weller and many, many, many more.

Given all these famous influences I have to say, very respectfully about them all – alive or dead – far more important to me are those who have not only inspired me to write but have helped me aspire to be a better person and regularly continue to do so.

These are those I yearn to please most of all…

Archie, Charlotte, Daniel, Ethan, Harry, Matt, Tyler and, last but definitely not least, the centre of my universe…

Jane (without a y).

I love you all. X

INTRODUCTION

As merely the story-teller and reporter of this, I feel that to fully appreciate the incredible events you are about to discover, it is necessary that you get to know a little bit more about our main character Brody before we start.

Knowledge of some of the events in his past that have made him the man he is at the point where we commence our journey together, will certainly be of benefit in the understanding of his personality and how it affects and shapes the outcome of the adventures as they progress. I am therefore going to take the opportunity, as has been the tradition since Ancient Greek and Roman times to, within the Prologue, give you a brief background and taster of Brody and some of the others involved in this amazing tale.

Some of this information may seem irrelevant, quite innocuous and some just plain stupid, but you may find that the old saying 'The devil is in the detail' might be worth keeping in mind as you explore deeper into the strange and complex happenings that are about to unfold before you. There is another old proverb of a more dubious heritage that says, 'Cometh the hour, cometh the man'. It may also be just as relevant and, as you may now be realising, not everything will always be as it seems.

Read into things what you will, take out of it what you can, but remember, the human brain is a very complex machine, capable of much more than we mere mortals usually allow.

Historically, some have tried many different methods to help expand this potential, such as the use of mind-altering substances or even dabbling with horrific internal modification. Our character Brody did neither and, like this very volume you now hold, was always an open book.

Metaphorically speaking, one of his main problems was that the handwriting in that very book was not always easy to define, making him personally a difficult read. With patience, some managed to enjoy more than a single chapter of his life, but others just gave up on page one.

I hope you fair better and make your own decisions about him. Hopefully you will enjoy my account of his adventures because it is safe to say that in a lot of cases, *he* did not!

PROLOGUE

At the time of the unusual events that get our story rolling, Broderick Edward Martins was thirty-eight years old. His original platinum blond hair had darkened and he was greying at the temples. 'Distinguished' was his line of defence when ribbed about getting old. To take you back in time, which might now be an irony in itself, life, love and death were all subjects on which he had strong views, especially his own. If the subject of life and/or death ever came up, his usual comment was that he would live forever or at least to over one hundred and fifty. "Whichever comes first," he used to joke.

Possibly as a self-defence mechanism because of the unusual nature of his own name, he eventually made certain that he was always referred to as Brody.

At school he was also well known as the class clown. As a growing lad he nevertheless became popular with teachers and pupils alike, having a great sense of humour, a loveable cheeky grin, sparkling crystal blue eyes, girlfriend jealousy-creating long eyelashes and a mop of golden-white blonde hair.

There were occasions when he crossed the line between having a bit of fun and being over the top and this would be something that would stay with him for most of his life. If nothing else, it allowed him to take a very positive outlook on even the grimmest of events, even if the recipients of his special brand of humour didn't always appreciate the levity.

As a youth, Brody always had an eye for the girls. He was very confident and comparably spent more time chasing them than on his academia. This was something he would eventually come to regret and consequently, in time he had to work extra hard to rectify the inevitable qualification deficit it left him with.

All through school he had male and female friends aplenty and when moving into his later teens he possibly had too many girlfriends at any one time. Shirley, Deborah Julie, Jane, Jennifer, Alison, Philippa, Sue, another Deborah and Annabel too. He loved them all, you might say, from the bottom of his pencil case. All these young ladies seemed to him at the time as if they would be the one – they all felt very permanent in the heat of the moment, but none ever really amounted to anything serious in the long term.

Brody knew all about lust but was totally inexperienced in love; he had trouble committing his time to anyone, male or female. It wasn't that he didn't care about them enough but his life was always so full on. He wanted to do it all and experience it all. School was a mere distraction from the importance of football, golf, motorbikes, swimming, table tennis, chess, reading, music, films, TV and, of course, chasing girls. As he got older, football, golf, tattoos, food, beer and chasing more girls were the norm; I am sure you've got the picture. Every single day was absolutely brimming with stuff that needed doing and it always needed doing right there and then. As you can imagine, this meant many unfinished projects.

Many trials as a would-be professional footballer, tenuous thoughts of pursuing a career as a golf pro and dreams of being a bestselling author all went the way of many other grand ideas and were not followed through. A shame really as he had great potential as a golfer in getting his playing handicap down as low as two. As for football, his aspiration to be a professional goalkeeper was detrimentally hampered by the deficiency of height and physical stature that he suffered in his early youth. "Very good, agile and sharp, but come back next season when you've gained a few inches and filled out a bit," being the favourite line trooped out to meet his many trial games. He wrote the first chapters of quite a few interesting stories in his rare moments of spare time but never completed any of them.

Quite ironically and gradually, as he started to mature, the slow development of some minor OCD traits prevented the procrastination from becoming too much of an issue. By the time he was over the age of twenty-five, he had progressed to a point of usually getting things finished… eventually.

His true friends just accepted him as he was, but strangely this never seemed the case for his many, more romantically biased female relationships.

Sometimes he would outwardly seem to lack commitment but, for sure, when he finally made up his mind to follow through with something, he was steadfast and always stuck to his guns. Integrity was always his ace in the hole, but he hid it well along with his birth Christian names and many other things. Although in many ways, as mentioned in the Introduction earlier, he was something of an open book, that volume was not always easy for anyone to fully understand. He played the 'What you see, is what you get' card cleverly but also guarded how much anyone saw. Those who got him understood and stuck with him through thick and thin, but those who didn't bother to look beyond the publicly visible, open but edgy exterior, never really knew him at all. Cash and Charley, his very best friends and two of our other main protagonists in this tale, were of the former mindset.

Brody would always stand his ground if he thought he was right with a 'do or die, fight to the death' attitude. Some would call it the Napoleon complex, although at five foot nine he wasn't tiny, but he would always be the bigger man and first to apologise if he realised he was in the wrong. He was a good judge of character but did tend to be a little over-trusting with his first impressions, always trying to give people the benefit of any doubt.

If wronged though, he found it very hard to forgive and *never* forgot. He sometimes couldn't remember what he had for dinner or where he'd left his keys but had a great memory for inane details of things long past.

After leaving education early to seek employment, his scholastic flippancy hindered his career-building opportunities so he made major efforts to return to night classes to fill in the gaps. Classically, those gaps were where his school reports read, in red pen 'Could have done better!' With regular evening classes and daily Internet study he made up for lost time, and more. By the age of twenty-nine, although he had had a string of failed relationships behind him, he had gained a very impressive clutch of qualifications: five A Levels, a PhD in Physics and a Doctorate in Astrophysics.

Whilst studying at that time, he was working mundanely for a small independent company as a domestic appliance service engineer. Without fulfilling his potential he topped up his income as a semi-professional goalkeeper at weekends as well as making extra money by gambling, fighting and privately gambling on the fighting. He was not addicted but, in truth, Brody would gamble on two drops of rain running down a windowpane if someone took the bet but was somehow reasonably successful in most of his wagers. He enjoyed betting on his own ability as a card player, a golfer, a chess player and very dubiously as an unlikely exponent of unlicensed underground street fighting. To say his life was eclectic was no exaggeration.

Amongst these 'hobbies' another of his biggest passions was heavy metal rock music – he followed his favourite band live wherever and whenever possible. He was also the very proud owner of two unique pieces of this very particular band's memorabilia.

One of these was Bruce... Even though it was basically a toy doll, it was one of his most prized possessions. Being one of a kind it did have considerable monetary value and he took it everywhere with him. Most people thought it was just an ugly toy, but secretly it contained a tiny digital recorder that allowed files or music tracks to be downloaded and played back through its own internal speaker system. Bruce could be linked to a PC to upload or download but looked quite freakish on the outside. It stood about eighteen inches tall and portrayed a facially disfigured zombie character dangling the strings of a puppet – a lizard-like devil creature – that in turn was holding a puppet of some other strange being. As weird as it looked it was a technological wonder.

When his mother had purchased it for him at a charity auction in 2011 he had affectionately named it Bruce as a loyal homage to the historically famous, regularly faulty, mechanical shark device similarly so named by the director of his all-time favourite feature film. It was also possibly a minor tribute paid to quite a few other influential Bruces.

Now you know a little bit more of Brody and his ways, let's move along to see how these and other idiosyncrasies develop over time and affect the complexities of the biggest adventure he has ever had, as he tenuously and unknowingly embarks upon it. Let's see who chooses to travel the same path with him and where those footsteps will lead.

BREAKING THE TRANQUILLITY OF SOLITUDE

PART ONE

CHAPTER 1

Time Passes, Decisions Are Made.

Brody had owned Bruce, his sacred rock star-worshipping, digitised toy for over twenty-five years and, at one point, had spent a considerable amount of time and effort (not to mention money) chasing his musical heroes around the world getting it signed and authenticated by all the band members. Due to this the band knew Brody quite well and his ownership of Bruce had gained him some notoriety within their ranks. The group's bassist and leader had desperately wanted to buy it from him, offering a considerably attractive amount of money. He had been its original owner and the very person who had commissioned its production, along with a book that carried the full lyrics of the first four albums that his band had produced. The toy had been retrospectively made to commemorate their achievements in the music industry at that time.

On occasions, Brody had been sorely tempted to simply return the toy to his all-time musical hero, but Bruce was one of a kind and Brody, a few years earlier had twisted his mother's arm and successfully managed to get her to purchase the commemorative lyric book as well. He was thus the proud owner of both, a fact that not many people other than the band themselves knew. The pair of rock merchandise goodies was of immense financial value to a collector such as Brody. He had twice been lucky enough to have his mother be able to make these purchases relatively cheaply; once at the charity auction and the other at a filthy, rain-washed, muddy car boot sale and both when visitors to these events, including himself, had not realised what was *truly* for sale.

The financial value didn't overly concern Brody now; he was far more interested in the status it gave him with his heroes and the uniqueness of the fact that they knew him. Unlike other star struck individuals, Brody didn't need to queue for hours on end for autographs. The band knew him and he was extremely proud of it. The lyric book looked much older than its actual years and additionally, being quite delicate was potentially far more resaleable and of much more historic collectable value. It was kept under lock and key, safe in Brody's loft. Bruce though, being more of a trophy, went everywhere with Brody. It was not overly popular though with the other two of the trio of friends that we meet early in the story.

Charley and Cash both saw it as part of his weaker side, basically a puerile waste of time and money as well as a source of some embarrassment if ever it was seen when they were out with Brody socially. Cash would often hide the thing to annoy Brody and Charley had even threatened to bin it on more than one occasion but to this point had not dared follow through on this. Beyond the banter, Brody really held this toy as an item of great significance to his own life and persona. It would probably even be buried with him one day for at this time it was his only family and Charley knew that the binning, if carried out, might just be one step beyond and too much for their friendship to sustain.

As Brody got older, as well as owning Bruce he also developed a minor tattoo addiction, having his personal interpretations of the songs of his favourite albums tattooed on his back. Charley, unbeknown to Brody, but heavily influenced by him, had recently got a tattoo and really wanted more.

There was a hidden envy of Brody's body art and Charley harboured a strange inexplicable need to see it in the flesh, but even after nearly two years of friendship, had never asked and had not seen any of the tattoos. The only knowledge that anyone ever really gained was from Brody's own, overly-detailed descriptions of what he had just got or what he was getting next, along with the deep and meaningful ramblings of how he had designed them all himself and what they represented to him. Anyone actually getting to see them was strangely not Brody's desire. He himself could only see them partially and, even then, only with the aid of a mirror.

Cash, however, having known Brody a lot longer, had seen them many times and in effect had watched them grow and evolve. He had in his own youth chosen to have a couple of football-related designs inked onto both his upper arms but he was not overly fussed on the subject as a whole. This was typical of Cash – all things in moderation. What with Bruce and tattoos, he was always amazed at how much time and money Brody spent on these two passions.

As I mentioned earlier, neither Charley nor Cash were overly keen on Bruce, nor on the music that Brody liked and were not particularly impressed that the two were intrinsically entwined. The wafting of a hand over the mouth and fake snoring noises were Charley's favourite way, when necessary, of giving Brody a clue. Cash had his unspoken, frowning, stare. "Really… Again?" being the unspoken but fully understood thrust of both.

In some ways it was a testament to the depth of their feelings that they did not more openly criticise his musical tastes – both saw it as a stage he would eventually get through.

When travelling in Brody's car you either enjoyed or suffered the journey, based upon your own personal appreciation of a few factors: the length of the bonnet and how low the front passenger seat was, the lack of space in the back seats and, of course, whichever of his favourite tracks, from his favourite album, from his favourite band was monotonously playing and replaying very loudly at that very moment. Unsurprisingly, whenever the three were planning a longer journey, either Cash or Charley would always insist on driving.

In contrast to their semi-judgemental but light-hearted feelings about Brody's choice of music and toys, the other two always seriously warned him about burning the candle of life at both ends, especially regarding the dangers involved in the fighting and gambling he liked to dabble with. Brody always joked, "Fighting or gambling is just like getting a tattoo – it has to mean something," but always added, "You don't have to be tough to make money fighting, you just need to be quick and know who is going to win. The bravery aspect is only relevant the very first time you do it. After that, backing the right guy is the skill." Usually he would finish off with, "You can easily make money and avoid bruises; you just have to learn to know how and when to lose safely."

Secretly and never admitted to, what Brody really liked was the sheer adrenalin rush of being in mortal danger. The being able to display his tattoos *without* need of lengthy explanation or onlookers' understanding of their depth of meaning was just an added bonus. Getting paid for it all at the same time was the icing on the cake. The feeling of accomplishment was a mini drug for him; if he could successfully gamble on the outcome of a fight he was involved in, come out unscathed and get to strut his art all at the same time, winning was immaterial. It was the feeling of being in control of a situation that he was not fully in control of that he relished.

Like any gambler, it was the thrill of possibly losing everything that made winning so exciting. In Brody's case, win or lose could mean the same, dependent on how carefully he had placed his wagers.

Brody took little or no notice of the 'naysayers' who disagreed with any aspect of his life but remained very loyal to a few of what he called real friends. To him, anyone else was just a mere acquaintance and had to go a very long way to qualify as a mate with very little chance of ever being considered a true friend. When we meet him just before the start of his amazing adventure, he only really had one such real friend, the aforementioned Cash. But Charley would soon join those hallowed ranks, as you will soon see.

About Cash, initially the name doesn't really make much sense but was the pet name christened upon him by Brody, very early in his life. His actual name was Kamylloxerajit Bashir, which was a ridiculous mouthful even for his Indian-born mother and mixed-race Jamaican-English father. Kids at school twisted the difficult to pronounce name and called him all sorts – some viler than others as I'm sure you can imagine.

Some of the more pleasant versions included simply Lox, Kam and Raj, but Cash was never fully comfortable with any of these or the proper version for that matter. As a child he didn't get physically bullied as such because of his size, but he never forgot the jibes and jokes. Mental cruelty is often worse than physical abuse, so Brody who did sometimes himself receive a bit of physical stress as a youngster and his friend Kamylloxerajit defended each other to the hilt. Brody thought the name tag Cash worked well.

It had started quite jokingly as a question he had once asked his friend about spelling. Out of the blue at the tender age of eight he had simply asked the question, "Your name is so long and hard to spell, are you an Indian Chief?" Out of the mouths of babes. This daft jocular question, once overheard by others, quickly morphed from childish naïvety into heartless fun poking. Various forms of Chief, some less complimentary than others, eventually became Chief Cashier. Brody started this, partly because he felt guilty and, having noticed it written on every monetary note he had ever handled, tenuously, linked his friend's last name of Bashir to Cashier.

It was only meant as a lesser joke than others were levelling at his friend, but Brody was a very thoughtful lad. Others started to revert to the term Chief without the Cashier, this didn't sit well with him. When some not-so-friendly kids were describing his best pal in this way it bothered him that he had been the cause of his friend's potential upset. Brody was quite influential in the starting of crazes that periodically surfaced at school, so set about making it well known that Chief was to be dropped in favour of the much more acceptable Cashier. This finally evolved to Cash because of the black country/West Midlands dialect that everyone at his school suffered from, and it stuck.

Perversely, by initially poking fun and then publicly protecting his friend's feelings, he had created a very positive reputation for himself around school and developed the name that Kamylloxerajit would be known by from then on. From zero to hero in one unwittingly naïve moment. By the time they were both twelve nobody even remembered the real name let alone the fraught, tearful and pride-hidden early years of name bullying he had suffered. Not even his wider family used anything other than Cash, except as in every young boy's life; Broderick's included… his mother.

"Kamylloxerajit, have you done your homework?"

"Kamylloxerajit, put your coat away!" etc.

Cash rarely mentioned it but silently thanked Brody eternally for this accidental identity change and seriously considered getting hold of the appropriate deed poll form to change it permanently, but never did.

Brody had known Cash since they were three years old in nursery school and had, since he was old enough to understand the concept, always considered him his closest friend, treating him like a brother in the knowledge that both he and his friend were, an *'only child'*. Cash was so laid-back and likeable that many said the same about him. "He's always been Mr. Popular."

The two never had the type of friendship where they were living in each other's pockets but their bond was strong. As adults it was hard for Brody to read Cash's feelings about his relationship with him but suffice it to say that well over thirty years later they still socialised together. Brody would do anything for Cash, any time night or day and if ever he needed help, all Cash would have to do was to ask. The theory had rarely been tested either way, but both understood the rules; if you need to ask it must be important.

Neither having siblings, both always sought to please. Brody had dim and distant recollections of stories about his parents having lost more than one child prior to his birth and as such, as a young boy he had always refrained from discussing the possibilities of future brothers or sisters. One brother from another mother became his lot and he liked it that way.

They both also had a distinct love of all things movie and music and were always quoting a lyric or two from a song or a line from a famous film of years gone by as a method of describing something else unconnected that was happening. Most people hearing them during these friendly banter-type sessions would usually become confused at these seemingly unintelligible random statements, quotes or partial lyrical outbursts. The two of them usually knew exactly what each other meant like some bygone era secret code.

A classic example of this was on an occasion a few months previous, Cash had fallen about laughing in response to him having been asked to do some unwanted extra shifts at work. Brody, when told about it later, immediately burst into song in the middle of the pub, belting out the lines of one of Cash's favourite songs which he felt epitomised the moment. Bearing in mind Brody was a truly awful singer, he crooned his best version.

"In my life. Why do I smile, at people who I'd much rather kick in the eye? I was happy in the haze of a drunken hour…"

Cash knew the next line and laughed while others laughed at the quality of singing.

Away from his propensity to find a film quote to match any occasion or his ability to badly sing a random line from a song as a subliminal message, (about something only *they* would fully appreciate), one of Brody's biggest problems in life was the taking of orders from people whom he considered not to be in a position to give them. His trail of failed jobs over his first thirteen or so working years being a testament to this issue and was longer even than that of his trail of failed relationships. His curriculum vitae was somewhat chequered to say the very least.

He would always argue the point if it was raised and usually turned things round to say that the diversity of the experiences he had gained in multiple trades helped him to be that much better in any one job he might choose in the future. To him, working as a greenskeeper on a golf course, driving lorries, working as an analytical chemist in a cyanide plating solution factory, selling insurance, working on building sites, being a motorcycle courier and a whole host of other jobs that we will come across within this story gave him an advantage in life. "Strength in depth," was how he always referred to it.

At the age of thirty, Brody made a bold move and decided to go self-employed so he would no longer have to be taking orders from anyone. He set about starting up not one but two of his own businesses based generally on what he enjoyed the most, workwise. By putting his head down, switching off completely from watching or playing football or golf, chasing girls, drinking, gambling and even the underground fixed fighting, he decided to try to make a reputation in these two chosen fields.

The companies he created were completely diverse; one being domestic appliance repairs and the other goalkeeper coaching. Brody even created the marketing and designed the logos in his spare time with very professionally sounding inspirational straplines coming from that melting pot of an underused brain. He did one job in the day and the other at night, five days and five nights a week, fifty-two weeks a year.

This continued for pretty much the next eight years straight – work, work, work – realistically only resting at weekends when he would allow himself small amounts of alcohol to help him unwind and completely crash out. Money was understandably building up nicely now and he was not spending much, having very little time for socialising with acquaintances, friends or starting new relationships. During this period even, Cash only saw Brody about twice a month for a friendly pint and the occasional sporting activity which helped them both to stay fit.

Brody wasn't one for saving and money was not an objective, so his mattress tended to be lumpy but his bank balance was usually flatter.

This not-preparing-for-the-future attitude was one of his more serious failings, but it didn't even occur to him. "Live for today" and "You can sleep when you are dead" being two of his regular rebuttals to any criticism of his happy-go-lucky, unplanned lifestyle.

Cash was and always had been much more conventional. He was a computer expert and circuitry genius straight from university going to work on developing systems, analysing computer processes and repairing infrastructure. He, like our not yet fully introduced third party, Charley, had worked for the same company for many years and led a relatively normal and quiet life outside work. He was an ex-national table tennis champion and a real sports all-rounder. His athletic build and tanned-looking, dark skin tone had long been the envy of many. Back in their youth, Brody had been platinum blonde and Cash black-haired, but more lately Cash was, by choice, shaven headed and Brody was gradually becoming pepper pot grey. In truth, he was rapidly approaching the legendary silver fox status that his own father had worn in all of Brody's living memories. His father had apparently been labelled Sylvie at thirty-five and Brody was only waiting for the inevitable.

Although they were the same age, Cash was cheese to Brody's chalk. He was a six foot plus Mr. Reliable, straight down the middle, laid-back and never upset anyone – Joe Cool. Brody was more of a five foot nine, speak as you find, tell-it-as-it-is, Jack the Lad. Cash liked the quieter life and was long-term married with no kids and no worries except the minor issue, which was his own personal concern of how Brody's life seemed to swing and change so much.

Cash regularly conjured the thought of Brody's life being like a huge pair of out-of-balance retro (life-monitoring) scales, mirroring the fact that Brody usually had so much to weigh up and balance regarding his future that usually he just left it all and got on with the present. He thought his old mate should try to settle down and consider the idea of giving up some of his more reckless pursuits, but Cash being Cash, he never seriously voiced his concerns publicly or to Brody.

It was on one very fateful day about a week before he had even met Charley that Brody was having a late drink with Cash. They got chatting about work and everything started to change from that moment onwards. On that very night, they were sitting drinking their usual two or three pints after Cash had, as was often the case, thrashed Brody at whatever sport they were engaged in; on this occasion it being table tennis. Cash happened to mention that the company he worked for was looking for someone with an open mind, free spirit, drive, determination and, as luck would have it, a PhD in Physics to head up a new full-time research and development project.

"What do you reckon, pal, is that for you?" he asked, smiling over his beer.

"It's got to be better than the Nobby-No-Mates eighteen-hour days you are doing now. It's about time you got some focus in your life; it's for living, not slaving. You know that, right?" he sarcastically jibed.

"I reckon we should play golf next time instead of table tennis, you shark," was Brody's sarcastic and dismissive response, but he was secretly quite intrigued and, after leaving his friend later that evening, spent the rest of the night silently weighing up the pros and cons of the idea compared to his current situation and decided to investigate it further. The next day he contacted the company and organised an interview for the following week.

CHAPTER 2

Love at First Sight.

Brody hadn't seriously bothered much with socialising outside of the occasional evening beer with Cash. For nearly eight years he gave all his time to work – even chasing girls had taken a back seat. When he entered the shiny offices of Cash's employer Brundle-Brown Incorporated in the late afternoon of Friday 6th June 2036 for his interview, he was most definitely not prepared for what was about to happen.

Cash was already at work that day and had been for about nine hours already, but he was deliberately delaying leaving for the day so that he could see Brody briefly to wish him good luck ahead of his interview. He knew only too well having checked the times with his colleague Charley who had set up the meeting a few days before that the interview was scheduled for five o'clock. He was deliberately stalling his visit to the reception area to try to coincide it with Brody's arrival. He had arranged for Charley rather than one of the other normal reception staff to handle the initial meet and greet for various reasons. He planned to pop in and say hello to settle his friend's nerves just before his allotted meeting time. He did not want Brody to know this so had told Charley not to mention it.

Brody arrived, as was his way, plenty early enough to scope out the place and ensure that he was mentally prepared for anything that may occur. The car park was like a beauty spot and detracted markedly from the huge modern six-storey glass structure behind it. He pulled up slowly and turned his car stereo down to a respectable volume from its normal cranked-up to eleven, position. Heavy metal music blasting out of the windows may have lowered the tone. Against all the other modern vehicles parked in the generous spaces, each lined individually with decorative shrubs and bushes, Brody thought that his skinny tomato red Capri possibly might have the same effect, but to him it was a statement maker and he loved his retro rust box – it was inaccurately adorned with a Starsky Gran Torino 'go-faster stripe' down each side that joined across the roof. It was a proper 1980s TV cop shows mix and match homage.

The very first thing Brody saw as he walked through the strangely unattended lobby of the plush six-storey, high-rise office block was a choice of three other doors to go through. After waiting in the lobby for a few moments he remembered that the person he had spoken to on the phone said that if nobody was immediately in attendance he should go to the secretarial reception office.

'Now for the first test… a bit like Neo,' he thought to himself as he stared at the three doors and contemplated which to try first. Would it be A on the right or either B or C on the opposite wall? The doors were marked in this very strange alphabetical manner and, although amused, he was also confused as to what it all meant. He would one day find out but for now, his curiosity got the better of him and he inadvisably and foolishly just guessed. All manner of cleaning products and other equipment fell and clattered towards him. Quickly slamming door B was the only realistic option. He hurriedly did so and used all his skill as a fleet footed goalkeeper to sidestep swiftly back to the middle of the lobby. He stood looking

around and hoped nobody had seen his Chaplin-style recovery.

Another few minutes went by. He was a man who, for various reasons, never wore a watch and whilst parking had noted on his dash clock that it was four-forty. Knowing that he had been there a good ten minutes by now and thinking that this was possibly an initiative test, he potentially only had another few minutes to pass it. He had to make a choice without much information to help the decision. Or should he just wait? He went for A – perhaps wrong – but there was now a fifty-fifty chance and he gambled that he couldn't be unlucky twice.

As the door opened he silently and nervously rotated it back revealing a corridor that led into another room that screamed out to him… "Winner!" Door C had been locked but he didn't know it.

As he strode down the short corridor, he now saw a large secretary-style desk and a three-seater couch at opposite sides of the room with a few filing cabinets and a large photocopier on the third wall. A water cooler and coffee machine stood in the far corner by an adjoining doorway. Next to the coffee machine he could see his car. He quickly realised he was looking through a huge glass window wall that gave anyone inside a nicer view than just four blank walls. Thankfully, not back outside, he noted that the reception desk seemed to face the other way by about ninety degrees, so it was possible that the view was preferred for visitor comfort rather than staff. He had not spotted the office from outside when he parked as he had reversed into the only free visitor's space, preoccupied with time and making sure he was exactly in the centre of the two white lines that marked the parking bay.

Little did he know at that very moment how many future hours he would spend standing in this very area, leaning against that very window, usually near that very coffee machine. The area was medium-sized, sparsely decorated but neat and tidy with an immaculately polished shiny tiled floor; the crisp reflections sparkling from it pleased his inner tidiness OCD.

'Very neat, very clean, very professional.' Whispering to himself even inside his head, he didn't speak aloud just in case, even though the reception was empty. He ambled over and sat on the couch to await his allotted time, perched precariously on the edge of the middle seat ready to stand quickly if anyone arrived. A few minutes passed and he was starting to consider leaving when a bittersweet aroma caught his nostrils.

'Wow, what is that smell? That is soooo good!' Still mentally whispering, his mind briefly drifted, concentration on interview techniques temporarily interrupted by this completely unexpected intrusion into his primary senses. He couldn't place it but felt that it was feminine and found it strangely quite erotic. An increasing pheromone response from within his body was starting and that began to worry him; he was unintentionally becoming uneasy and nervous, such was the potent effect of the fragrance he was experiencing. He even felt a tiny bit light-headed and aroused, but since he was there for an interview and was otherwise very focused, he was able to reassert his concentration and those feelings did not yet further surface, but they were undeniably there. He felt them; he didn't understand or like the idea of them much, but he could not fully ignore their existence. Another few seconds that seemed like hours passed and then Cash sauntered in,

"Hi mate, what time is your interview?" he enquired in casual pretence of not knowing.

"Five o'clock," Brody replied. He sprang up offering his outstretched hand, rigidly trying not to appear too relaxed or stressed, but professional, even though at this point nobody but Cash was there to see. Cash casually slapped the hand Brody had informally offered. It was always assumed by most that these days someone can see you, wherever you are, and Brody glanced up and around fervently as he re-perched himself and tried desperately to look comfortable. 'Big Brother is watching...' was his fall-back line when such subjects were debated. He was not a conspiracy theorist but understood how technology had advanced. Just as Cash was about to wish him well and go out towards the car park, Brody could restrain no longer.

"Can you smell something, matey? I have roses, marigolds; I don't know what else but it's making me dizzy and I find it strangely compelling." Cash looked at him completely puzzled.

"No, pal, nothing in my hooter, you must just be nervous." He winked and wafted his hand by his nose in a 'Was that you?' sort of way.

"Phew, DO NOT go in there," he further joked, going straight in to surreptitious film quote mode, intimating further that Brody himself may be the cause of any such odours.

"He who smelt it, dealt it..." Cash stifled his own laughter.

"Yeah... yeah... but, mate... it's making me excited in a way you don't want to be excited just before an interview... Do you get my drift?" Brody whispered for real this time, very quietly, as if trying to keep a company secret. Cash just laughed aloud.

"You're a complete nutter! Lucky you caught me; I was just on my way home. Call me later, let me know how you get on. My colleague, Charley, who you spoke to on the phone will be here any minute to sort things out for you. Good luck, pal." As Cash disappeared out of sight the redolence which, apparently up to now, only Brody could detect and of which was having such a profound effect on his senses, seemed to increase in its intensity and wafted past him making him feel physically dizzy.

Then it happened...

From the far side of the office near to the coffee machine and water cooler, the adjoining door started to open. Slowly, the door rotated its full ninety-eight degrees of possible travel and the handle nudged the side of the coffee machine. As Brody held his breath a vision of female perfection stepped into his life. Space and time completely froze and his jaw literally dropped open. Ten yards away in front of him, in his now glazed eyes, was a goddess of such amazing beauty that it left him completely tongue tied. All his normal, ever ready, quick-fire chat up lines completely left his head. Metaphorically, they deserted him like rats from a sinking ship, chat up birds flapping and panicking to escape the slowly prowling cat next-door. They flew straight up and out through the closed and sealed window wall, turning only to wave goodbye and laugh as they looked back and saw him, like some sort of stroke victim, staring blankly at the young lady who had just entered. Still with his mouth open looking completely dazed, he was momentarily unable to do anything but gawk.

Aided by his earlier dizziness and the shiny floor, his teetering position on the couch suddenly failed him and, as his gravitationally affected body pushed the couch towards the wall, he slipped to the floor with a slap that reverberated around the reception area. So loud was the noise of his backside hitting the tiles that the young lady who had unintentionally caused the slip, looked over as she approached the desk.

She spotted the now uncomfortably seated interviewee and smiled, a sweet sexy smile that made Brody embarrassed, relieved and quite horny all at the same time.

Possibly a mere two seconds elapsed as she prowled cat-like past him and took her position behind the desk. In those two seconds within his recovering dizzy blur, he saw the possibility of the rest of his life becoming much more meaningful and completely meaningless simultaneously.

She had burnt auburn red hair that glinted like fire. She shook the mane around her shoulders accentuating her pale skin and slender neckline as she rounded the desk.

Most men if pushed to be brutally honest, will eventually admit that the one thing, or more accurately things, that they initially notice when meeting a girl for the first time, are usually her boobs, tits, knockers, hooters, norks or any of a thousand other such derogatory terms that 'blokes' tend to banter to each other on a far too regular basis; usually over beer.

Brody wasn't thinking that way these days and he started to realise that he hadn't really been looking at all for the past few years. However, even now, as he became aware that he *was* noticing things, it was not a randy bloke looking at a gorgeous girl but more an art critic viewing a masterpiece or even a blind man miraculously re-gaining his sight.

He had always loved the normal flirtatious glances he used to share with girls, centred usually on their physique, but... not today. In this case, the first thing Brody noticed was that apparently invisible and undetectable to others perfume, then it was her hair and those amazing eyes.

'Bright green emeralds set in creamy smooth perfection, surrounded by fire,' he thought to himself. A hint of rouge on her cheeks and full pouting lips glinting with lipstick of a similar tint, the reflections from her hair came next and then... Well, then there was the body!.. Her crisp, white blouse was perfection personified. Its inability to cope with her amazing curves was mind-blowing; she blossomed in all the correct places and the buttons of her blouse temptingly struggled to cope with the pressure exerted upon them in holding that perfect hourglass shape.

All of a sudden an image of a famous singer came to his mind but the vision, although relevant, was not as impressive as the reality he was beholding – not even the thing he was mentally attempting to process. The picture of the singer was accurate in every detail but swiftly gave way to the lyrics of a song she famously wrote and sang. In a flash, Brody was silently singing within his swirling confused thoughts.

'Your beauty is beyond compare, with flaming locks of auburn hair. With ivory skin and eyes of emerald green. Your smile is like a breath of spring; your voice is soft like summer rain. And I cannot compete with you, Jolene.' He saw the mental picture of the historically enhanced singer again, remembering her diminutive stature and outrageously huge baps, but his mind centred on the current aptness of her absolutely undeniable genius as a songwriter. He could even recount the oh-so perfect lyrics, but could not bring her name to mind, such was his brain-addled, fantasy-driven predilection at that moment.

His eyes scanned the new office arrival walking closely by him. He could not, and did not, fail to notice the tight pencil skirt clearly showing the telltale signs of thin clasps bulging through the material, not too subtly giving away the presence of suspenders which led down to the hidden tops of white stockings emerging at mid-thigh height. His eyes travelled further on to the relatively sedate three-inch red heels via firm athletic thighs and toned but smooth calves. It only added to his current predicament. Not only was Brody now sitting on his backside unable to move or speak, but also other areas of his body were now starting to respond in kind. Now he was feeling unable to stand even if he could summon the co-ordination required to do so.

Never in all his living memory had meeting someone of the opposite sex affected him in this way and he was becoming quite scared. He had never experienced a feeling like it; his heart was racing, his pulse was smashing his temples and sweat began to bead on his forehead. He felt faint, struggled for breath but couldn't move for fear of embarrassing himself further. The mere four seconds or so that it took in total for this siren to slide from the door to behind her desk seemed about a year and Brody was thinking that he might actually be having that stroke his mind had conjured seconds earlier. She sat down and turned to look at him again. He dipped his eyes, worried she might realise he had been so obviously transfixed.

"Are you OK?" she enquired with that sweet, quiet, summer rain voice.

"Yeeerrraguessso, thanks," was his level best semi-stuttering response as he fought his emotions. He was trying to be his normal confident, calm self in the presence of this girl who, in his confused state, was potentially ruining his interview possibilities with her completely unintentional display of what was to him such obvious perfection.

"My name is Charley, short for Charlotte but everyone calls me Charley, a bit like the boy's Charlie but girly with a y. Are you Brody, here to see Mr. Harris?" she asked softly but with complete confidence.

"Yes, that's me… Sharley… Charles… errrr… I mean, Charley, sorry – bit flustered," he blathered. His eyes wouldn't focus from flitting from hair to eyes to lips to bosom in a completely random order, not stopping long enough to seem to stare but not staring long enough to seem to be paying any attention. In the back of his dizzy head he suddenly pictured Marty Feldman and he tried to sober and control his eyes. In a now desperate subconscious attempt to avoid looking rude or weird he locked his quivering eyes on to hers and a few seconds passed as he gazed, looking deep into the green pools of her soul.

Souls were not something he particularly believed in. Usually scorning any religious conversation whenever one reared its head in earshot, at this moment he felt a distinct connection to this stranger that he had never experienced before. Those few seconds felt like forever; he started to think that both time and his heart had stopped.

"It's OK," she replied softly.

"No need to be nervous, he isn't an ogre, you know." Her naïve follow-up broke the tension a little and made him smile.

"So, *YOU* are Charley. Sorry, it must have been a very bad line when we spoke on the phone yesterday and I had thought you would be a Charl*ie*." He emphasised the masculine apologetically as he scrambled to his feet and dusted down his trousers even though they were not dusty, trying desperately to stay in control and not ramble into a pit. He knew he was tightly holding the shovel but desperately wanted to lean on it rather than dig any deeper.

"No problem, Brody. Cash has told me a bit about you." Cash had very much done just that, telling Charley a lot about his old friend in a nice, pleasant but blatant match-making sort of way. Cash knew Brody wasn't particularly looking for romance, but he felt it might be the very thing that would wake him up and bring him back to humanity again. Brody had, over the last few years, drifted to a work only zone and it concerned Cash that his friend was possibly burning himself out and needed a fresh perspective.

He had set about whetting young Charley's appetite with talk of his friend's boyish good looks and fun sense of humour. He had the advantage of knowing she was into older men and Brody liked...well, everything that she was, in spades. Cash had even surreptitiously logged into her computer and left cookies and tags all over the place so that over the last few weeks she was continually reminded of the name and the possibilities of meeting this person; it was reaffirmed regularly. Cash even glorified the name by leaving a link to a names website which extolled the romantic background to the derivation of his friend's name. Truth and facts were largely irrelevant, but he succeeded in creating an air of expectancy and intrigue even before Brody had even applied for a position. His plan had been a match made accidental meeting on a night out, but a workplace romance could work even better.

"Errrr, OK, so what has he been saying?"

"Oh, nothing really and all good anyway." Charley was glad she was seated as Cash had described Brody quite well and her anticipation of who she would be meeting had excited her. She was by no means disappointed and felt a strange attraction to this apparently shy bumbling character, known to be slightly older but a young-looking guy. An internal feeling that she did not quite understand bubbled and simmered. The web page she had read only the previous day, thanks to Cash's trickery, had described…

BRODY: The sweetest guy you will ever meet in your entire life: you can't help but fall in love immediately. He is so full of compassion and kindness and has such a caring heart. He is extremely hilarious and will make you laugh and laugh. He is also very sexy, adorable and handsome – all at the same time! He has a great body, wonderful smile, gorgeous eyes, etc. He is so very smart/intelligent and can do anything he sets his mind to. He will make you so very proud. He'll also make you the happiest girl in the world. Whoever has him is the most blessed girl ever. He is just so completely and totally perfect in every single way.

The girl's own magazine description had probably been used a thousand times in hundreds of magazines to describe Andrew, Brian, Carl, David and Brody as well as an alphabet's worth of others, but Cash surreptitiously fed it to Charley and she failed to look any further. Subconsciously she had fallen for the rouse and subsequently was more than a little interested in who she would now meet.

Glancing nervously down to avoid further eye contact, beneath the desk she held her own hands as her fingers were shaking uncontrollably. Inexplicably she felt very excited, nervous and her knees were trembling. She had deliberately dressed a bit on the sexy side as Cash's last few days of bigging Brody up had caused something of an air of anticipation within her and she was now realising that she herself had been quite attracted to this newcomer even before she had even seen him. Now meeting him for the first time she saw a not overly tall but well-proportioned man that she knew full well was approaching forty but looked about mid- to late twenties. She saw short, tightly cropped hair with a distinct scar running through it from the left temple to behind the left ear.

She didn't need to ask what had caused it as Cash had already relayed the long version of a story of a foolish accident that the two of them had been involved in on their pushbikes at the tender age of seventeen. She saw firm muscles with tattoos on both arms just barely visible beneath the white, short-sleeved shirt. It looked like it had not been used for a few years and was a little creased.

It was a hot day and he had left his suit jacket in the car. She rolled her eyes to deliberately look, keeping her head slightly bowed, but cracked a nervous smile on seeing his comical, perfectly knotted and neat cartoon festooned tie. As she looked up properly, the whole picture was completed by his cheeky but anxious smile. She saw steel blue unflinching eyes and strangely compelling feminine-length beautiful long eyelashes. It was all merely concreting the preconceived feelings into place. It was magnetic, hormonal, electric and weird but the two just gazed into each other's eyes for the next few hour-long seconds and the silence was deafening.

Eventually Brody recovered his composure, they made embarrassing small talk for a few minutes and he ended up having his interview with one of the other research executives in a side office, as Mr. Harris had strangely not been available.

'*I bet he saw all that on CCTV*,' Brody mentally speculated as he was 'treated' to a thorough two-hour long tour of the company facilities by various high-ranking employees. As far as he was aware, the only places they did not show him were the sixth floor and the contents of door C. He was given coffee from the machine in the reception area but did not see Charley again that day. This point bothered him somehow, but he could not immediately work out why. He went home with mixed feelings about his success possibilities but could not get the images of Charley out of his head. Even if he *had* failed the interview, he knew that he needed to return there soon.

Amazingly, after all the trepidation, when he received a letter a few days later he was surprised to find he had been offered the job. He accepted and started the process of winding up his other businesses over the next couple of months.

This is the point where our story truly gets started. Brody at thirty-eight had, at that very pivotal moment, entered a new stage of his life. With a new job in the bag, working for a huge professionally-run organisation and alongside his best pal Cash, it was like finding the proverbial cake with an 'Eat me now' permission slip attached. He had also now met and, even though he was not fully aware of it yet, already fallen head over heels in love with the icing on that very cake, the beautiful and enigmatic Charley.

CHAPTER 3

Not All Mistakes Are Obvious.

So briefly, before we go any further – what of her…

Apple Jane Christina Rose Charlotte O'Brien was a mysterious girl of remarkable intelligence, maturity and startling beauty. Like Cash, her name had been changed from its birth version. Her parents were a little on the hippy end of life's spectrum and Apple, having been both plump and rosy cheeked as a child, had inevitably been labelled 'Rotten Apple' amongst many more cruel descriptions that were all very upsetting for a young child to deal with. It got that bad that she moved schools more than once before a house move for the whole family was seen to be the only solution, such was her parents' naïve inability to see that it was their own mistake which had caused all the problems.

When the family finally settled into their new home and she re-started school, the administrators of this learning establishment were placed under pain of legal action if they revealed her true name and she was henceforth known as Charlotte O'Brien. The shortened Charley was a strange and unlikely derivation of a pet name for her, bestowed upon her by an ex-boyfriend. He had insisted on calling her Angel, which she absolutely hated. His over the top personal fascination/hang-up about Cheryl Ladd was always a concern. She eventually ditched him for that very reason amongst other maturity issues. The Charley part stuck; she was though, quite comfortable with it, even knowing that it had originally come about from a childish three-girl fantasy. To those who didn't know, it was a natural shortening of her own name anyway.

Nobody now, not even Cash or Brody, would ever know these deepest of secrets unless she was to mention them – her family house move had been global. They had uprooted and moved from her birthplace of Utah, USA, to not-so-sunny middle England.

The day she met Brody nearly eighteen years after having arrived in the UK she was just over twenty-six, so about twelve years the junior of her new-found admirer. Neither knew the exact age gap, or even the age of the other at this point, but it truly didn't matter. Brody had always coyly joked about liking younger girls, a joke Cash would regularly cringe at as in these times of political correctness it could so easily be misconstrued. Charley liked older men as she found them easier to relate to on an intellectual basis and preferred the more mature conversation. Although Brody was perfectly capable and plenty intelligent enough for that, projecting maturity outwardly was something he historically struggled with. He had become used to flippancy and it came naturally to him – joking was his default position.

Charley had worked at Brundle-Brown Inc since it was formed by the amalgamation of two large competitor companies that had occurred some years previously. Before this she had worked directly for the man Brody had been meant to meet at interview, Mr. Harris, owner of one of those companies – The Brundle Corporation.

She was outwardly a very confident young lady but privately slightly naïve and insecure. Having to fend off unwanted young male attention practically daily because of the positive affliction of her amazing physical looks was tiresome and, naturally, she craved a more meaningful relationship. Consequently, she had not done much dating over the past few years whilst waiting for Mr. Right to come along.

She had met Cash through work and they had become good friends. He talked about Brody a few times over those formative years and a lot more recently; the prospect of him working alongside the two of them intrigued Cash and he had set about the task of pushing the two towards each other. Charley, even without the encouragement Cash had secretly been edging her with, would now quickly form a new and even closer friendship with Brody. The three bonded well. Consequentially, they would see a lot of each other in and out of work. Charley yearned for commitment at this time in her life, not machismo, and Brody was not properly sure he was even looking, let alone know what he might be looking for. Both had found each other and neither fully realised it yet.

Due partly to his sabbatical away from the courting world, he managed to convince himself that she would not be single for very long. It was slowly dawning on him that in the last eight years or so he had not even kissed a girl let alone shared a relationship. In an emotional turmoil he was unable to contain himself for long and asked Charley out on a date the third week into his new job as head of future transportation development. However, regardless of his persistence of asking in complete earnest or even in jest nearly every day from then onwards, although they saw each other socially with Cash and without, not once did she agree to see him for what he considered a proper date. 'Just friends' was the cliché and romance seemed to be far from her agenda, much to Brody's frustration. They often socialised together with Cash and his wife. Not once did they fall out, but the proper date had so far never materialised. Brody comforted himself that it was his age. Charley just pushed her true feelings back and denied the inevitable. Both were aware there was something between them but neither realised just how powerful it might yet be.

Brody's new job kept him from getting too frustrated. It was based around an attempt to solve the theoretical issues of transportation of living matter through multiple phases of reality that, if successful, had the potential to massively increase the range, ability and speed of the current normal site-to-site molecular transportation devices. It was a complex and mentally taxing task and enough to distract the most lovelorn. Normal site-to-site transport was commonplace and had been in regular use on a global scale for years. Over the months and years to come, Brody worked on and developed these theories and, after some small interim successes, came to affectionately refer to the new development ideas as his 'baby' "My amazing discovery of a new inter-phase travel system." If he could contain his bravado and make it work, access to the Universe as it currently stood would literally change within the next couple of decades; cars, trains and other such forms of multiple passenger movement were already used solely for entertainment and recreation these days and freight had been transported by site-to-site for fifteen years or more.

What people wanted now was the ability to reach out into space and be able to travel to distant places, not just within their own solar system or lifespan, but anywhere and instantly. Not as a one-off journey that would take up most of a person's life. Not as a one-way trip, but as a jaunty day trip or holiday. The time factors had always been the big issue back in the rocket era.

Cash was the one who put all these theories Brody was trying to develop onto a PCB, so they could enter the physical world. Between the two of them they were very close to making the breakthrough that might change the future and make history.

Let us now fast forward to Saturday 3rd April 2038; just under two years since Brody joined the company.

"Morning, Charley," called Brody as he entered the reception area, having already spotted his heart's desire from outside the building. He had seen her stunning outline sitting at her desk through the huge viewing window, way before she saw him.

'*I am only* 'nearly' *forty*,' he thought to himself with an air of self-reassuring confidence while gazing intently into those hypnotic green eyes that were, as usual, so desperately trying to avert his stare.

"You are looking even more gorgeous than ever today! Dinner later tonight at seven, then a concert." It was a statement with acuity to try not to give her any opportunity to refuse. He knew only too well that would be her default, as usual.

"My treat for you having to come in to work 'specially, on a Saturday, because of me." He never missed a chance to work on her resolve; having met and fallen in love with this girl just under two years ago, it was now his mission in life to get her to fall for him. As is the way, the things you want most are often the hardest things to get so he had pretty much resigned himself to the fact that she would never see him in that way.

He had patiently used his boyish good looks, cheek and charm continually since first meeting her, to get her to go on a serious date with him – so far without a single meaningful success. Charley was used to him rolling his ice blue eyes at her when asking her to date him. By now she always witnessed the little furrow appear on his brow moments before he let slip his latest opening gambit – it had become like a little poker tell.

Naïvely, he still didn't really know why she continued to play hard to get because she flirted regularly and always dressed, in his eyes, completely provocatively. It always ended up with a polite 'no' somewhere in the day, always leaving him feeling like she wanted him to keep trying.

Charley was always flattered but had been in quite a few no-hope relationships in the past with guys who obsessed about her body and never challenged her mind or were just control freaks not wanting her to even look at another man, let alone talk to one. She tended to rebuff him as a matter of course if he was remotely trivial in his approach, waiting patiently for that moment when he showed his true colours and gave her the impression that he was in fact properly serious. She needed to know for sure that he was not just after the usual things that most eager men were after when asking her out.

Deep down she knew he was serious but not sure how much. Cash had sold her the goods but described the sell-by date incorrectly, so to speak. Brody had unfortunately not been in on the deal so was not aware he had been match made, and thus constantly bigged up his fun side and downplayed the serious guy that he was totally capable of being. Typical of Brody, it never occurred to him that he might be wrong and that another approach might be more successful. He just assumed, as any good salesman would do, that a 'no' today is only a 'not now' and that sooner or later his charm, charisma, persistence and continuity of approach would prevail.

And then out of the blue…

"If you would just take a chill pill, dump Bruce, listen to some less evil-sounding music and generally lighten up a bit about work, you may eventually, possibly notice that I might just actually be quite interested. So, how about you take my provisional yes and work with it…" The reply was a little more aggressive than normal, but to Brody's blinkered way of thinking, it still seemed to be leading to a hidden, later to be revealed, 'no thanks'. He consulted with his precious Bruce with the merest of glances at his left hand, which held the little monster, secretly smiled to himself and decided to try and call her bluff…

"OK, I'll do it. I'll get rid of him once and for all, I promise."

Without saying another word, he triumphantly turned on his heel and walked out of the reception area, not allowing Charley the chance to call him on his feeble, weakly played and hopefully bluffed hand. It was a classy but cheaply executed partial close. He whistled as he entered the corridor but promptly gave up , as it was as tuneless as ever. As usual, he decided to pop into Cash's lab on the way up the corridor; he glanced at the twin wolf logo on the door as the auto mechanism slid back and he entered.

Cash was a big football fan, but they supported different teams; a subject of many a debate, but not right now.

"You won't believe it, mate!" He excitedly went on to explain his latest apparent failure *or* triumph with Charley and the attempted bluff. Having received a humorous, laid-back and casual response as normal from Cash, he left and continued up the corridor towards the lift and his potential destiny. His thoughts that day, although coloured deeply with all things Charley, were mostly centred on his pre-arranged meeting with the owner of the company, Mr. Harris, to discuss the latest developments and his very close proximity to a final solution.

Cash, Charley and a few other staff members had been called in to open the offices and labs especially on a Saturday to facilitate this potential ground-breaker of a meeting Brody had scheduled with the owner of the company.

The meeting was only three minutes away and since he hadn't, in all the time he had worked there, actually *met* his boss, he was naturally on edge. He was sure he'd seen the elusive executive more than once in the last few months but whenever he tried to touch base with him; he just seemed to disappear...

'One more test,' he thought and darted into his lab. The annoying little squeak of his door sliding open was not even noticeable on

this occasion as he concentrated on getting every detail perfect. As he considered, "I certainly don't want any schoolboy errors creeping in to spoil the triumph or steal my thunder"; it occurred to him that this was exactly the way his father used to say things. He hadn't thought much about his parents over the last few years, work had blocked even sentimentality. He heaved a sigh as much for their memory as for the fact that he categorically didn't want *any* mistakes at this extremely late stage of possibly the most important game he had ever dreamt of playing.

The lab was as usual, immaculately pre-set up – ready and set for a full demonstration after the planned meeting, but Brody being very fastidious wanted to test everything one last time – he still had just about enough time to do so. He adjusted everything on the calibration board by memory, stepped into the transportation pod and whispered to himself,

"What does this button do?" Without a second glance, he hit the remote commit button…

Moments after hitting the button, the external commit switch activated and the mag-lock spun and clicked, locking him inside the transportation pod and initiating the travel programme he had previously meticulously set. As he glanced out of the inspection window his office looked strangely different to normal and somehow empty. He couldn't place it, but it sat niggling in his mind. A moment of panic hit and he flashed a glance over to the return pod which sat only three metres away, but his fears were instantly allayed when he saw the glow of the red light in the return window that told him all systems were on and functioning normally.

After more than a year of running backwards and forwards calling either Cash or Charley to come and flick the commit switch on the control panel to help him travel and continue testing, he had recently decided to forgo some of the safety aspects of this system and had rigged up an internal red tooth wireless laser remote. This enabled him to work alone and not have to wait for Cash to finish his coffee or Charley to get off the phone.

His big red button was designed as homage to all the post-apocalyptic movies of his youth and a nod to a literary publication by the lead singer of his favourite band who had recently released their autobiography.

He loved both Cash and Charley dearly in very different ways but wanted to push on and break the coding issues that were holding back the progression of his inter-phase transportation theories. He had continually, for many months, felt only moments away from the breakthrough but for the past few weeks was beginning to doubt his own resolve. It seemed that often the data that returned from each new transport test, although physically perfect and fully successful, strangely uncovered more inconclusive evidence that the process was not completely stable. It was as if someone was in the workings, laying traps for him, trying to test him or trip him up.

Brody was struggling to get his head around these extra pieces of information that were so small and innocuous but all of which needed to be fully understood. They must all be proven to be completely extraneous and not worthy of any further research before he could safely put hand on heart and go to his boss with a watertight suggestion.

A suggestion that might, if accepted, lead to full production prototypes of his ground-breaking phase transporter pod system being manufactured. Suggestions that may, in fact, change the world. He had vague recollections that when the first site-to-site molecular disruption transporters had been put into general localised usage, poor pre-launch safety protocols had been implemented.

Brody was no historian but did remember that a company called Newman-Phillips Tic-Toc Industries had proceeded far too fast back then, trying to leapfrog others to lead the field but with catastrophic results. He had read about their even earlier tenuous experimentation with direct time travel that was equally fraught and was eventually cancelled after only one year. He felt that if his ideas were to revolutionise the site-to-site travel industry as he thought they would he *had* to get things perfect. There must be zero risk to human life, so although he had done this proof of the pudding experiment over twenty times already this week and well over six hundred and fifty times in the past year, he knew that it was not just he that was a little on the OCD side; well, he knew he was, but…

'One more test couldn't hurt.' Momentarily, he allowed his mind to drift, thinking,

'What would the good doctor say?..'

"What am I, a doctor or a moon shuttle conductor?" As he repeated the famous line to himself a smile spread across his face as he readied himself for the slightly nauseous feeling that came with inter-phase travel. As he glanced around, he felt certain in his periphery that he had seen the shadow of someone leaving his lab. Could it have been Mr. Harris checking on his progress? He gritted his teeth and hoped not, he wasn't quite ready. Just another thirty seconds or so whilst he travelled a few thousand million miles and back just to prove a point to himself… again.

The theory he had been progressing was based on the now common belief within scientific communities around the world that the Universe was multi-phased. It was generally agreed that every single event had infinite possibilities and outcomes, all of which were linked to the physicality of the original event itself. It was also a relatively accepted surety that alternate planes of existence would be the result of these phases shifting within the fabric of space and time. By attempting to manipulate these temporary but regularly occurring phase shifts, it was considered possible to move objects between reality planes instantaneously using a drastically modified narrow path or beam of molecular distortion. This would glamorise the near perfect accuracy of the term "Beam me up", an overused line from an infamous sci-fi drama.

'It's way deep, un-comprehendible shite', he remembered Cash having said, the first time he had explained it to his friend over a beer. But belief in parallel planes, alternate universes, so-called wormholes and the dynamic forces they all exerted upon each other over the years, had led scientists to reconsider whether breaking the speed of light was ever going to be the cure-all for travelling long distances that most had assumed it would be.

Brody had been trying to unlock these mind-blowing secrets and possibilities using his newly developed ideas on multi-phase technology, combined with the more standard molecular transportation devices in use. These had been further developed and virtually perfected years ago by the Brundle Corp; the horrors of Newman-Phillips' failures that surfaced previously ensured they had been ultra-cautious.

All of that had not happened overnight and certainly not without its own issues. Most of these developments had occurred before the amalgamation of the aforementioned Brundle Corp; with one of its main competitors, Brown Science Developments.

'I would have loved to have been a fly in the fan for that negotiation,' he mused and smiled to himself for his clever working in of a mixed metaphor and an inane film reference at the same time. The joining of these two companies had not only ushered in a worldwide ban on time vortex technology development. It had also led to the creation of the scientific industry giant Brundle-Brown Incorporated, for whom he now worked, alongside his old friend Cash and new challenging friend and potential life partner, Charley.

It had long been believed that incredible leaps in man's ability to transport himself over massive distances were literally only a single innovation away. Brody now genuinely thought he had discovered the final missing link in that innovation chain, the link that all other striving scientists had been searching for over the years – the holy grail of transportation theory. Could he now possibly ignore the conflicting data as insignificant minutiae and just go to the meeting with Mr. Harris regardless?

'One more test will do it.' He was fully convinced this was so and braced himself for the meeting more than the transportation itself. The sickly feeling he was pre-empting stemmed from the main issue with standard molecular transport. It is not possible to disassociate or reform memory engrams at the same speed as normal atoms, molecules and physical DNA. Memories have no physical form so react totally differently when dissociated from their holding vessel – the brain itself. Thus, a feeling of travel sickness tended to occur for a few seconds as the brain, in effect, was being reprogrammed with the same information that it had before transport initiation. For now, his expectation of this common nauseous experience was the least of his concerns.

One of the major planned off-shoots of the transport technology, which Brody was so excited about, was the potential to use this stomach-churning temporal lag to develop a method of curing all cancers. The simple collection of a person's dissociated particles mid transport could theoretically filter out the disease. Reassembly of everything held in flux minus the offending malignancy was the hope. He grimaced to himself as he considered the word – 'simple'. It seemed so inappropriate in any sentence that described molecular transport. This was one of the main reasons why Brody was so completely consumed with getting things exactly right because he had extensive personal experience of the ravages of this terrible disease. Even in today's advanced world of high technology it still haunted him that nobody had yet cured this monster that had robbed him of so many friends and family in the past.

The ramifications of his success and how else it might be used were meteoric in their potential future influence on mankind's development and actual survival. He wanted to be the one to lead these developments forward. It had all occurred so fast, even he was amazed some days at how far his work had progressed in such a short space of time. "Inspired" was how he had described it when asked at various press conferences over the past few months.

The feeling he was expecting started to well within him and he mentally braced himself again. He knew from extensive experience that it only lasted a second or so on a transport of this distance. The fact that the two transportation pods in his lab were only a few metres apart was, by the technology of the day, largely irrelevant. Physical distances could now be measured easily. 'Phasically' – this word wasn't even in the dictionary but was the term Brody decided should be used to describe it and he repeated it to himself aloud now as if to reinforce its validity.

"Phasically…mmmm…phasically…I like it."

Transported items could theoretically be moved millions or even potentially billions of miles in moments by using the temporary creation of conduits between alternate planes of reality, wormholes and the boundaries between parallel universes. In his tests, no destination was required or even possible as, via Brundle-Brown Inc, he owned the only two pods of this type in existence. His total physical travelled distance was still a mathematical equation only fully provable as and when new pods could eventually be placed at other appropriately distanced sites. He had already amazed the scientific community nearly as much as himself with the speed of these developments over the past year.

The use of single pod transport had been perfected some years ago by using a similar system to the now outdated and ancient mobile phone networks and, with millions of old-style pods placed around the globe, external travel was now commonplace. Although transportation pod to pod was considered to be the safest method, the current network of pods meant that external travel was the general and convenient norm.

All Brody's new innovations were strangely beholden to this existing technology. His new suitably modified pods would at some point, if proven completely successful, need to be transported to their new locations using old-style transporter beaming or the comparatively slow-moving impulse drive space vehicles. The pod networks of the earth were naturally restricted by gravity. Transportations of this type over greater distances than a few thousand miles were classified as unsafe due to the networks themselves not being stable enough to hold the patterns of the item being sent in stasis, long enough for accurate re-integration.

If interstellar phased transport was to become the new thing that Brody was striving for, breaking out of Earth's gravitational pull was one of the major technological hurdles he must leap.

To help things along with speed over distance issues, the sci-fi films' fabled warp drive had many times been attempted by other scientists but had not yet got anywhere near its historic feature film success.

Brody always marvelled at how many of the current science facts seemed to have been initiated by forward thinkers and were based on TV programme content. Brody thought of himself along these lines, "If it could be dreamt up it could be made to happen," he always used to say. With one of his own mottos ringing in his ears he knew only too well that his calculations and theories had to be completely accurate. With only minor data return question marks that needed ironing out, Brody was supremely confident, but he knew even a single error would probably not be acceptable to his bosses and if he were to succeed towards commercial development, perfection would be expected.

Cash holstered his steaming soldering iron, picked up his internal phone and dialled '1' for Charley's office extension. She answered within one ring having expected the call.

"Has he gone up?"

"No, I think I heard his lab door squeak, so I reckon one of his compulsions has kicked in and he has gone to tidy up or reorganise his files. Don't worry; I'll let you know as soon as he comes down. Chill a bit and trust me – he is going to nail it."

"I pretty much said yes to a date for tonight and he genuinely sounded like he might ditch Bruce." Her trailing voice gave away the questioning lack of confidence in the last four words.

"Yeah, I heard, but I wouldn't bank on the Bruce bit. You two need to get sorted. I'm getting bored waiting for the engagement party." Cash laughed quietly and could hear Charley sigh softly in response.

"I don't want to affect his work right now, it's very important to him." She dragged possibly her most feeble excuse out yet, especially for Cash.

"You can keep making excuses; I know you, Charley, and I know you two will be perfect for each other," Cash responded firmly.

"Yeah, I know, but I just want to hear some commitment in his voice. I know it sounds stupid, but as you well know, I have had my fair share of show boaters, tough guys, sex-obsessed idiots and control freaks. Since you did the sales job before we even met and all the nights out with you and Allia, I have seen many sides to him and I love them all except this false front he seems to want to protect himself with. I know it isn't really him and all I want is a bit of good old-fashioned love and attention. I'm scared he might only want to be casual," she questioned herself now more than Cash.

Allia was Cash's wife. She and Charley had become close friends over the past couple of years, the two regularly gossiping about more interesting things than astrophysics and transporting a molecule here or there.

"You can trust me, girl, as far as you are concerned, casual is not even a word he knows exists. He absolutely loves the bones of you." Her cheeks flushed red and she hesitated, not sure what to say next.

Back in pod one, Brody believed wholeheartedly he was ready. As on all six hundred and sixty-five previous tests, regardless of minor resultant data conflict, he had always got one hundred percent categorical physical success.

Why then was he suddenly feeling sick to his stomach and reeling within the pod? Before he could answer this question or his gut could regurgitate his breakfast, he passed out cold and fell to the floor. An unknown period passed… He eventually awoke and got shakily to his feet.

CHAPTER 4

The King and Others.

The sweat was dripping from his brow as the mag-lock on the transportation pod door spun, finally clicked and the door slid back. A wave of emotion coursed through his system and he felt faint again as he realised he was not back in his lab or even in the return pod where he should have been. He was still in pod one and the outside environment seemed to have changed, a fact that contradicted all his understandings of the science he was trying to further. Both pods were bolted down to their earthing plates and so could not move.

"I can't hear much but reckon I saw someone milling about through the glass a second ago. Better go, I'll call you if I hear anything else." Cash comforted Charley knowing that she really wanted to progress her relationship with Brody, but he knew his friend was very prone to flippancy when not head down at work – it was his way of coping.

"Thanks, Cash." She blew her friend a kiss down the phone and gently replaced the receiver. She was anxious because after many casual relationships that had gone nowhere, she had become guarded about letting anyone in to her true feelings. Brody had broken that on day one and she had fallen for him very soon after meeting him. It was a little primordial and she was not quite sure why, but he intrigued her. Physical attraction aside, she wanted to understand him and saw a frightened man hiding behind humour. Not for over a year had she realised that the disconcerting pangs she felt whenever he entered the room was her growing attraction to this enigmatic anomaly that was Brody Martins. After all Cash and Allia's partisan encouragement she loved him now for certain, but she was holding back because she knew he was right on the cusp of a big and important development. Excuses were easier than letting her guard down and openly admitting to herself that if they had a future together, she might need to change as much as he, in acceptance of who they both were and what they truly wanted, if nothing else. Mentally, she promised herself to let him in on her real feelings next time.

Brody tried to comfort himself with humour and spoke to himself with a mixture of sarcasm and worry.

"Did the Earth move for you, babe?" He couldn't even muster a smile in response to his own frivolous question and stared blankly out of the pod. Neither his normal predilection for humour or the habitual thinking about Charley and her apparent unwillingness to fall for him as he had done for her two years ago, were of any comfort now.

He heaved a huge sigh of 'no going back now' proportions, then very tentatively took his first Armstrong-esque small step out of the pod. He was not mentally prepared for the giant leap into the complete unknown he was just about to take…

Incredibly, what he saw in front of him as he stepped outside of the pod was a wide beach scene with what looked like a huge Viking ship in the distance.

"What the f…?" he said out loud, but his words trailed away to nothing.

Taking a moment or two to steady himself from the dizzy

experience, he stepped cautiously further out. With his feet in casual loafers he sank into the crisp sugary sand.

'It's real'. The mere thought was astounding let alone the reality.

"It is actually REAL!" His anxious thoughts spilled from his lips but still he bent and touched the sand in disbelief, running his fingers through it like an excited child, a child at the seaside for the first time, having never seen the sea let alone a Viking ship. It wasn't excitement he had felt though. He had been to the beach many times with some happy and sad memories, even one particularly hilarious seagull-related incident flashed through his head.

Just as his family's completely over the top reaction to the accidental seagull injury was, all those years ago, there was no time now for hilarity. He was certainly not as amused by the flash recollection as he usually would have been.

This was just not right. He shook his head to clear his thoughts of the past. He knew only too well that he should, by rights, still be in his lab returning from a twenty-five second, two-billion-mile phased transportation that he had successfully completed so many times before.

'What has happened? What could possibly have gone wrong?' As he started to try to compute the possibilities while thoughts were randomly jostling for position in his mind, he was promptly interrupted by the sound of the transportation pod door beginning to slide shut behind him. Letting go of all the computations as he turned to see the whole pod fading from vision, he desperately dived goalkeeper-like; clutching at the disintegrating image he grabbed only air as he landed firmly on the soft, warm sand where the pod had previously stood.

Panic now began to edge into his mind.

'You have got to be shitting me; is this for real? Where am I? How is this even possible?' Uneasily he felt that, given enough time, his

self-questioning could have been infinite, but at that very moment another distraction saved him from the endless possibility of eternal wonderment – a voice calling, seemingly loud but audibly faint, as if from a long way off. Turning to his left he immediately saw a large long-haired figure running full pelt towards him looking very agitated and excited, waving his arms and pointing out to sea.

"We must run to get help. The Norsemen will be here before the day is out; the tide is against them, but they hoist sails and make ready to land. I only see one ship but who knows how many are on their way. Run now; come on. Come with me," the big man called in an authoritative way as he flew past at full sprint. As if there were an echo, Brody thought he also heard another voice.

'Do not trust him,' it whispered in the background but it sounded as if it was shouted from inside his head and he realised he had not really heard the words but felt them.

The apparent sincerity in the big man's voice was enough, however, to encourage Brody to follow him, if nothing else but to have someone to talk to about where he was. How he got here. And more importantly, now that the pod had disappeared, how was he going to get home again? All these questions needed answering but as he looked closer at this new and unusual arrival's attire it did not fill him with confidence that he would be able to supply any meaningful answers.

This man looked more like a high-ranking Anglo-Saxon warrior dressed for battle than any scientist he felt he needed and his agitated mention of Norsemen seemed to add weight to that supposition.

'But surely then, this must be a dream.' He felt sure that no parallel plain or alternate phase could reproduce this era so accurately and concurrent to his own – at least not by any science he understood; not without time travel and that was currently

way beyond the human race's capabilities or, even to some degree, logical comprehension.

'How can I be here? How can this be real?' As he began to run he glanced out to sea and saw the big square-shaped sail of what now looked most definitely like a Viking longboat, starting to furl. It seemed to further indicate that he was witnessing a historic event or some weird off-shoot of something somehow created hundreds of years ago in an alternate plain to that which he regarded as Earth's history.

"What year is this?" he called to his now more distant running companion as he increased his pace to catch up with the stranger. The long-haired man halted and spun round to face him with a spear in one hand and shield in the other.

"What year? That seems an unusual question to ask a stranger. Why would you need to know?" At least he spoke the same language.

"Have yea lost your mind?" the tall man barked in further reply. Brody momentarily considered Kyle Reece and felt like saying 'yes' but thought better of it and quickly retorted,

"Errrr, no, I was hit on the head weeks ago accidentally by a friend and sometimes unusual things spill forth. Please forgive me, My Lord." His quick-thinking, weak attempt to mimic an olde English Anglo-Saxon accent and style of speech seemed to have gone unnoticed. Internally he breathed a sigh of relief as he had no real idea of how he should try to sound to this apparent historic character who, if nothing else, undeniably now stood before him as a reality of at least flesh and bone. As unbelievable as it seemed, they were both there and what might happen next, he could not even dream to imagine.

"What makes you think that I am a Lord?" the apparent warrior enquired. Thinking quickly and taking in every detail Brody replied as confidently as possible,

"Your shield, Sir, it has your crest on it so I assumed you must be a Lord." His blustered reply was hidden by years of experience in confident sales patter and a love of Jeremy Brett as Sherlock Holmes.

"My name is Alfred, King Alfred," came the incredible and high-toned reply that scrubbed some of the shine off Brody's outward confidence.

'He lies,' the Echo whispered loudly into his very consciousness. Brody hesitated a second, confused. He shook his head slightly as if to dislodge the echo from his mind and quickly dropped to one knee. He knew vague snippets of history and one thing he now remembered from his grade E GCSE fail was that kings usually had guards nearby and impertinence could quite easily be considered treasonous.

Servility seemed a good choice whilst he tried to hatch a plan to learn more and ultimately get out of this crazy situation. Although his attempt to talk in an old-fashioned way had probably not held water, his body language might have covered the cracks.

"Arise, friend, we are all at war together and I have no need of such platitudes, they serve me nothing. Where is your shield and spear?" Now he was struggling, apparently standing in front of King Alfred the Great dressed in chinos, a T-shirt and loafers.

"Stolen," was his best and quickest comeback. The light breeze blowing in from the sea wafted the apparent King's long hair around. that was, for some reason, the wrong colour in Brody's mind. He stood well over six feet tall. His face was young of colour and complexion but had an older look of experience. Brody couldn't fathom it and felt uneasy.

"Matter not, come back to the village with me and my men will equip you. The Norse approach and, after the recent episode at Lindisfarne, we know they take few prisoners." Brody was now in a tricky spot and had a decision to make, and fast. He didn't want to leave the beach and risk losing sight of the area where he might at some point relocate his missing pod, but he certainly didn't want to potentially be plundered, raped or pillaged by marauding Viking warriors either.

The two had only run a few hundred yards away from his arrival point but he noticed the tidal wash had flattened the ground somewhat and ensured that he dragged his feet deep into the firm damp sand to tenuously mark the spot. He reluctantly fell in behind this rather laid-back self-proclaimed King as he turned and headed inland.

'Laid-back.' The thought made him consider his other life for a moment and his best friend Cash.

'Would he be worried? Did he still even exist? What about Charley?' His day-to-day thoughts usually ended in thinking about Charley in one way or another but now a new pang was evident, something he had never experienced before. He had the sudden realisation that he may never see her or Cash for that matter, *ever* again.

The two strangely mismatched travelling companions climbed up the steep dunes and walked along the coastal track that led up to a cliff top path. They left the breezy beach behind and Brody thought he would try asking him the question again as he had not seen a single guard on their travel so far.

"Apologies, Your Majesty, and no wish to offend, but what year is it, please?" He asked very cautiously this time.

"Your head troubles you more, I see. Eight hundred and sixty-eight is your answer for what good it might serve you." The reply was curt and slightly sarcastic.

'Did they even have sarcasm in the year eight hundred and sixty-eight?'

"How is it that Your Majesty travels unguarded in such times of trouble, may I enquire?" Brody ventured, thinking that, although this looked and sounded like Anglo-Saxon England it probably wasn't and, in this alternate reality, he might benefit from learning the protocols of the day.

"King is but a title these days, young Sir. I carry it like a stone weight on some days and with pride on others and although I have royal privilege, no monarch for centuries has set themselves aside from those whom they serve," he answered in a tired but proud sort of way. This was very interesting to Brody and totally different from today's monarchy, well *his* today at least, which now, ironically, might be his future or his past, dependent completely on how the scenario eventually panned out.

"I see, but it still seems quite a risky way to travel. I mean, I could have been an assassin and you would have been defenceless," Brody probed with underlying questions, just a little deeper and with slightly less caution.

"I said that King is a title and kings do not set themselves aside. I said nothing of travelling unguarded or being vulnerable. If you had been an assassin or in any way, a threat, you would already be dead. Did you not see the others that protect me?" His response and question were both sharp and seemingly very cryptic.

"Errrr, no. I saw nobody; they must be amazingly well camouflaged, Your Majesty." He attempted to cover his indiscretion with the transparency of a poor compliment.

"You will see them when they wish to be seen," Alfred further confused Brody with his quick riddle-like rebuttal. They travelled on in silence together for the next few hours and it started to get darker as the oddly large and crimson coloured sun started to set behind them. He felt sure it had been more orange earlier and puzzled at this stark change on a clear day. Brody had not noticed this anomaly before but, as it dropped behind the horizon spreading a pinky-gold hue across the outstretching countryside, he glanced over his shoulder and realised that this celestial body was certainly not the sun that he was accustomed to seeing from the beaches of England, Earth.

This fact seemed to reinforce his growing belief that this was not England or even Earth. In the bright haze he thought he could see a lone horseman silhouetted against the golden black horizon and was not sure whether to be perturbed or comforted by this sight. Another human being, at least.

'Is that one of the 'others'?' he thought to himself. Turning back towards the path they were walking on, he enquired more carefully,

"Begging your pardon, Your Majesty, where are we heading to, please?" He was being a little more guarded, trying not to further antagonise his new companion.

"The village," was the now somewhat expectedly cryptic and unrevealing answer.

"Not far to go now and we will be safe for today, at least. The sea is our defence but it will not be long before a ship of that size moors and landing crafts are despatched," was the swiftly added detail delivered with an air of complete confidence.

"More longboats have been sighted; the evidence of war has begun," the King announced moments later, very matter-of-fact. Brody was once again lost.

'How can he know more boats have been sighted? We haven't seen anyone along this whole journey.' His thoughts had hardly registered in his own mind when they were answered.

"The others speak to me without speaking aloud – that is how I know." This reply shook Brody to the core as he realised this incarnation of Alfred the Great or whoever he was, was truly great and able to read his thoughts! Without consideration for the potential new audience he had just been told about, he started mulling the possibilities this had uncovered.

'What other surprises are in store?' And he wondered how he could explain himself safely if every thought he had now was to be an open book to this alleged King.

"I sense you are not of this realm and are seeking transport to another place. If we survive this latest invasion..." he paused for a second as if reconsidering telling a secret, "...ye olde sacred book may hold your answers." The stutter in the King's inexplicable sentence did not register as anything important but did spring another shock – not only could he definitely read Brody's thoughts but was apparently advanced enough to comprehend the situation he was in. As if to deliberately further confuse, he stopped in his tracks, turned towards Brody and made a loud and seemingly quite random proclamation.

"Gort, Klaatu, Barada, Nicto... Remember these words, my strange new friend. Later, things will become clearer and when the time is right, with the *Necronomicon* open, recant them aloud. Consume them to avoid the others gaining knowledge of these powers." The statement was completely lost on Brody, he was baffled and had to mentally search for understanding as the King continued and reiterated his peculiar statement even louder.

"**Gort, Klaatu, Barada, Nicto**...Recant and consume and you alone will gain the power that you require." With this seemingly completely unintelligible and random group of statements the King fell silent and stayed that way for the remainder of the journey.

Brody had never before met a King but this seemed the strangest King he had ever met and he tried his best to hold on to blank thoughts to save confusing things further as he attempted to mentally decipher and understand the conundrum that the strange monarch had bestowed upon him. Above all else he was now intrigued as to why the weird statement was to be kept from the elusive and yet, unseen, others.

'If they were so trusted to ensure the King's safety, why would there be a worry about them hearing something so easily passed on to a stranger?' It seemed somewhat suspicious.

'And also, who and where, actually, are these, 'others'?' As they arrived at the village the strange-coloured large 'sun' finally slipped below the still visible cliffs behind them. Darkness began to enshroud the pair but before pitch black arrived, an eerie glow started to rise to both left and right horizons.

"The twin moons will rise and the Norse will rest for now but tomorrow we must battle to survive. Many Nordic fighting men will come, their swords and shields will gleam in the sun." The King spoke confidently in what seemed more like a public announcement than a silence-breaking friendly comment. It also felt to be in some way a semi pre-emptive explanation, as Brody had just been deliberating the possible causes of the increasing light at either side of him.

"Will you call your people to arms to defend yourselves? Should I get ready to stand and fight, or will you try to negotiate a treaty for your lives?" Brody enquired all this in his best olde English questioning drawl, trying to get information to build a mental picture of his new surroundings and future possibilities.

"I am unsure what it is, that you think that you mean, by saying, 'my people' in that way," Alfred commented. Brody attempted to explain himself. The concept was strangely lower in complexity than those that he had already seen evidence of being understood. Simpler by far than any that this strange being who claimed to be King Alfred the Great had already exhibited a full comprehension of.

"People, Brethren, Citizens, Populous, Community," were the best suggestions Brody could come up with and the explanation of his earlier statement was easily understood by Alfred, but he himself did not immediately understand the next reply.

"There are no people, my friend, only us two and the others together now, safe in the village." Alfred had obviously understood but the answer to Brody's explanation and his various descriptions of his new acquaintance's unseen countrymen were perplexing to him.

"How can it be that there is only us two and some random others whom I am yet to see? You mentioned earlier 'my men', didn't you?" he asked, accentuating the other man's earlier apparent continuity error and risking a progression of his cross-examination, now not even considering his rightful place or status.

"Why would the Vikings send armies and boats to defeat one man and his private guard – surely they cannot even know of my existence?" He probed deeper, throwing caution to the wind with anxious impatience.

"It seems I lost you. Trust me, I am not in contradiction. It merely seems you struggle to comprehend my fuller meaning," came the contrary reply that sounded more like a weak cover story for an earlier mistake.

"Friend... A king is merely the conduit from whence the others draw strength. My life wanes and what was left of the people, as you call them, have all been dead or dying since the Vikings' last attack at Lindisfarne. The sea defends but the others and I are all that remain." He seemed to be rambling, perhaps deliberately to confuse.

"The Norse seek our powers for their own ends, the others and I are the last of m–... our kind." His explanation seemed weak and he had started to say 'my' not 'our', but then he switched down another track completely throwing Brody into a new complexity.

"If we can survive until the next triclipse day we will be able to regenerate ourselves again, but I doubt we can survive that long. The triclipse is nearly two years away and the Norsemen know this only too well so plan to defeat us before then and take the power we control." Brody was initially dumbfounded by the new information but then strangely started to grasp the concept, not because the explanation had been a good one or because he was super-intelligent to work it all out for himself but more as if it was being slowly placed into his subconscious for him to draw on as a weird new memory of his own.

He now started to understand and half-remembered that Alfred was apparently some sort of a host for a mentally connected symbiotic race who had nearly been destroyed by their Viking enemies. They desperately needed to survive until the two moons and sun coincided their orbits for some celestial event to regenerate the remnants of the species. This completely blew the reality of him being the real or even phase related alternate version of Alfred the Great. Still, he was here and Brody needed to find more information, but how could he help to fight a whole army of invading Vikings, and either way…

'How do I suddenly now know all this? And what was he on about earlier with the Gort, Klaatu stuff?' After contemplating in the pregnant pause left by his inability to reply to the now doubtful King's statement, he thought he had pieced the puzzle together, or perhaps subconsciously it was being pieced together for him. With perfect timing, the Echo whispered an explanatory but equally cryptic message of support for his developing feelings about these ideas, directly and vociferously into his now spinning head.

'You cannot trust him, he plants information in your mind for you to find and not much of it is accurate.' Brody glanced around looking for whoever said or transmitted the thoughts he heard in his head. He was distracted from the pursuit of the answer as he started to notice tiny dots of white light in regular patterns of two appearing in the undergrowth and around the building edges of

what, by now, he assumed to be the village meeting rooms.

'What next, rabid dogs?' He questioned himself and wondered where the thought of dogs had come from. It worried him and he started to move away from the bushes and seek the safety of open ground, which was confusing in itself as he didn't usually scare easily.

'Can it get worse?' A cold feeling of foreboding swept over him as he reached Alfred's position by the meeting room doors. He desperately wanted to barge in for the safety of a more sheltered and civilised surrounding, but the strength of his ego held him back.

"The others have arrived," Alfred announced. Brody relaxed, realising his error. Not dogs after all, so he relaxed more as if instructed to, but he felt uneasy and not in control of himself.

The two pale moons, one a warm pink and one contrasting with a cool blue were already both past their zenith and morning sunlight approached fast. This strange new world he found himself in seemed to move very quickly. He had only been here for a few hours of daylight and what seemed like a mere few short minutes of night and it appeared that the sun would soon rise again bringing with it war and carnage. If Alfred was to be believed, was it his judgement day that had arrived? He wanted to stand his ground but, based on what he had seen and heard so far, he felt he would soon have to be prepared to run.

"They're coming in from the sea," Alfred announced commandingly. He paused as if for effect, then spoke again.

"They've come! The enemy will soon be here. Beneath the blazing sun of this new morning the battle must be fought and it has to be won…Invaders! We must defeat the Invaders." The King's tone had changed from a bold confident proclamation to one of a considerably more frantic feeling. Outwardly, he now seemed to be panicky, but Brody somehow felt this was just a façade for his benefit.

As he turned to see the sun rising, he realised his royal compatriot was now surrounded by the owners of the previously glinting lights in the bushes. Certainly not dogs, they were what could only be best described as a group of seven 1960s-looking school children. They were standing eerily and completely silent around his new King, all with platinum blonde hair…

'The 'others' were children!' Two add two made four now, but here they were as the plus one. It then struck him that they were possibly the originators of his earlier echoing companion.

'We are not children, we are the children of others.' The whispered thought from within his head screamed quietly and unsettled him by its content, but it further confirmed his suspicions and, as if to further explain that it was *them* who were warning him earlier, 'it' spoke again.

'Trust us, not him.' Brody was inexplicably sure he could, but obviously could not communicate back to these new arrivals. As he was trying to think of a way to get a line of dialogue going with these new, others, or children of others as they had described themselves, he stood and watched the silent monarch who seemed to be resigned to the impending defeat and his own potential death. His mind drifted and involuntarily washed clean and the thoughts of the children's communication were gone.

CHAPTER 5

Slaughter. And Learning.

The King slowly raised his arms above the children's blonde heads in a comforting way as they surrounded him, flock of sheep-esque. Brody let go his attempts to untangle the confusion and shouted across to him.

"Your Majesty, should we set ablaze some campfires to alert any remaining men from inland? Surely a warning must be given. There are certainly not enough of us here for a meaningful last stand." The different tones in his own voice sickened him, as he was unused to sucking up and pandering. He somehow felt that a vain attempt to communicate in some ninth century olde English or Saxon twang might help. Considering that the King was probably not even a King and neither of them may survive the next few hours, it suddenly sounded like a stupidly futile pursuit and, in his own head, he was embarrassed by it. He tried to bring his growing panic into more modern terms.

"These Vikings will likely be far too many for us, way too powerful to take on our own. We must get reinforcements, we surely can't dream of **trying to fight this battle alone!**" Brody had started to shout frantically even though he had not yet seen any foe to worry about – he just felt scared as if he had been told to feel that way, again.

He didn't have time to fathom why he was so torn in this way. In stark contradiction to the way his emotional state seemed to be guided, the King spoke but this time more calmly.

"Fear not, my friend, the others will help us. Prepare yourself." An unexpectedly confident response was received, followed by a more rallying cry of preparation.

"Pillaging and looting. They will come over the hill and have come to attack – they will soon be coming in for the kill! There is no turning back, now we must fight!" he boomed, but Brody was at a loss as to how he could do anything meaningful that might help.

He turned back towards the area Alfred was describing but saw nobody and remembered the hill was over two miles away; they had climbed it just before sunset last night, less than two hours ago. The King's arms, no longer just the public house where Brody and Cash sometimes met, were now outstretched; his palms were down. Brody had the strangest feeling as if Alfred was drawing power from the silent children. Their eyes now appeared to be glowing brighter than the cat's eye effect he experienced on their arrival – fierce red – like fires in their expressionless faces.

The children all turned in unison and to Brody it was like watching a flight of the Red Arrows display team creating a flat line ready to peel off at any moment into a final fly-by. But these were not jet planes, they were possibly the remnants of some peculiar race that seemed to be gearing up for the last stand against a superior enemy.

In the distance, as Brody ran over to hopelessly join the King's final display of bravery, he started to hear the rumbling and chanting of the impending enemy attack, obviously as predicted. The sea had apparently not slowed them much and the Viking warriors were now nearly upon the village.

Alfred stood statuesque with eyes closed and seemed to be

concentrating some unseen power via the flame-eyed children. Brody turned helpless, weaponless and scared to see the arrival of thousands of marauding Viking warriors as they charged down the hill. Although they disappeared for a moment in the flat valley they reappeared again en masse, much larger now, spilling one hundred abreast over the village green and heading towards the main hall with the certain destruction of anything in their path being imminent.

As he watched crouching, waiting for an axe, arrow or spear to whizz in and pierce his body, he thought that at least it would be all over quickly and soon. He closed his eyes and thought to pray.

'Don't be ridiculous.' He couldn't succumb to the idea of a higher power, one even capable let alone willing to step in to save them at this their eleventh hour. The screaming and thunder of feet grew and welled in his ears and his imagination; he couldn't look and, for the first time in his life, was truly afraid.

"Not forever, not one hundred and fifty. Not even forty." Brody spoke aloud as he steeled himself and forced his eyes open.

Completely unexpectedly.

Just as if Richard Burton himself had commanded it... Abruptly, the sound ceased.

Immediately the desolation and solitude became unendurable. The scream he was about to release stuck in his throat as he saw before him only metres away as if frozen to the spot, hordes of Norsemen standing mid-charge with pained expressions on their faces, completely unable to move.

The thousands of angry warriors were now all silently held motionless by... Brody looked sideways and was amazed to see Alfred who was now hovering three feet from the ground like some Blaine show or homage to *The Exorcist.* The others, as he had called them, stood beneath his outstretched arms, eyes flaming and heads aloft, pouring their unknown, unseen power through their symbiotic host king and out into the oncoming enemy's path like some sort of force field or invisible deflector shield. As the power emanating from the others reached a pinnacle, the King dropped his arms. The others' flaming red eyes fell cold and black in some eerie kind of 'stare to scare' expression. The silence was deafening and then, without warning, all hell seemed to let loose. For a split second Brody ducked and cowered again, fearing that his new allies had run out of their mysterious power and that momentarily it would all be over.

He cringed on the floor ball-shaped in anticipation of the bloody end but realised he had not been stabbed or cut in two by sword or axe and was still unharmed. All the commotion was due to the Viking warriors frantically battling each other. He now realised what had occurred.

Alfred's ability to mind-read and simultaneously communicate with the symbiotic others had been utilised to create a whole new thought pattern which the others had then transmitted through him and out to the onrushing horde. The result was that the fury of the masses had been channelled back at them and even though they were not aware of it, they were, with their historically well-known aggression, tearing *each other* to pieces and not their enemy.

The sounds of the Vikings' axes grinding together and maces clashing were nearly as painful as the sights he beheld as wounded fighters fell to the ground. Severed limbs, fatal wounds and bloody corpses were aplenty. The smell of death and burning flesh was nauseating but the battle-weary continued to fight to the bitter end. These men seemed not only controlled to attack each other but possessed of greater than normal resilience to injury. Many fought on with cuts and gashes that would normally lay low even the strongest.

One wretched soul shoulder-charged another to the ground but couldn't finish the attack due to his gruesome lack of arms. His confused and angry adversary recovered from the charge and beheaded his countryman with a screaming thrash of a hefty sword. Only then did the intrepid armless soldier rest and fight no longer. Hours later with bodies strewn all over the place and blood flowing in the main square's gutters, silence again reigned as the Vikings had been overpowered – victims of their own mighty Norse aggression. Some scattered and tried to run but the battle was already lost, not won. They tried to escape but inevitably only one could survive this savage slaughter as they were mentally driven to destroy each other.

A single soldier escaped to fight another day, but he was severely injured and would possibly not survive his journey back to the boats that brought him to this, his own personal hell. If he managed to reach the fleet, he would surely be unable to explain how two thousand or more of his marauding countrymen couldn't defeat two old men and some children. No raping. No pillaging. No plundering, just devastating bloody murder. Where would he go next? Valhalla or Fólkvangr.

As Brody looked around he saw death at every turn; blood seemed to stain every wall within his sight; it had been a complete slaughter of the innocents, although to describe them as innocent seemed somewhat misplaced in this context. The Ruben's related term meant little or nothing here but he briefly remembered where he had heard it; another of his father's favourite one line analogies.

'So, who are the good guys?' With such ultimate power exhibited it was hard to tell and seemed unlikely the Vikings would not have experienced this before. It then occurred to him that even if they had seen it all before there would never be anyone sane enough remaining to report the reality of what had happened. It mattered

very little now anyway in the current situation as the 'others' and their king seemed to be the only hope Brody had.

Since his pre-battle relations with Alfred were of a relatively positive nature, he hoped to learn more of Barada, Nicto and the book called *Necronomicon* so that he might seek to escape this growing weirder by the minute alternate state.

Alfred now lay sprawled on the ground looking completely drained, his head resting on the side of the main hall steps. Brody rushed to do whatever he could to assist his apparent saviour. As he approached, he heard from deep within his head,

'Kill him now whilst you have the chance, we cannot do it, but you can.' He spun to see who spoke but realised again that nobody was near and the idea was being planted within him. He didn't know, or even realise that he had ever known who was responsible. He had somehow now forgotten the identity of the owners of the Echo and consequently shrugged and turned back to the prone king.

"Your Majesty, a monumental success, I think," Brody called out confidently as if trying to curry favour.

"How may I be of assistance to your recovery?" His question was phrased in a semi-grovelling tone and, again, it sickened him, but ingratiation seemed a better ploy than just having fingers crossed for a positive response. Alfred forced himself up to his elbow and looked across at Brody.

He was concentrating hard, trying to keep Brody's thoughts from centring, knowing his own subterfuge could only last so long. He knew the children would be trying to undermine him given the opportunity, but for now confusion worked in his favour.

"You did well, my friend, your will is of iron, made on an anvil of glory. Many who witness our transmissions go out of their minds or get mixed up and join the mêlée." Pleased to see he was not portrayed as either the enemy or weak, Brody helped Alfred to his feet and led him over to the others who were all equally disassociated and laying about in various exhausted states.

"Please, you will stay with us for a while whilst we regroup. Triclipse is a long way off but when we regenerate you will be like a new father to the new others; such will be our stories about this famous victory," Alfred gloriously suggested.

"But I did little or nothing, though." Graciously he started to contradict, but Alfred jumped in and the seemingly over-complimentary interruption amused Brody.

"You stood with us when you could have run away – that is enough to earn our respect. You have qualities we all respect." With the feeling that, if they thought so much of him he could perhaps chance his arm, he enquired further as the others started to recover.

"I hate to ask right now at this very moment, but you previously mentioned an incantation of some kind that I could use to help me return to my home that involves some pages of a book I need to read or even eat. Can you fully explain this, please?" His enquiry was confident but shaky and was initially met with no reply from Alfred. The others were silent throughout the whole ordeal.

After a minute or more of this silence, which Brody presumed was spent by Alfred in unheard communication with the others, the King rose and gestured to Brody to follow him. They all trooped towards the village hall. Alfred ascended the six steps, pushed the door open and walked in. Brody followed to the front door, the others remained outside. Alfred went over to a high bookshelf in the corner of the reception room and lifted down a huge volume that looked very old and gnarled. Its cover seemed more like a leathery version of the bark of a tree which had twisted and split and vaguely resembled a tortured face, not too dissimilar from a famous painting Brody remembered.

That image was commonly made into a mask at Halloween and

was used in a series of comedy horror films that were prevalent in his youth. But this was more gruesome than comic. Regardless, he felt he had seen it before.

"You have, by now, probably realised or considered at least that I am not the real King Alfred and that the others, these children, are not biologically related to me. Allow me to explain a little further as I feel we owe you that much." The revelation was no surprise to him, but Brody was intrigued to hear it and wanted to learn more.

"You owe me nothing, Sir, but your explanation may help in more ways than you realise. Please continue," he urged, encouraging Alfred to elaborate.

"With due respect to what you may be able to understand, we are, like you, currently in an alternate phase of reality to our own natural state. Your race's research into this science is extremely close to opening rifts in time and space that, once open, will not be easy for you to close." As Alfred paused, Brody was, not for the first time, realising that he had already had suspicions that this was not a Saxon king and certainly more likely to be a highly advanced alien being of some sort. Either way, he or possibly it, was possessed of great intellect and scientific knowledge and he questioned himself as to how he had forgotten such an obvious thought but his mind retained no explanation. Alfred, on cue, continued.

"Not only will these discoveries allow your improvements in travel, which is what you, like myself have been seeking, but as with any open two-way door, they will work both ways and allow other things access to your phase of reality." Again, he paused for what Brody read as dramatic effect as if his speech had been rehearsed.

"This, my friend, is not a good idea. You are, as a species, not aware of what lies within these other phases and not yet suitably able to deal with them." His explanation was not something that was completely fresh news to Brody. No physical proof or evidence to support widely held theories that touch upon similar ground, had ever been found. Most scientists had long since ruled the possibilities as negligible. Science itself proclaimed that any such phases would be barren of any intelligent life.

As such, the use of these phases as a resource to forward Earth's scientific advancements had always been justified without cause for concern. If these temporary or even permanent phases were not as previously believed – just conduits containing only reflections of alternate realities, but were in fact home to sentient life – all things would have to change. Alfred's next statement completely confirmed all that had just struck Brody, in one almighty lightning bolt of a revelation.

"These phases that you think will just merely facilitate your improved transportation are not as basic as you conceive them to be." As if this was not confirmation enough, the now apparently fake king continued to unravel and embellish his story.

"They are not just opening and closing temporary alternate versions of your own reality, they are in many cases, actually, completely independent and permanent states of existence, some where your physical laws do not even apply."

Brody was astounded at the similarity between what he had just surmised and what Alfred or whatever his real name might be, was now informing him of. For a moment he briefly considered one of the earlier Echo statements, but as he couldn't justify them as real, forced the thought to the back of his mind. Surely this was not just simply confirmation of his own thoughts.

Alfred's mind was working ten to the dozen in trying to restrain the silent others' mental interjections, so that he could verbally coerce this potential new ally. The children were doing just the same; they did not resort to what to them was a crude form of communication but patiently tapped away at Brody's subconscious. Both parties had their own agenda and at this point one was stronger than the other. Brody had only heard one side of the incredible story. The diametrically opposing views and the memories of previous successful transmissions blurred as if they had never occurred.

Brody was altogether suspicious, confused, intrigued but blissfully unaware of this behind the scenes battle of wills. He had initially felt something, but now heard only Alfred.

"I apologise for probing your memory engrams, but it was necessary to find out your original intentions. When *we* realised that you posed little threat to us, we only desired to help you back to your own phase." His seriously toned and more formally delivered statement amazed Brody.

"OK, I think I get all of that now, but how does chanting from a book help me get back?" Brody asked somewhat flippantly. He leaned forward intently as if he was likely to be unable to hear the reply.

"Please sit down, my new young friend, and allow me to comprehensively explain." Brody sat and listened intently as Alfred described in minute detail how the race he was part of lived a symbiotic life with those he had referred to as the others. He learned that the others retained youthful physicality from the exchange and were able to channel their extremely powerful psychokinetic energy through him and, more of his kind, like him. In return, this endowed them with the ability to read the thoughts and probe into the memories of any being they encountered, especially those like him who were not mentally equipped to stop them. It seemed a fair exchange and made them potentially very powerful allies.

He also learned that similar experimentation to that of his own had thrown them into a time vortex very similar to that which had thwarted the work of Newman-Phillips and the Tic-

Toc project all those years before he himself even got started in the industry.

In this reality, the apparent variant of Vikings had taken over the whole of one continent and were threatening world domination; not really a concern to the accidental tourists who, like him, just wanted to return home, but an inconvenient fact, nonetheless.

'More lies!' The echo attempted further disruption but its message was once again strangely soon forgotten. Brody just had to ask and was now clearly informed that his new acquaintance was obviously not King Alfred, but that his name was Evetzzirrah. He and the others had been trapped in this phase for years with only the sacred parchments and books to use as tools of possible escape. The name sounded very Greek or even Egyptian to Brody, but he didn't recognise it.

It also became apparent that none of them would actually have been of any real interest to the Vikings, but for the fact that Alfred or Evetzzirrah had, on arrival, tried to blend in with the locals and they had then initially appeared to the warriors as human Saxons, causing the Vikings who were until then blissfully unaware and happy in their own reality, to just see them as another part of the race of people that they were currently attempting to conquer.

To Brody, Evetzzirrah was quite a mouthful and after hours of complex bantering back and forth, the abdication of Alfred was completed by much procrastination over the proper pronunciation of a new shortened version that Brody selfishly foisted upon him. "Eh-vet, Ehhhh-vet, Evet... EHVVET... Certainly not Yvette or E-Vet, but just Evet." It all seemed overblown but Brody put the former monarchs insistence down to pride, remembering his own feelings about Kamylloxerajit or even Broderick Edward. Eventually satisfied with the more masculine Evet – finally he got around to the book he had been nursing.

"This, my very insistent and astute friend, is the *Necronomicon Ex-Mortis* or *Naturom Demonto,* literally translated in your Earth English as 'Book of the Dead' or 'Book of Souls,'" he announced very grandly. The complicated, suddenly went from the ridiculous to the sublime…

"It has allegedly been in existence for centuries, carried back and forth through multiple phases by various folks who have, over the years, desired its secrets." He lowered his tone, which seemed to add sincerity and fear to his voice.

"It is by all accounts omnipresent in all realities we have ever visited and is rumoured in your history to have the power to harness things called Kandarian Demons. It also allegedly has the ability to control both the dead and the Deadites, as well as the power to summon the Kandarian itself." Brody believed things were getting out of his scientific realm and more into belief systems that he had always steered away from as another form of useless religion.

"We found it here in the roof rooms of the village hall library; it is dated seven hundred and thirty-eight." The detail in the explanation was by now fascinating and strangely seemed to sit quite comfortably with him, but Brody nagged himself as to why.

"Since our experimental scientific work back in our own phase accidentally landed us here, like yours did with you, we have been unable to find our transportation vehicle which, also like yours, just disintegrated after our arrival. This, at present, is our only hope but we have as of yet been unable to make it work." Things began to make more sense, but Brody was still left confused as to how. Once again, his understanding of all this was, in realistic terms, far too clear.

"We understand that the recanting of the phrase I mentioned to you should do something like opening a rift in time and space and we had hoped it might be a way home but, as I say, we have yet to get any more from it." This closing statement seemed to answer his own mental misgivings, which was quite unnerving.

'Lies, lies, more damned lies!' The Echo suddenly whispered, directly into his subconscious.

Brody was completely stunned by both the revelations of Evet and the harshness of the contradictory Echo. Where *were* these inner echoed voices emanating from?

He felt he should know but just couldn't place it. His mind drifted to the thought of the day he met Charley and how he could recite the lyrics of a song but not remember the name of the composer. In his mind, an image of Charley blurred and faded as he listened to Evet give masses more information, much of which seemed to start to contradict itself, but he tried to understand and fathom how he might potentially use it all for his own ends to escape this situation and just go home.

Evet's speech patterns had now seemed to soften and he sounded less regal, friendlier, even more black country and Brody thought that this was also very unusual. However as he himself had a tendency to accidentally mimic accents he just glossed over this unlikely change.

Evet saw the thoughts in his mind and an inner smile spread his subconscious as he realised how the soft image of a female form of great importance could be of massive assistance in getting Brody on side. The others saw it too but their ideas on how to use the information were totally different to Evet's.

Confused completely by the conflicting information swimming around his tired head, he flipped from optimistically thinking some super powerful being could help him return to his own phase, to the very pessimistic and desperate hope that the random reading of some magic words might somehow help. On top of that he was apparently hearing voices like some prospective serial killer in waiting.

'I like it... not a lot,' he thought, and even though his humour was, as usual, quick and relevant, again, it neither amused nor comforted him and did little to change his current feelings of complete despair.

"How long have you been fighting these Vikings and trying to decipher this wretched thing?" he asked, pointing at the *Necronomicon* book.

The stony silence created by the answer hit like a drop kick to the head.

"Six hundred and sixty and a few more of your days!" Brody slumped back into his chair deflated, trying to take it all in. He needed sleep but felt anxious to try in case he should awake in an even worse scenario.

CHAPTER 6

Who Tells Truths and Who Sells Deception.

From the trepidation and horrors of the first couple of days after meeting Evet and the seven children now just known simply as 'the others', things became a lot less exciting straight after. Whilst Evet and Brody collaborated to try to crack the meaning of various sections of the *Necronomicon*, the others seemed to just mill around contributing little or nothing. Brody, however, assumed they might be delving into the problem mentally and transmitting their findings to Evet silently. Pretty much every day was spent in the same manner. Get up, forage, read, discuss, read more and sleep.

After spending six long months with his new companions, reading and re-reading the *Necronomicon Ex-Mortis* from cover to cover, Brody was starting to regularly contemplate the long-term reality of his life. With this group of weird and quite probably alien beings, he started to consider that the alternate title of *Naturom Demonto* sounded more of an accurate description for the book and its effect on his current state of sanity. Deep in the recesses of his mind he considered Evet was somehow just biding time and waiting. Many discussions held with him over the book and its contents had been completely fruitless and unrevealing.

At this point, Brody still had no idea of the true intentions of these unusual people that he had been thrown together with and only one of them outwardly spoke to him. He also had a continual uneasy feeling that the Echo warning him was possibly the work of the others trying to communicate without the knowledge of their cerebrally symbiotic host. It was not a nice feeling and it worried him greatly. It drifted in and out like a fading memory but periodically nagged at him as if he knew for sure but was not being allowed to know, either *what* he knew or even *that* he knew. If *this* thought was even close to being accurate it could surely only realistically be Evet that was holding back the knowledge and, if so, how much of *his* revelations could Brody safely believe? Why would Evet be going to such extreme lengths to cover things up or could it even be the work of the strange outrider he kept seeing in the distance? It was like they were patiently watching and waiting for a chance to approach.

As he awoke on any one of a hundred similar days, it took but seconds for the harsh reality of his situation to hit home yet again. Another hot morning, more reading and trying to find some hidden cryptic clues within the covers of the damn *Necronomicon*, probably followed by a scant meal of leaves and shrubs; long since had the larder in the deserted village store run empty and it was weeks since he had eaten meat.

Evet entered the room after knocking but had not waited to be asked in. He sat down on the chair by Brody's bed and announced,

"The others feel it is time to leave this place and search for more options. We are very powerful in our own way when linked but we need the triclipse to regenerate our energy and, after the drain of the latest battle, we may not be able to withstand another raid if they return." For six months the Vikings had been silent so Brody was surprised at this sudden change of tactic and, since the others did not speak and he had also heard little or nothing from the nagging Echo for a while, he resigned to listen to Evet's side of things, again.

"They may return soon, so we think it best to move on now. We hope you will come with us. If so, we will protect you as best we are able." Many things had gone through Brody's mind in the past six months in the village and this had not been one of them and he was unsure what to feel. For certain, the best plan was sticking with Evet and the symbiotic others but moving from the relative safety of the village to an unknown destination seemed ill-advised. Travelling in the ironically searing heat of this alternate phase of English countryside did not seem the best option to him, but then again, what other ideas had he managed to come up with in the last few months?

The triclipse event that Evet and the others allegedly so desperately needed was still apparently over sixteen months away – sixteen months of ninety-minute nights and thirteen-and-a-half hour days. This fifteen-hour cycle and the strange coloured twin moons had taken a few weeks for Brody to become accustomed to. He had since developed a habit of finding a dark place to sleep for a few hours in the day or to just go to bed three or four hours before sunset, effectually having a two-to-three-hour lie-in every day.

In one of the longer drawn out philosophical discussions Brody had gone through with Evet, he learned of how this apparently all-important triclipse would help them. By Evet's complicated account of things, he and the others had virtually been at death's door after their accidental incarceration in this phase.

He explained that their normal physiological regeneration cycle was controlled by regular solar events in their own phase which would release so much energy that they could absorb as much as they wanted for days on end, which was stored in glands deep within their strangely configured bodies. It seemed to Brody that they were similar to a very efficient rechargeable battery and his acquaintance seemed to like the comparison.

Evet had explained that when they were approaching the anniversary of their accidental arrival in this phase, their life energy had not been regenerated for the whole of that time and they had become nearly completely depleted which, in human terms, would have been akin to total starvation. They had literally been at the mercy of the Vikings' very next attack. This phase's regular twin moon and sun triclipse that they had until that point been completely unaware of, then just happened to occur. By sheer good fortune, the massive natural twin corona generated during the event, gave off a burst of solar energy which was very similar to that which they needed. In effect they were saved and regenerated in that very fortunate celestial moment.

The new others that Evet had previously referred to were actually the same symbionts, but on the regeneration of the energy stores they had, it could only be described as morphing their bodies to give, in effect, a developed rebirth as the same childlike beings. The silent foreboding, sometimes flame-eyed others were, physically at least and according to Evet, perpetual, young children; children of an unknown age from some other strange dimension. The larger being that they followed was also still somewhat of a mystery to Brody. He quirkily wanted to start calling all the children Doctor, and Evet, Master, but refrained. The thought was convoluted and to those who might at some point *have* to use it - confusing. But *all in good time,* use it they would.

With the Echo still occasionally bouncing around his head in warning, he was still unsure of the amount of trust he should bestow upon the taller long-haired host of these so-called others and which aspects of his extensive and detailed accounts of them he could safely rely upon. He felt sure of only one thing and that was that if this confusion carried on, he would certainly go mad juggling the paranoia they were all slowly developing within him. Maybe a change of venue would help.

Not all the times and dates seemed to match up in Evet's stories, but Brody had initially put this down to his own obsessive need for closure and his desire to tie up all the loose ends. In any case, who was he to contradict a super being from another phase? Evet informed him that the Saxons of *this* phase had formulated methods of calculating future triclipse events. By careful use of this information, combined with details from the complex star charts within the *Necronomicon*, he knew that they could be relatively certain that the next event was due in about four hundred and eighty of their shortened days. After much discussion it was finally decided that leaving was going to be the best option and Brody had no coherent reason to argue with their superior knowledge of their murderous potential opponents. He capitulated to the popular opinion but could not ratify the vote, being only able to take Evet's word for the fact that it was a unanimous decision. He gathered together as many supplies as possible before the agreed departure time.

Brody had never witnessed Evet or the children eat anything. Thus the supplies consisted of just a few pieces of remaining fruit for him and some vegetable stock. He had rustled up the stopgap soup using skills gained in a previous one-week job as a sauce chef that he was employed as, in the summer of twenty seventeen. He decanted the soup into a spare water container and found a huge leather bag which looked like a giant's school satchel to put everything in. Water was realistically all there was for the children to carry. Between the nine of them, they gathered as many water bottles as they could and filled them from the well in the courtyard beyond the village green. Although they did not seem to eat, it appeared that, as with all species Brody was aware of, water was a universal constant and without it, nothing could survive. Luckily, in this phase it was not in short supply. When everyone was loaded with at least their two canteen bottles they were ready.

Immediately after the first sip was taken the huge water cooler in Charley's office sprung to Brody's mind and he fondly recalled the hours spent leaning on it drinking its contents trying to convince her to go out with him on a date. He enjoyed copious amounts of coffee from the adjacent dispensing machine that he drank daily just so that he could spend more time doting over her. He compared the two situations of coffee vs water against Evet vs others. Perversely, he thought of the life providing water also being present within the coffee that he could not live without. He shook his head hopelessly in view of his current situation and jogged the few paces to catch up to the group.

Evet saw everything that Brody thought and so did the children. What they respectively chose to do with the information was very different. Their agendas were entwined but of very differing integrity.

As they all left the war-battered village, Brody stopped and turned. Looking back, he considered,

'Although it's not been much use so far, we really should take that Necronomicon *thing with us.'* He hurriedly ran back and picked it up from the table, wondering that if it was so important, why Evet had not taken it. As he placed it in his satchel the cover seemed to move and, for a second, he could have sworn that it winked an evil-looking eye of the scream-like cover directly at him. His surprised double take would have impressed even James Finlayson himself let alone being appropriate to grace his all-time favourite black and white TV comedy double act. When staring back again at the ugly cover, nothing moved. He shook his head again, pushed it into the satchel and ran back to the group without mention of this paranormal experience.

The question of carrying weapons on this journey had been raised before they left but it was decided very undemocratically, two to none (the other seven not having been consulted) that it would be futile with a maximum of eight swords in action versus potentially thousands. If the mental abilities of the others channelled through Evet were not sufficient, the carrying of such implements would only delay the inevitable.

Brody had managed to smuggle a small but very sharp knife that he took from one of the slain Vikings as a keepsake. He hid it carefully into his belt ensuring the sharp end was protected in its decorative sheath. He felt a strange comfort from this small act of defiance.

After three long days and four short nights travelling, they came upon an obviously very deserted settlement; tumbleweed was blowing around the yard and gates rocked in the breeze.

'No doubt ravaged at some point by the Norsemen,' was the thought that immediately popped into Brody's mind. The children looked as solemn as ever and still did not speak or seem to transmit any thoughts to him – he was still unsure of their ownership of the Echo. Evet shifted uncomfortably, looking around nervously; Brody assumed it was caution.

Evet had his reasons to look slightly nervous; the children knew but neither commented verbally or mentally. Although the smallholding was deserted of humankind, or any such being, there were a few livestock roaming around and the fields looked full of crops. So, if the first indications past the gloom of dereliction looked prospectively good, Brody reasoned that if there were still animals and crops, the raid was probably recent – but where were the fallen bodies?

He soon found the answer to that question behind the barn and cowshed. In the sty amongst the pigs were the very mutilated and semi-consumed bodies of what must have been a family of five adults. The main clue to this fact was the size of the skulls remaining as the omnivorous pigs had been unable to get them into their mouths. However, it looked like they'd had a very good try as nearly every piece of skin was missing from each skull. Brain debris, hair and eyeballs were everywhere congealed in the mud that the large boars were still rooting around in. Most of the larger organs and a good percentage of the skeletal mass had been consumed and Brody, although disgusted but somewhat fascinated, could not help but to think of a character from one of his favourite movies… Brick Top.

The stench from the rotting corpses was disgusting but seemed to have no effect on the others who largely ignored the site. Evet was similarly disinterested and was most surprised when Brody finally succumbed, vomiting violently. He turned a strange version of yellowy-white before finding a shady spot to sit down, restore his composure and drink some water.

Evet gave him a moment before he wandered over to him and enquired, "Your consumption of food and the processing of it to create energy to fuel your body is a very crude method, but from our experiences seems relatively efficient and easy to control. What was that you did then? Human ejection of waste is, to my knowledge, usually done rectally, so why did you expel from your facial orifice? I mean – your mouth." Brody explained the process as best he was able and the two laughed a little before picking up shovels and digging shallow graves for what was left of the previous inhabitants of this smallholding.

Brody had not noticed a splinter in the shovel handle he was using and, by the time the work was done, the handle was wet and red with his blood where it had blistered his palm. Evet gave Brody a piece of cloth to wrap it with. The wound was only minor but bled profusely and hurt far more after he'd noticed it than when accidentally inflicted. It now seemed obvious to him that as well as water, injury and death were also universal constants and the respect for the dead might possibly resonate within multiple phases. Perhaps he had more in common with the mysterious Evet than he had originally imagined. Evet's concern for the minor wound and apparent compassion for the dead comforted Brody until the mood was completely rubbished by a stark echo inside his head, '**He** *did it! He murdered them all!*'

'*Where is that coming from?*' His frustration with the intermittent mental messaging and his now far too regular mental block as to their origin was growing. He felt angry. Was his impending mental instability the issue causing the confusion or was the seemingly foisted confusion causing the growing mental instability? He seemed to have found a mental impasse.

Outwardly, it seemed that at night the others would regularly huddle together and communicate the day's happenings in a mass silent vigil, but in the day, unless summoned by Evet, they would tend to wander around independent of each other but would always be instinctively aware of each other's presence. Brody thought that other than the golden hair they did not particularly resemble each other, so it was a quandary to him as to how they were *what* they were purported to be. They seemed to be more a part of some sort of collective hive mind controlled loosely by Evet, rather than symbiotic partners – it was more the tail wagging the dog. He was still unsure and further unconvinced if asking was a good ploy.

The group set up camp and took over the house at the centre of the smallholding. It had been decided by Evet that since there had obviously been a raid there recently it was probably as safe as anywhere. It did seem unlikely that the warriors would have any need to return any time soon and so Brody, having forcibly forgotten the identity of the accused murderer of the previous inhabitants, again, looked around and rummaged through the belongings of what would have been some alternate phase of an Anglo-Saxon household. His understanding of how these phases were constructed in the fabric of time and space and the rationale behind what he might expect to find next always seemed to contradict itself. Every time he thought he had formulated a theory to explain it all and potentially work out a way home, something new occurred to prove him wrong. It was weirdly reminiscent of his research glitches back home.

Yet another coincidental constant in all of this was the strangely all too convenient meeting of himself and Evet – the more he thought about it the more it seemed so unlikely that a being of such obvious intelligence and power would endanger itself to go down to the beach moments before a hostile invasion. Was he trying to generate some form of synergy and trust between them? Brody even started to consider the question of whether he had just simply been conned and that perhaps the Vikings were the good guys, trying to rid themselves of the space-time travelling foreign troublemakers. It also occurred to him that the others had made a major contribution to what had saved him – he had seen it with his own eyes. Without them and Evet for that matter he would have been chopped meat – that much was certain.

After a couple of days of merely surviving at this new abode with not much else going on, Brody was getting very frustrated at the apparent apathy within the group. Was everyone just going to sit and wait for the mysterious and miraculous triclipse event to save them? Spurred on by the latest intermittent niggling Echo in his head warning him of Evet's untrustworthy nature, he thought playing devil's advocate might bring up something new. He tested the water by asking Evet a direct question.

"Evet, I need more information..." He paused before diving into the unknown pool of cross-examination, "Individually they look and walk like small children, but I have watched their eyes burn others away, like black holes in their golden-haired stare. They transmitted great power and they certainly are *not* children, as I understand it. I would appreciate you telling me a little more." Evet; possible conman, paused a moment before answering, "I understand you have difficulty comprehending our very existence but that is no different than us finding you for the first time, only we have abilities that you do not and can better survive this phase. You must believe me, my motives... err, and that is to say, our motives are sincere." Again, his alleged sincerity seemed tinged with the possibility of deceit, but Brody continued to listen with interest as he continued, "We want to get home equally as much as you do and, for over seven hundred and fifty of your days now, I have searched for a solution. The others are damned to be perpetual children anyway and God knows, I want to go home." Brody so wanted to believe all he said but found nothing particularly viable offered in his convoluted statements and the mention of the G word further perplexed him.

'Can religion be a universal constant misnomer?' Everything seemed far too convenient and he felt there was a desperation creeping into Evet's tone. Each time his mind was clearing and getting to grips with things it seemed to haze over as if he were being made to think down certain lines against his will. It was both disconcerting and confusing, so patiently he listened, hoping for a bigger clue to explain his misgivings more than the Echo that periodically badgered him. Evet continued:

"Some days I am walking around like a dead man. Some days I feel that if I could, I would crucify us all and get it all over with. I constantly feel like I am standing on my last step... and of oblivion?

Well, it beckons us all." He paused before lamenting further, "But then you arrived and things changed for me – my mind became clearer. I think you are here for a reason. I think you are the key, my friend." Evet's detailing was still as blurred but had raised the bar in its level of intrigue as if in clever response to Brody's unspoken doubts.

Although more positive in its finishing tone, this statement was also still quite random and was of little comfort to Brody. By now his suspicions were starting to overpower his ability for logical deduction and thousands of possibilities were racing through his head.

"You originally said chanting those strange words at the correct time and then consuming them would possibly help me. What did you mean by that?" he further probed, looking for definitive answers rather than another brush-off.

"I have read that volume thousands of times and the only positive thing I have found in it is the continued reference to that verse, but we have never managed to get it to do anything. I… well, we, genuinely believe it somehow opens a rift in time and space where all phases intertwine and if opened could somehow allow us to travel back to our own phase." The complex but not particularly revealing answer was of little help to him and his head spun with the stress of all the conflicting information swirling within it.

Brody withdrew the *Necronomicon* from his satchel and laid it firmly on the table like Exhibit A from a murder mystery and, in a much more accusatory tone, asked a question that had troubled him for days.

"Why did you leave it behind then?" he challenged Evet strongly.

"No reason, I just forgot, I suppose. Actually, I thought you had it anyway," was the completely feeble but extremely confident reply. Brody was unconvinced and was starting to think that Evet was hiding a lot more than just his true intentions. Once again his thoughts clouded and he had to start reconstructing his next plan. In the clearer moments it felt to him as if it was like having a condition such as Alzheimer's and he started thinking about how many times he had felt dizzy or had passed out lately. This, at his age was not much of a concern under current circumstances, but if nothing else it served to distract him from Evet's evasiveness. Suddenly he had a piercing revelatory thought that time had seemed to have become static and maybe he was actually in some infernal temporal loop or worse still, already dead. After a few seconds, hours or even months of silence Brody decided to push on with his interrogation.

"Let's try it out again, right now," he suggested and flipped to the page where the passage was written. He slowly read aloud the four words to the best of his ability.

"Gort, Klaatu, Barada, Nicto." Nothing happened and he riffled the crusty old pages in despair.

"Anyway, what did you mean by 'consume them'?"

"If you look at the passage in the previous chapter, it suggests that the consumption of the words at the right time stops others reversing the power of the book once you have unlocked and harnessed its ability to control the Kandarian – whatever that is... I am unsure if consume is translated correctly, we can hardly test it out but once." Evet, as usual, answered in depth without really revealing much.

"I was just relaying what I had learned myself. I think if you read something enough times, after a while it starts to sound real." Smiling to himself, Brody mentally compared this last statement to his own experiences with religion and the total belief that some people he knew and respected had in the mere words of what he considered to be a purely fictional book. Words, that when analysed, would not stand much closer examination without appearing to be as watertight and very similar in value to any decent tea bag.

He was still no historian but seemed to remember some ancient Egyptian, Mayan or other such deep folklore, saying something about the Kandarian being the biggest, baddest demon – the one you would never want to meet.

"Maybe this is just a story book, like the Bible or Harry Potter – it could be just down to interpretation and shouldn't be taken so literally. We could be looking at the puzzle from completely the wrong angle; perhaps it all means nothing at all."

This idea was met with a wry smile from Evet. Frustrated, Brody grabbed up the book and started walking indignantly outside. As he got near the open door of the farmhouse there was an ear-splitting scream emanating directly from the twisted face on the book cover. A liquid that looked like yellowy blood started dripping from what might best be described as the thing's eyes and mouth. He dropped the volume in shock and, as it landed on the dusty floor, the sunlight streaming in through the doorway hit it and the cover seemed to flex and twist; the face-like shape contorted as if it was made from actual skin and not what he had originally assumed to be some sort of animal leather. As the book hissed and gave off what looked like steam the screeching noise continued to fill the room, he realised the thing was moving, slowly inching itself away from the sunlight.

Brody grabbed it quickly and pulled it back into the darker area of the room. The still-twisted face looked fractionally less pained and the blood-like substance abruptly stopped flowing and disappeared as if it had never been there. Brody wondered if he had imagined it all. He shook himself from the spine-tingling feeling that it had evoked.

"Did you see that? Sunlight! Wow, this book actually doesn't like sunlight." Evet did not reply but looked very pensive.

"Surely you have, over all this time, read it in the day at some point?" Brody asked incredulously.

"In the daytime, yes, many times, but amazingly enough, although I had never considered it until now, never in direct sunlight, believe it or not. (Brody considered not.) No, we were always cautious not to be seen with it publicly, so all our reading, contemplation and examination of the text has always taken place indoors." The unrevealing reply only added fuel to Brody's doubts. He decided to press on and call this weak excuse and hopefully expose more of his suspected reality.

"So, let's try it outside at night then… tonight!" Brody proclaimed triumphantly in a somewhat challenging tone, as if to dare Evet to find yet another excuse of an answer.

'Could something as simple as the rays of the sun have had this much relevance?' As he considered it more, he mentally cross-referenced the triclipse and its apparent significance and felt sure he had accidentally found the very key that might unlock the mystery and get him and the others home again at last.

Both Evet and the others extrapolated this information, direct from Brody's thought patterns. Literally, as he thought it, they all saw it and, once again, what they chose to do with the knowledge would vary drastically. Later, someone also picked up the now dry but blood-soaked cloth he had discarded at the graves site days before and they did not dispose of it as would normally be expected.

CHAPTER 7

A Damning Revelation.

Outwardly there was much excitement between Evet and Brody at the prospect of potentially being able to uncover the secret of this ancient text and possibly both being able to find a way back to their respective points of origin. They had many hours to wait for sunset and the arrival of the short night that would follow, allowing them a brief chance to experiment with their new ideas.

To be more precise, there was about twelve more hours of waiting so the book was put safe in a cupboard away from sunlight for the time being. Apparently, alerted by the commotion of this new-found possibility, the others gathered, huddling, outside the house so Brody knew that they knew what was going on and, for the first time since meeting them, he thought he saw an emotion in their faces… fear, to be precise. This worried him to some small degree and his thoughts of Evet being the liar were now being questioned. Could it be the others that had been playing him all along, planting information to make him suspect Evet?

"Where were you going with the book, anyway?" Evet asked in an intrigued and engaging tone.

"I was just literally going to throw the damn thing in with the pigs," Brody replied, looking a little sheepish.

"I understood why you were hiding things when we first met and

I get that you have been stuck here a damn sight longer than me, but since we have got to know each other over the last six months I really don't think I have learned that much about you other than your thought-connected symbiotic relationship with these so-called others outside." There seemed no point in hiding his feelings any more. Especially now that they might be getting closer to a solution, and Brody had always been taught that honesty is the best policy.

"I feel that although we are working towards the same goals every day, I have somehow actually never met the real you, have I?" His questioning statement received no immediate answer. Evet glanced up but, as was often the case, looked pensive and even worried.

"Whilst I'm on about the others, do they ever speak? And why do you reckon they looked so scared? Was it because they heard us talking about reading the *Necronomicon* at night?" Brody was pushing hard now, pushing for answers that had not been forthcoming in the last few months. If there *was* to be trust, these other beings from a different phase needed to be more open with him before he bestowed them with any more of his trust – it all affected his only chance to get home. With these new thoughts in mind he had decided it would be worth the risk to push even harder.

'What can they possibly do to make my situation any worse?'

"All in good time, friend," came the ridiculously ambiguous and defensive reply to the earlier enquiries. It was as if it was meant as a deliberate delaying tactic to answer or tease his inner thoughts but to completely ignore the outer questions. Brody fell silent and mentally admitted to himself – yet another confusing defeat. He sat thoughtfully considering his next best course of action.

'If I'm going to get any proper understandable information, I'll need a bloody crowbar to prise it out of this one. Oh well, if that doesn't work, I could always use it on his skull!'

The others and Evet sensed Brody's rising internal anguish and one party knew it spelt hope, the other saw it as a distinct danger.

Sporadic conversation about nothing much was all that broke the silence of the frustratingly lengthy, watched pot; the long wait for nightfall. The prolonged silences were only broken with Brody poking questions about the true nature and desires of Evet and his smaller companions. His elusive counterpart managed to dodge most of the probes like a true politician on election night. When all the votes were counted it was still a hung parliament. Who could he truly trust? Eventually, the sun began to drop towards the ocean and the two started to prepare for their ritual reading of the *Necronomicon*'s verses outside at night.

Brody fetched the volume from its darkened cupboard location and headed for the door. As he approached it with outstretched hand he noticed through the adjacent window that the others were standing outside in a semi-circle. They were all linked hand in hand as if playing some school yard chain tag game. He pushed open the door and, as the last rays of sun fell upon the cover of the *Necronomicon*, it twitched in his arm as if to attempt escape. The others stared blankly at the door where Brody stood; they looked defiant as if trying to make a statement.

"What's the problem with them?" he asked over his shoulder.

"They think I will abandon them if we unlock the mystery of the *Necronomicon* tonight and find a way back to our respective homes." The unusually forthright and apparently first honest answer Brody could remember Evet giving, came as something of a surprise and it came from further inside the house than Brody had expected. He spun round to see that Evet had stayed back in the lounge area and had not followed him through the reception passage to the front porch as he had assumed. Very nearly, before Brody had even asked his question of, "Would you?" he received the reply,

"Possibly." Evet quickly proceeded to explain as if to cover up his suspicious pre-emption of the original enquiry.

"You see, as I explained to you before, the individuals of my race generally live more than one thousand years by regenerating themselves regularly. Our ability to live symbiotic lives with those you know as 'the others' is non-essential to us, but it is completely essential to them. They are of our descendants but, like on your planet and in your phase, evolution changed certain species – they remained symbionts but we evolved. We still utilise them for their strengths but do not actually need them." Suddenly, the world was turning the wrong way and Brody felt the pangs of guilt, thinking that all his fears about Evet might have been unfounded. Evet continued to verbally spin the globe.

"They are very powerful, when linked, which has helped me… I mean, us to survive this ordeal stuck here. But I'm getting old and just want to return to my family. If we can find a way my need for them will be gone and they know it." Brody retreated into the room and slowly closed the door in front of him as he backed away, dumbfounded, unable to immediately fully comprehend this unexpected change in circumstances and complete reversal of what he had been expecting.

"They look as if they are about to channel their energy just like when they helped you defeat the Viking warriors; can they do that without you?" he asked. The reply was not what he was hoping for.

"Oh yes, indeed they can, and what you saw with the Vikings was just them playing; they could literally have just killed them but wanted to watch the sport of them killing each other." Brody stumbled, fell into a chair and started to dizzily mull over the options. It seemed as if normal negotiation or even running would be out of the question. Any chance that the *Necronomicon* might be of help by opening the rift and allowing passage tonight was now apparently determined by the flimsy theory of the passages working at night, outside and, even then, hinged on safely passing the others without violent confrontation. The others now menacingly seemed to be guarding their only exit.

"So, what do we do now? Will they believe you if you tell them you will take them too?" he asked hopefully, but more in desperation at finding anything positive.

"Unfortunately, they already know that I am considering their destruction. If I leave, they will need a new symbiont within days, so they definitely do not want me to leave either way. If I do, they will want desperately that you most certainly will not! They want me, but…" he paused dramatically and Brody held his breath a second.

"…no offence meant, but *you* will be better than death until they can find themselves another way back. They also know that the chances of us all finding safe passage is very unlikely now."

'Lies, ALL lies, ALWAYS lies!' The Echo was right on cue and screamed into his head. He was now certain that all his previous suspicions of their origination had been confirmed. It was surely the silent others that had been communicating to him all along and now he became concerned as to whether Evet knew this and had been somehow blocking him from that fact. He also wondered if he would perhaps know what they had said to him. Either way, who could he trust from these contrary argumentative and alien strangers?

"So, what do we do now?" Brody reiterated his earlier question.

"They… We are getting close to regenerative exhaustion again and the recent confrontation with the Norse has brought that closer. They rely upon each other as a collective but I do not. If we can distract and separate them… I can kill them all," Evet said coldly and very matter-of-factly.

Brody was shocked and stunned at hearing such a radical solution and, having moved to a more eager position to listen to

Evet's revelations, he now rocked back into the chair again, taken aback and deflated at how insensitively it had been proposed. Emptiness washed over him that felt quite sinister; it left him momentarily speechless. His jaw nearly dropped open before his reply could be formulated. Eventually, it fell sorrowfully out.

"You have been linked mentally to them for all this time and would kill them without a second thought. That seems somewhat, if you pardon the expression… inhumane." Brody had said this before thinking things through. He suddenly realised that he probably shouldn't have antagonised the only other person that could, at this point properly, communicate with him. Especially when he or it was probably saving his very life right now as they continued there debating.

"Well first, Brody, I am obviously, as you know, not human but if I were, would I want to keep rabid dogs just because I had owned them from pups?"

'Rabid dogs...' How strange but familiar an analogy it seemed, but Brody found this logic inescapable and smiled at Evet's ability to make as swift and measured a decision without any sign of emotion.

"You are not from Vulcan… are you?" he joked. It was apparently wasted on Evet who merely looked bemused and ignored the comment. They talked a while longer as the moons rose. It was decided that leaving was not an option tonight but if they could somehow distract the others to split up in the morning it might help. The potential was for Evet to then carry out the allegedly necessary, but horrendous to consider, act of multiple filicide! It seemed to be a step beyond his conscience, and all just to allow them to re-try with the *Necronomicon* on another occasion. There surely must be a better solution. Evet had one but kept it to himself for now.

'He just wants you to help release **them***; you won't realise you are doing it, but it is all a trick.'* The others' echo chimed in to put further doubts and confusion into Brody's mind.

Although he had not become close to the others in any way and knew they were not his or even Evet's children, he knew they merely resembled youth and were a lot older than children as he understood the concept – he still couldn't shake his complete discomfort with Evet's radical and murderous escape plan.

Once again he quickly forgot the echo and had to start afresh trying to work out who was what and how, when or where it would all lead.

Evet seemed to intercept his digression of thinking and explained that it was highly beneficial to try to empty his mind of direct thought and attempt to concentrate on inanimate objects to avoid the others probing his mind and making a pre-emptive first move. Under the unknown danger of the others' intent, he agreed to Evet's suggestion that the best method of blanking the mind was to sleep, so they did just that. Brody was tired and fell asleep quickly, but his dreams were horrific and laden with murder, blood and guts. His subconscious mind had a better memory and was trying to warn him of the impending dangers.

Only a few hours later as morning drew closer, during his last throws of REM sleep, one particularly nefarious image jolted Brody awake. His newly conscious sight was bombarded by the first rays of sun blazing through the gap in the curtains that hung heavily but failed miserably to shield the lower section of window in his room.

'Why are they not blinds?' He liked blinds in his bedroom. For a fraction of a second he was tucked up in bed aged around twelve, his mother was just about to burst in and draw the beloved blinds and pour coffee down his dry throat. He was immediately and

sombrely reminded of his current location and predicament by the unusual warmth and vibrancy of this new sun's colour, but was quite relieved to see it and to know that he was still trapped in an alternate phase with a potentially murderous partner in crime. It was, if nothing else, proof in his own mind that he was not already dead – killed in his sleep for dreaming of the death of the others.

With these paradoxical thoughts, he promptly got up and approached the window where he found the disturbing sight of the unusually menacing-looking seven, extremely blonde children still standing in the exact same spot as they had been five or six hours ago. They were all still in a semi-circle surrounding the porch, hand in hand as if picketing the building, on strike against the potential of being left behind by their previous counterpart. Brody was unsure whether they were aware or completely unaware of Evet's heinous intentions.

His thoughts drifted to a scene of a movie where extreme patience and waiting on a similar porch in all weathers and for an indefinite period was a prerequisite of successful entrance to a secret club held within. His mind locked onto the statement of the film's main protagonist when they said to one such club applicant,

"You're not coming in, you are too... BLONDE!" This extreme nonsensical reasoning resonated in his head but was then washed away by a more pertinent and pressing enquiry.

'*Where was Evet?*' The thought clanged around his still semi-conscious head like a lone cookie in a jar and he couldn't believe that he had possibly been duped and left to become the new symbiotic partner to these strange beings who now menacingly surrounded the porch. They did not look overly patient now. Running around the house searching every room, he soon realised the former King was gone. Not Elvis, but the real liar and deceiver had... left the building.

The option of Evet being the real danger that the Echo had been continually warning him of, suddenly became a total reality. Suddenly it all became crystal clear and serious. He *had* been tricked. Furthermore, the realisation now of how *much more* serious this could really be, hit him like a runaway train. He rushed over to the cupboard, opened it quickly and his stomach tightened into a knot as his worst fears were shockingly realised… The *Necronomicon* was also gone.

Full-blown panic now started to set in. '*What would the others do to him? Would there be any physical or psychological effects on his joining their collective, if he was forced to do so? How could he ever hope to get home without the* Necronomicon *or the ability to locate his transportation pod?*' The clanging solitary thought of being conned had been replaced by a jingle-jangle of a thousand insidious connotations to this horrendous, brown-coloured and odious scenario that his former ally had now apparently dumped him deeply into. Self-preservation was his first instinct and as he considered his options, he weirdly found himself feeling that if the roles had been reversed he might have done just the same.

Evet had obviously seen an opportunity, learnt new information – thanks to him – and took the chance to slip away and experiment with the *Necronomicon* when the opportunity arose. If the shoe had been on the other foot and *he* had been trapped, would he have chosen differently? Again, he found himself reasoning that this person he knew very little about and obviously could not trust, was not so different from him at all. Maybe back home he could learn a lot from this, but to get home he really needed to find Evet and quickly.

With his knowledge of the others' mental powers and an idea of what they might want, he tried to calm himself and reasoned that direct communication would probably be the best choice of next action. Perhaps he could appeal to them and use Evet's deception to his advantage. However, he had never heard any of them speak and knew they communicated with each other mentally, so was unsure on how successful he was likely to be – what other choice did it leave him? If nothing else, at least they would know he was sincere.

Opening the front door and allowing the sunlight to pour into the lounge, he stood at the front step and looked out, feigning confidence.

"Can you speak? I know that you understand my thoughts, but I cannot respond in that way, so I need to physically talk with you," he announced as steadily and clearly as he could. His very nervous inner self was struggling to cope. What came back shocked him further.

'YES, WE CAN but it hurts us to do so, thus we choose not to, but we will listen to your proposals as we now know the other has deserted you. We feel his link to us has been severed and we also need your help. We can take your help if we must but would prefer it to be given.' This was the rasping of all seven voices at once; it hurt his head and he was physically shaken by the volume and tone of their reply. However, it was not as menacing as he had anticipated. Whilst contemplating how to respond, he realised that none of them had spoken – none of them had moved a muscle – their mouths still closed in a pursed frowning state with furrowed brows and slightly glimmering eyes.

He also remembered what happened when those eyes glowed brighter, thus he tried very hard to phrase his next statement extremely sensitively.

"If Evet has informed me correctly, you will need a new symbiotic external being for you to channel your energy through – is this true?" He attempted to sound unafraid.

'NO, HE LIED! He used you to manoeuvre and we tried to warn

you.' The trumpeted reply hurt and he stumbled backwards into the door frame; head spinning from the powerful response. He held his head and blurted out:

"I let him manipulate me like a pawn, I was a fool." The reply indicated that the comprehension by the others of chess, was nil.

'We do not know of pawns, but foolish? NO, he manipulates and controls the thoughts of others to confuse,' came the understanding but brain freeze-inducing response.

"Please… I do not want to anger you, but can you select a single spokesperson or lower your power levels somehow? I must be made differently to him." Their next reply was measured and singular in its voice, tone and volume.

'We apologise but have been communicating as one for nearly two years and he never had issue with it, so we did not realise you might be harmed. Are you OK?' He was, but then again he wasn't, so he explained how his recent situation had originally started and how it had further developed overnight, frustrated that he hadn't managed to communicate with them directly before now.

He explained how he had arrived in this phase and how he only wanted to return home, thinking to appeal to their seemingly benevolent nature that he now felt via their direct mental projections. He asked if they could survive without a host and how the arrangement with Evet started in the first place. The children already knew most of what he had to tell but listened politely and then tried to explain the other side of the complex coin that Evet had flipped so casually by leaving.

'Much of what he has told you was correct in principle, but he always twists the details and full truth for personal gain. The earlier reference, we did not understand it, but can read from your thoughts the rudiments of an ancient challenge game and now see with his attempt to be King, how it could have seemed somehow appropriate.'

The singularity of the soft voice entering his mind was strangely soothing and the non-humorous similarity of focus on comparing things just like he did was astounding. The descriptions they or she transmitted in the next few minutes gave him an overview that was very disconcerting.

He scanned the seven faces to work out which the voice belonged to. The tallest of the children locked his gaze and, as if winking, flashed a tiny flame in *his* right eye to answer Brody's unspoken question without breaking *his* own thought pattern.

'Legend has it that his and our ancestors were joined in their history. A long time ago the evolutionary process was deliberately meddled with by a leading but unstable scientist who believed that we as a race, could soon reach out to other phases of reality, travel in space and time and move from place to place with no physical form of transportation device.' All the information he was receiving seemed to flow into him rather than being heard – he just seemed to understand.

'With these new eugenically developed powers he surmised we would be able to control other races, take power over the Universe and make grander, more devastating plans such as ruling the whole cosmos. This scientist was an inspirational but radical revolutionary.' Brody was drawn intently to this amazing history lesson. He had received it or heard it; he could not yet discern which.

'Nobody could ever fully trace his lineage and rumours of him not being of our race at all were rife, but still he was held by our ancestors as a genius and was given cursory support in the beginning.' The earlier feelings of trepidation that Brody had experienced were being replaced with complete ease and interest as he listened without the use of his ears and started to feel comfortable with this process of telepathic communication. In the back of his mind he was starting to feel envious that he could not respond in kind.

The tallest continued and Brody realised it didn't matter who was addressing him, they were definitively individual but of one mind.

'He carried out strange experimentation on many of our people. These experiments led to a long-term genetic mutation and some developed a larger, more useful physicality while others withered and stayed childlike. The offspring of both followed these traits and we ended up with two distinct factions of population.' As the thought patterns arrived into Brody's consciousness, the tallest child gesticulated towards the others and said,

'We children evolved to become, forever small but with amazing mental abilities allowing us to regenerate ourselves periodically and control the thoughts and actions of others with what you might term as psychokinesis. The 'others' became more physically able but reliant on us for regeneration.' Brody smiled and wondered if John, as he had named the tallest, would know why he had done so.

Brody was amused by the feeling that, without even moving a muscle, John had perfectly accentuated part of his thought transmission with raised hands to make the inverted comma motion around the word 'others' and it was *so* visible to Brody within his mind, but at the same time felt natural at not having actually occurred. He was pleased by this feeling of deeper understanding of such minutiae.

Additionally Brody was comforted by, and felt empathy for these strange beings that he now wished he had indeed paid greater attention to. He now realised that the reason he had not done so was a self-proclamation of the truth of their earlier warnings. Evet had blocked and re-blocked any realisations for he had been desperate to delay Brody from discovering the truth.

Evet had obviously not allowed him to pay them that much needed and greater attention and, although the children had also been delving around inside his head in the same way that *he* had, it now seemed that their intentions were far more honourable.

His amazement and pleasure were completed and reaffirmed when, without even the slightest pause or change in tone, John continued with, '*John is fine for now, and you weren't to know – how could you? When he caught on to us trying to warn you, he started to block us by twisting your mind. We had to pick our moments and we know he tried to confuse you and called us the others. In our phase, the larger ones are the others; we are known as the children of others.*' It seemed such an insignificance of a difference in wording but obviously meant a lot to them. Brody mentally made a note to refer to them accordingly from then on.

'*Others couldn't control things like us and needed us to regenerate them; they were physically bigger, however, relatively powerless and struggled to survive over time without us.*' This complete reversal of details seemed obvious now and Brody was slightly embarrassed at how easily he had been misled.

'*After only a short time the others all died and only the creator of this horrific eugenic experiment remained. He further experimented on himself and totally changed his own DNA to retain his larger physicality and to attempt to possess all our powers.*' As Brody continued to listen intently to the children of others through John, his melodic, gentle and harmonious-sounding voice (which he had accepted as having emanated from the male appearance of John) still sounded strangely female. The distant thought of Talosian adventures flicked in and out.

It, she or he continued and laid out the complex history of how, over centuries, these two joined but genetically-modified races had been forced to co-exist as harmoniously as possible due to the horrendous experimentation of one seemingly mad scientist of hundreds of years ago.

"Your history is very harrowing but also absolutely fascinating," Brody verbally complimented John who had vicariously become, as Brody thought of it, the singular voice of the children.

'Children of Others,' he mentally corrected himself and John smiled. Brody realised the obvious – they heard every thought.

After learning all about their trials and tribulations through the generations, it felt strange to physically speak. He had been listening to a non-speaking conversation within his mind for so long, he felt he should respond the same but was obviously unable.

"So, what happened to this maniac in the end then?" he asked naïvely.

'It was normal for one of the others to co-exist with only one or two of us children of others to safely balance the power trade-offs, so we were sent to bring him back to justice after he used his experiments to escape our phase centuries ago. He has eluded all the children of others sent and us also, thus far,' John explained.

"So, how can he still be alive after all these millennia?" Brody queried the timescale discrepancy in their story.

'The others could live a long time, hundreds of years if linked to one of us periodically. Their normal lifespan, without being linked, would be relatively negligible and, if you pardon the term, quite humanesque. We, on the other hand, live about eight hundred of your years if not connected, but if linked and regenerated regularly we can share virtual immortality. This is what he wanted – our ability to live on without the need to link to us.' John went on to further explain how, periodically, it seemed that Evet had managed to link to various individuals of the pursuer children of others, sent to capture him and thus had managed to regenerate himself and live an, *'on the run, search for immortality'*-style, precarious existence.

'Although we have never been certain of his heritage he was the last but in effect, now modified, is the first of his kind. He killed and changed himself and his whole lineage in the name of this sought-after immortality. He will stop at nothing to get it.'

"If he linked to some of you now and again, this guy must be hundreds of years old by now then," Brody outwardly surmised.

'Yes, we seven have only been on our quest to bring him to justice for about two years, but many more have sought him before us for many hundreds of years without success,' John confirmed in a sort of disappointed tone.

"With so much riding on your success, this Evet character has really let you down then. He seemed closed, defensive and only interested in just getting home." Brody tried poorly to sympathise with their plight, not having fully grasped what he had heard. All he thought he knew now was that Evet and the mad scientist were both stuck in another phase with a limited timescale to find a way home – like him, really. Two and two had made three.

'He did not *let us down, we let ourselves down and he merely escaped AGAIN. He used your mental patterns to disengage from us during the night – that is why they sent all seven of us to apprehend him in the first place, to avoid this very tactic, as previously only two or three have been despatched.'* The penny creaked and started to slowly drop within Brody's normally sharp, but currently very confused mind.

'He is old, cunning and wily. We will prevail eventually; although his powers have grown over time, we do not believe he can travel far without re-connecting to at least one of us fairly soon.' The verbally silent but mind-blowing response explained what Brody had missed like a mini explosion inside his head and, as the idiom hit home, he was physically shaken in his realisation.

"EVET is the one who did all that, which you have told me of." Brody had heard it before, but the light switch had flicked and only now could he put two and two together and got four instead of his earlier failed attempt. Still, he couldn't fully take it in.

'Evetzzirrah is but one name he has used over the years. Our history

lists many alternates: Dybbuk, Hellion, Erinyes, Mephistopheles, Djinn, Lucifer, Kandarian, Beelzebub, Satan and many more.' The absoluteness of this final statement, which literally made Brody's blood chill, echoed around his consciousness. He felt a twitching pain between his shoulders, became dizzy and had to relax right back to lay flat on the porch decking. His understanding of nearly everything he had ever known or believed in had been decimated by receiving this terrifying and damning revelation.

CHAPTER 8

The Children of Others.

Brody was physically and mentally stunned. As he scrambled back up to a seated position on the porch he thought to himself that crying or praying might be the only options. Had he, for however short a period, truly, in effect, been in league with the Devil?

'Ridiculous; it just can't be!' His thoughts beseeched nobody in particular and were of arguable desperation. Whether he could accept it or not, there was no longer any wonderment about why he couldn't fully believe all that Evet had said and done. Most of it had certainly been deception and lies and he had exhibited mastery in these departments. Brody now considered he was in some way to blame for his escape.

'No, it was not your fault,' the patient melodic voice of John interjected into his thoughts.

'We could not tell you about him in any greater detail whilst still connected to him; his power was developing to mimic ours and was too great when tapping our abilities, even with our seven minds controlling him he could still exert enough influence to make us help him kill the Vikings of this phase and *hold us from communicating directly to you. In* this phase, *those you call Vikings seem to attack anyone; we don't know why. We hoped to merely avoid them until we found a way to get home. He seemed to* enjoy *the killing. DO*

NOT blame yourself, but please help US.' The statement was firm but pleading.

'*How?*' he thought openly, still not used to the lack of mental privacy.

'By allowing us to connect to you periodically and helping us track and recapture him.' The reply to a question he did not outwardly make reminded him of this point, but before he could debate the rights and wrongs of the issue, John continued as if in his own desperation.

'His random transportation to here, with no proper method of return may not have been random at all. He always maintained that it was due to some sort of failure in his transportation method. It apparently *marooned him here, but he definitely and deliberately destroyed* our *transport vessel when we arrived in pursuit. Since your simple discovery of how the night influences the* Necronomicon, *he might now choose to escape this phase and leave* US *trapped here forever. We now believe he always knew how but was waiting for some reason... For YOU. As you seem to be his only reason for staying, we really need* your *help to recover him.'*

Brody didn't need to speak; his reply needed no words. It was said with a smile and a flameless wink towards John. Of course he would help. After all, his own ability to get home seemed to rely upon it also.

For the rest of the day the children of others untangled his brain and laid out how Evet had time and again laid plot over subplot to confuse and manipulate him into thinking whatever he needed to be thinking. As they gradually got all the information to him, they also managed to educate his mind in the methods of unspoken communication.

"I had genuinely thought that all this time the mystery echo I kept hearing was you lot trying to warn me. He must have known and was holding back my thoughts and stopping my decision-making process because I am usually a really good judge of character. Well, I'll be damned!" Brody finally had all the information and realised that, even with it, he still knew next to nothing about what Evet might do next. He certainly didn't wish them dead, it seemed. Not yet, at least anyway.

'What did you mean when you whispered to me, 'he wants you to help release **them***'?'* Brody thought-asked, testing out his new ability.

He was very pleased with his raw new skill which allowed him to communicate directly to the group.

'The Necronomicon *was not found here as he told you, he brought it with him from wherever he had been hiding before we relocated him here. We had sadly lost him temporarily a few years ago, but we managed to find him again because this place is of his doing. Its sudden materialisation out of sync with the rest of our known science drew us here. As of yet we are uncertain of its purpose or stability. We do believe his distant ancestors, if not ours, may have originally written the volume and we think he might be attempting to release the demons which it mentions, right here as some sort of controlled test.'* Another bombshell landed and Brody started to fully comprehend the size of the task ahead of him and his more honest companions.

'We always knew that if he could get you wound up tight enough that you might try to help him and unfortunately you did just that by simply sleeping as he suggested whilst he was craftily sneaking away. His powers are obviously more developed than we had anticipated as we were also duped on this occasion.' The children replied virtually but softly through John to ease him into his new-found ability.

As Brody became more accustomed to multi-communication from his other six, as of yet, unnamed new compatriots, John did most of the unspoken talking and explained how they, as a group, wished they had been allowed to execute Evet to save all this trouble. Their high council had dictated years before that he must be returned to them to be tried and sentenced accordingly; the council wanted his knowledge.

Apparently, the power of the high council members combined could extract it from his living brain and, as such, a potentially exhaustive font of information could be invaluable to them in terms of trying to rectify some of the genetic physical weaknesses which he himself had bestowed upon them centuries ago. Brody didn't disagree but thought to himself that this potential extraction of information was ironically only mirroring in some way what Evet had done to them originally. The children knew his thoughts but did not allow him to realise that they knew; knowing it to be true, being somewhat embarrassed of the fact and not wanting him to mistrust them.

The group got much better acquainted and exchanged much of each other's personal histories over the next few days whilst planning their next move. The children often described a horrific death that apparently they regularly dreamt of en masse of bestowing upon Evet.

'*We would certainly like to slowly burn him alive for all his deadly and dastardly deeds... Just imagine the smell as his skin melts away from his bones. Picture it now, it's burning his hands, he's turning to laugh, he smiles at us as the flames sear his flesh, its melting his face, he is screaming in pain, the skin is peeling from his eyelids.*' The images swirling around Brody's head satisfied him but were also quite disconcerting. He was slightly perturbed at the violence they wished upon Evet, but balanced it off against the centuries of pain Evet had apparently caused them – it now appeared justified if a tad barbaric.

'*We would watch him die according to our plan, his dust*

staining the ground and we would be rid of him forever – but what would we have learned from it?' The fact that they had held him captive without attempting to realise their dream execution was a reassurance of their inalienable humanity.

'It seems our backs are against the wall, so now we turn to you and look positively towards the light at the end of the tunnel, to use one of your Earth colloquialisms. Sadly, there will probably be no burning in the night, but more like watching candles burn just for the light. Like a beacon of hope, perhaps you too can burn along with us tonight and help us avoid being the seven children that are damned to remain here for the rest of our extremely long lives.'

Their mentally transmitted case was completely compelling and he readily agreed to do everything that he could to help them, although deep down, after hearing all of his new adversary's pseudonyms he sincerely doubted the chances of their success. The doubt in his mind was no secret to the children.

After much debate with the now correctly titled Children of Others, over the next few days, following Evet's unannounced departure, it was decided they should all travel together and remain linked. Being as one at least during the night periods and never out of visual range of each other during the day, linked or not was decided upon as the safest option. As Brody was getting to know and understand the group, already more informally referred to as 'the children', the feeling of being part of their collective minds had initially felt most strange to him.

For the first day or two it quite often made him feel nauseous but, like most things, once they have been done repetitively for a long period they start to become second nature. Brody soon got used to the feeling.

One big advantage of being linked in that way was that now he could speak to them all together without having to physically speak or even be in the vicinity of them. They could individually talk to him without the need for an en masse conversation. This was the part that was very weird for Brody as, although they didn't have names or at least hadn't told him what they were, he instinctively knew which one was speaking when the thoughts were transmitted and received – it was like some sort of internal mental homing signal which equated to a human brain and ear's ability to discern who was speaking in a crowd. In this case it was without the need to even be able to visually see the crowd.

He could, however, not hear their inter-group thoughts and was unsure if that was to protect him from the complete mêlée of noise it would create in his brain or if it was just the last threads of secrecy between them.

Their plan now was not only to re-link to Evet to control him when he was found but also to attempt to physically incarcerate him in some sort of mobile cell, thus enabling them to take as long as necessary to decipher the *Necronomicon* in relative safety. Deciphering the book sufficiently to find a way back to their own phase of reality was merely the minor hiccup in an otherwise extremely tenuously conceived plan.

Their idea being (assuming the book worked as surmised) was that on finding Evet, he and they could switch links at some point giving them full control over Evet again. Then if it all worked they could send him to his own phase and Evet would be forced to go with them to theirs. It was unanimously agreed that this would only be seriously achievable with Evet as a permanent physical captive.

With their transportation vessel having been destroyed, Brody's confusingly inexplicable 'pod three' somehow hidden and with Evet's own form of transport allegedly broken (but either way a complete unknown quantity anyway) it appeared that *Necronomicon* was everyone's best hope.

That was the extremely tenuous plan that was completely reliant on myths and legends. How they would actually achieve it was even more fraught with uncertainty and, as such, it was all still under daily discussion.

'Forgive me for seeming rude, but with all his stories now pretty much rubbished as stretches of the imagination and twists of the truth and – I do actually understand most of it – but for all this time in this phase, if it was that easy for him to escape your mental link, why has he not done so before?' Brody transmitted to the whole group this question, one that had been troubling him for as many days as had passed since Evet's abscondence. Falling for a con once was relatively understandable given the complexity of the situation, but he did not want to fall for another one now.

The children explained that they had always believed that Evet, being only able to survive long-term by linking regularly, was unlikely to want to stay unlinked for too long. Although technically they had been controlling him seven to one, they hadn't ever felt the need to worry too greatly about his desire to escape in this phase, as they believed he would have eventually perished here without them.

That was a logical and sound explanation, but it seemed to Brody, based on his restricted experience of the man and the multiple historic stories he was now in possession of, that over the past few hundred years Evet might possibly have evolved and drawn new abilities and strengths from the long-term links with all the children's various predecessors. It also seemed logical that he might have secretly desired temporary captivity as it would have allowed him to make further gain of his own strengths until the time was right. It was now Brody's firm belief that he had been fuelling up, so to speak, for one big future push in the knowledge that eventually he might be able to survive independently without them. In effect, he had possibly been leaching their powers for all this time with the full understanding that at some point he was always going to dispose of them.

If Brody was correct and this was the case it remained a mystery to him as to why he had not done away with both him and the children already, if able to do so.

Things went round and round his now much more capable mind and he felt sure the answers to all these questions would only be found by recapturing Evet and attempting to decipher the riddle of the *Necronomicon*. He didn't really wish to consider the alternatives if it did not work. Further to all this, it now appeared to Brody quite naïve of the children to believe that they were always more in control than it appeared. They had stubbornly held onto this belief and were apparently sentimentally blinded with the thoughts of their own superiority. Possibly hundreds of years of hand-me-down pursuit of this one person had created a routine that did not lend itself to change. Brody was now realising that in *his* life he also always had to change and adapt and possibly, back home, had been equally naïve when it came to Charley.

Another thing he had learned in his multitudinous and varied career choices was a small amount of animal tracking when he had worked very briefly for the local forestry commission doing livestock surveys of unusual and endangered indigenous species. When they finally departed it was therefore not difficult for him to quickly pick up the tracks in the dirt, to get an idea of the direction that they should head in. Much to his amusement and delight, the children's thought patterns expressed pleasure and Brody assumed they were impressed.

None of them seemed to notice the transparently obvious fact that, of their group, Evet was the only one who had overly large feet within the region of a UK size eleven shoe. Brody's feet were a considerably smaller size nine and the children were all barefoot, so he enjoyed the plaudits and was quite entertained at the fact.

The only other marks he noted were some that looked like sheep or goat tracks, which seemed to follow the same path and, after a while, obscured the shoe prints completely. Although he had not seen any animals in the area, he felt confident of his fake bloodhound show not being sussed out and thought no more about it.

The trail was initially roughly heading west away from the coast, which seemed to support his ideas of the direction Evet had probably gone. He wouldn't have wished to encounter any vengeful Viking hordes whilst not linked to one or more of his kinsmen, especially in his suspected weakened state. Even if he had developed greater powers than they were aware of, the west still seemed the obvious safe bet.

In addition to the evidence of the original size eleven trail in the sandy path leading that way before becoming obscured, there were only two main routes leading west. The debate as to whether to split into two groups of four did not get off the ground when Brody was happy to announce that he had found fresh tracks on the upper trail. Apart from the sheep or goat markings, in truth, he hadn't. He had gambled on door A again and decided it was safe to assume that anyone wanting to be unobserved would probably choose to take high ground to get the best vantage point of increased defend ability. It would also be harder to be spotted by followers with the sun at your back most of the day. He blagged and gambled, feeling sure his choice was good. He remembered door B with a wry smile and concentrated solely on A. His mind wandered briefly, glimpsing forlornly, a fluttering mirage of Charley.

The children experienced his fond recollection and saw compassion and love. They were heartened and pleased. Evet saw weakness and opportunity and was similarly pleased but for different reasons.

They carried only water and communicated infrequently as they followed the rocky higher trail that gained altitude all the time. Even with his amazing tracking abilities, the footprint trail was by now useless as the hard ground didn't even reveal the surefooted goats' whereabouts. Brody thought he saw the quarry on quite a few occasions, but it always turned out to be reflections or shadows.

A Homer quote came to mind: *"Are we in India yet?"* and it repetitively tickled Brody on more than a few occasions when he thought he saw the children glancing expectantly in his direction. They had not yet become fully comfortable with the concept of human humour and showed no sign of amusement.

'Are we way behind, way in front, or just on the wrong track?' was another much more relevant question that Brody worriedly posed himself. The answer turned out to be none of these as they were all to find out very soon. The silhouette of the lone horseman was spotted again on the far horizon, but Brody and the children had more than enough to worry about without considering stalkers, shadows, lost souls or the possibilities of ghosts.

The high country path they had chosen to follow based upon the tracking skills Brody had discreetly not talked about in too much depth seemed to be, more by luck than judgement, bearing fruit, when on the third day of their trek they met a lone traveller coming in the opposite direction and learned that, not only had this particular person not seen any Viking raiders for months but he had seen a lone, tall, long-haired stranger who was heading for the next village.

The quietly spoken traveller informed them that the tall man seemed very stressed and tired and was carrying a large satchel. Of course, the description was too much of a coincidence to be wrong and, by all accounts, he was only just ahead by possibly half a day so his travel time since his escape was seeming to be very slow. Brody and the children had, in effect, given him nearly a week's head start. The information lifted Brody's spirits.

The man travelling in the other direction was wearing a large shrouded cape, which looked three times bigger than it needed to be, but he had genially taken the time to stop and chat to Brody – derogatory comments about his sense of style seemed inappropriate and unfair, even if sorely tempting. The shabbily-cloaked traveller told them that he was only too happy to help with directions to the nearest place to stay at the next village but advised against the visit. Before his departure he left them with a complete Scooby-Doo of a warning by half-whispering,

"I told the other man, the one with long hair and deceptive eyes, the one that you seek and I will tell you the same… Remember this… Trust nobody and if you take my advice, don't even go there. There is an evil in that village. You may feel welcomed when you first arrive but leaving may be much harder." His tone was shaky, foreboding and he sounded genuinely frightened. Brody considered telling him how lucky he had been not to have encountered the man that he had described as having deceptive eyes – more formally – but thought better of it. Better to let him continue uninterrupted and so he said nothing and just listened to the man's foreboding lament.

"People there say one thing and do another. I tell you now and can't reiterate it strongly enough – trust nobody in this area as most are not what they seem." If ever a warning sent shivers down a spine, this one did – but they were undeterred. If anything, all eight were now spurred on by the cryptic statement combined with Evet's potential proximity.

Brody chose not to reveal the complexities of Evet's nature and their inter-relationships to this helpful individual. He thought it unnecessary to burden him with such knowledge or to waste more time with fruitless tittle-tattle. After a few more minutes on polite pleasantries, he thanked the traveller on behalf of himself and the children and they moved on. When they had parted company, Brody felt two inches taller and as the eight of them strode on towards their new goal, he attempted to whistle a tune. It was no better in this phase than his own and he did not persist for long, but he smiled to himself as it brought fond memories of Charley frowning sexily as she always did whenever he tried to hold a note.

Perhaps Evet was not as powered up as they had imagined. The children noticed Brody's quickened pace and straightened stance and were, in turn, heartened and moved on in anticipation of catching up with Evet, perhaps even before he could get to the next village. If possible, ideally intercepting him before he could settle to his continued work of deathly disruption, would be best. The twisting of the community with his inherent untruthful deceptions or far worse, in yet another settlement, would only further complicate things.

They needed to stop him coercing others into helping him in some way; hiding or defending him. Certainly, they needed to try to stop him employing an even more permanent tactic as with the family at the smallholding they had left a few days before. He had, after all, merely just callously murdered them to silence their possible communication to others and to provide a convenient place to stay whilst leading the group.

By the setting of the sun on that day they caught sight of the village that lay ahead at the lower part of a steep bank running down to a beach. This made the direction and transparency of their arrival an easy decision as a small inland sea or larger lake was protecting the village on three sides, leaving them only the downhill winding path to approach on. The houses were painted in bright colours of varying shades, each one different to the next; it looked a very cosmopolitan society although at this distance no people were visibly evident. The only clue to a population was the occasional sounding of a siren that reminded Brody of an ambulance but, as more of an announcement than a warning, perhaps an ice cream van. They decided to wait until nightfall and try to get into what looked like the community area under the tenuous cover of the ninety-minute twin moonlit night, thus allowing some small potential for a surprise element to their arrival. Brody had become used to the darker first fifteen minutes or so of night and led the group in silence during this time knowing that the fast-approaching, brighter moonlight would more easily give away their arrival.

He gave some slight consideration to the fact that the moons rose at roughly the same time each night and had done so every night so far since his arrival. This seemed both unlikely and strange but could not be disputed as he had witnessed it himself first-hand. The thought drifted away as trivial and not important.

They entered the village square and approached an ornate fountain pool in front of the main structure that resembled an old clock tower of about seventy feet in height, but without a clock face. The unusual building was deemed, very likely to be the town meeting hall. Brody thought it might be a good place to make first contact.

He climbed the few steps leading to the huge, brightly coloured front door that was shaped like an arch and decoratively detailed. The doors creaked and swung open in what seemed to him to be a very melodramatic, Addams Family or Munsters type way. He was surprised by the lack of persons behind these doors and it seemed they must be automated in some way; nobody appeared to be present.

Part expecting an ambush of some kind and feeling more nervous, he tentatively took a step inside. The room was approximately fifty foot high with what appeared to be stained glass domed windows at lower roof level. These windows spanned the entire ceiling area allowing the moonlight to refract in, causing the room to appear to be virtually lit. Bright reds, yellows and blues bounced off the stark white walls creating an amazing and captivating collage of blended colours. He scanned the room but saw no evidence of life and the feeling of potential ambush drifted away.

Taking a few more steps inside he realised the walls were completely smooth with no windows at lower level. They were painted in some sort of fluorescent white material adding to the overall brightness. The others followed him in and filed around searching for evidence of any inhabitants of this strangely quiet village. Even though it was night there was literally no sound, it was too quiet, as if the whole village was holding its breath waiting for some amazing revelation.

As they stood in the eerily bright room looking at each other for inspiration, the double arched doors swung closed with a metallic clang. The stomach-churning noise revealed the simple fact… Easier than a mouse with cheese they had been trapped. Their curiosity and interest in the light refraction had completely blinded them to the blatantly obvious trap itself. As they began to frantically mill about, attempting futilely to find a way out they soon discovered that the double doors they had so naïvely entered through were made of some sort of solid metal-based material and were, in fact, the only obvious way in or out.

With the walls being so high with no windows below forty-five feet it seemed too incredible that they had entered without much suspicion of what might happen next – just a simple bit of light refraction acting as the rather embarrassing but irresistible cheese, to eight foolish mice.

The words of warning from the cloaked stranger rang around Brody's head and he blamed his lack of patience for placing everyone in this new 'told you so' type of danger.

'Not your fault, Brody,' thought the one that Brody had named John.

'We think that someone – guess who – has managed to create a brain impulse dampening effect around this structure as, just before we entered, we all felt somewhat less connected. We sadly paid little attention and in here we are now completely individual in mind and body.' This revelation did not surprise Brody as much as it latently worried him. Up until now he had felt comforted by the protection supplied and the power commanded by his new childlike friends. He felt a lot more disconnected in this captivity of eight. John continued the transmission unaffected by the resonance of Brody's inner fears – perhaps he had not detected them or decided to gloss over it to act as comfort.

'I am sorry to say we are relatively powerless in here; he seems to have won this round.' The rather weakly transmitted thought was like having the rug pulled from beneath him. Brody's knees buckled as his initial feelings of trepidation welled within him. He slumped to the floor tantrum-style in a cross-legged seated position.

Complete silence reigned for the next hour and it wasn't until the sun's rays started to filter in through the roof windows that anyone spoke or even transmitted any further thoughts. The strange up and down, high-pitched *der, dur, der, dut* siren noise they had heard when approaching now woke those sleeping and aroused interest from those sitting contemplatively as it repeated its twin bursts of pattern. What next would this unusual confinement throw at them?

CHAPTER 9

Confinement.

"WELCOME travellers!" boomed an unseen voice. Brody and the others rose from their resting positions and looked futilely up and down the walls of their new prison cell for any sort of amplification or speaker system. The words had seemed to originate from within the room and were received audibly, not transmitted to mind.

"We accept you here to our humble village," continued the grand announcement, "but we require information." It paused, then repeated the word 'information' twice more to accentuate its importance. Without waiting for further announcements, Brody shouted at the top of his voice, "WHO ARE YOU?" Another pause of what seemed like an hour but was only ten seconds, followed with… "YOU are the eight, WE are the village and we want information." Anger rose inside Brody's chest that gave him a feeling of bile rising after a heavy drinking session. Partly out of frustration of their whole situation he screamed, "WE ARE NOT **JUST** NUMBERS, we are free-willed individuals… We *do* have information, but you must show yourselves to share it!" As he shouted the words it calmed his anger and reverberated around his head. For an instant he felt as if he was in Portmeirion itself. Silence filled the room for the next long, drawn-out seconds and then a near-deafening booming laughter reverberated around the chamber.

"Ahhhhhaaaaahhhhaaaahaaaaahaaaaaaaaaaa!" It sounded manic, uncontrolled. It was full of emotion and confusion.

"The PREVIOUS one told us you would try to confuse us." At this moment, initially unnoticed perforations around the bottom of the walls were now clearly seen. They looked like minute air conditioning vents and were distinctly and suddenly very noticeable as appearing from them was a spray of fine white mist which clouded as it hit the air in the room and created a layer of low-lying, heavy gas that looked like thick fog or dry ice. Brody spun around to witness the shorter children who were closer to the gas, start to drop down, and one by one they fell onto the now hidden floor. Brody was also falling. Hitting the deck, already unconscious, he did not feel the impact of his head on the stony shale floor, which probably added to the fact he was slowest to recover. As he started to come round, he realised the others had already risen and looked unharmed. His head was throbbing and he noticed small spots of blood on his t-shirt.

Brody realised they were no longer alone. At the extremities of the square-shaped room stood eight, fierce-looking six- to seven-foot-tall Anglo-Saxon warriors – three along each wall surrounded them, all with various weapons in hand grimacing and snarling as if ready to jump in for the kill.

Virtually in unison the eight captives took a blind step back towards each other to the centre of the room creating a huddled group that, to an outsider, might have resembled the reaction of sheep to a sheepdog. They all had eyes darting in every direction to ensure maximum distance from the nearest Saxon collie that guarded any potential of straying from the invisible pen. Instinctively, the group cowered back further bumping and jostling each other for the position furthest away from any one of the threatening warriors and their sharp implements of death.

Brody stepped out of the crowd and headed towards the largest of them. His advance was met by the swoosh of a huge, double-edged sword coming to rest only inches away from his chest. He stopped in his tracks considerably quicker than he had started. A silent impasse was momentarily created with neither Brody nor any of the children confident enough to move further.

'*What next?*' they all thought to each other simultaneously.

'*The best we can achieve at this point with this damping field affecting our mental strengths is an annoying buzz that might break a window or two but not much more – we are relatively powerless. Any ideas, Brody?*' The children had unintentionally communicated to him what he already knew, that he had let them down badly and he himself needed to step up to the plate to get them out of this predicament.

All of a sudden, as if stepping out from another plane of existence, a short, stocky male appeared from behind the largest warrior and side-stepped like a goalkeeper, quickly placing himself between Brody and the monstrous Saxon. It was as if he was there to save the inevitable loss of limb that was at that very moment threatening him. Strangely, but not over surprisingly, Brody's mind locked on to a thought of a vertically-challenged TV character famous for his dubious interventions in all sorts of trouble. With only a wine bottle in hand – this little man could have been his double.

'*Tyrion,*' he thought.

"Who are you?" he enquired much calmer than the last time.

"I represent the village. Are you the leader of the eight?" was the expectedly unhelpful answer. Brody took the bull by the horns and, after flashing a thought around the group to indicate his plan to test their new captor's true intentions, he answered,

"Yes, I lead the eight. Why do you hold us here? We only came searching, possibly for the one you referred to as 'the previous one.'" The little guy stroked his beard and looked puzzled.

"You are not as the previous one had described, you seem civilised and polite and he assured us you would be heathens, treacherous and violent." It now seemed obvious to all that Evet had been here before them and convinced this village en masse that others of a danger to them would follow him and that, to incarcerate them to save themselves from a fate undisclosed, would be the best course of action. He had, in effect, used this place as a decoy to at least temporarily if not permanently stop the children from recapturing him. If nothing else, it was certainly going to slow their progress. Now it only remained to be seen how hard it would be to extricate themselves from this situation and get back on his trail.

The children reinforced Brody's concerns that if the triclipse came and Evet was able to use the *Necronomicon* successfully, his travel through space and time, using alternate phases in a fully energised state, could potentially have incalculable detrimental effects on the balance of the universe and reality itself. And as if it couldn't be worse, it would be virtually impossible to track him, as the destinations available to him were infinite. They MUST convince their captors of *their* sincerity and stop him at all costs.

"As you can see and have realised for yourselves, we are none of those things. Please release us and we will leave your village in peace the way we arrived to continue our quest to find the one you call 'the previous one' and bring HIM to justice for the crimes he has committed," Brody requested in a confidently reassuring manner.

"Mmmmmm. That is exactly what he anticipated you would say, so unfortunately I don't think we can trust you just yet. I will leave the guards here to ensure your safety and behaviour and consult with the elders before deciding our next move and your fate." To Brody's amusement, in his periphery the little guy did his little goalkeeper-like dance, side-stepped a little jig and then seemed to disappear behind the biggest warrior and in a flash was gone – into thin air. The children and Brody looked at each other in amazement. They were all bemused and intrigued but did not feel overly safe after witnessing this apparent ability to disappear exhibited so blatantly.

'Where has the little guy gone? He was like a tiny but irresistible force and now he has vanished behind this giant immoveable object.' Thoughts reverberated around the group and much non-verbal communication was bantered back and forth to try and explain the incredulous disappearing trick.

The small man that Brody and the children had not yet decided to trust was of a similar disposition having been visited recently by a powerful and seemingly benevolent King who promised many things for the capture of his currently not-so-comfortable house guests. The man wanted to trust them and felt an affinity with them but had been severely warned of underlying dangers they brought with them. How could he be sure who was being truthful?

It was difficult for Brody to keep up with the conversations flying around now; all seven were thinking and communicating independently and no longer co-ordinated via one or other's lead thought pattern. He did his best to interject a few ideas, one of which was the embarrassing fact that it was highly likely that the pleasant, quiet, warning-giving, cloaked stranger they had met on the track a few miles outside the village had probably been Evet himself. Somehow he had been hiding his identity from the thoughts of the group and disguising his physicality in the crudeness of the extra-large shroud. The whole group felt partly ashamed at having been that close to *his* capture and not having been able to see through the deceptions that led to their own. None of them so much as had a clue who he was and even as he warned against it; very craftily and quite deliberately he had blatantly goaded and sent them to their fate, right here. The possibility of him having chameloid abilities was discussed at length, but as there was no proof the debate ended without meaningful conclusion other than Brody's startled introduction to the reality of the existence of *shapeshifters.* Although amazed by his resultant gain in knowledge, Brody was naturally worried by the chances of Evet having a propensity for this annoyingly useful capability. They were *all,* also slightly amused, but to the best of their individual abilities, concealed their admissions of being mildly impressed. The raw, obvious and blatantly deceitful nature of their capture was a point of shared but denied embarrassment. They had to hand it to him, *however* he had managed it. He had completely played them for fools. Unfortunately, the three-times-too-big coat he was wearing not only helped disguise him but had also certainly been hiding the missing *Necronomicon Ex-Mortis.*

The children discussed the possibilities of Evet having leached these additional powers from any of a plethora of other beings in the different phases that he had travelled to. It seemed highly possible and even likely, if he met and coerced them during the years that they had been in his pursuit. It explained many things but they came to no definitive conclusions. Could it have been a natural evolutionary change in his DNA or even a result of his own self-experimentation that they had previously been unaware of?

Brody busied himself by intermittently testing the water with their silent guards. On the few occasions that he probed, any move towards the door or walls was immediately met with a drawn sword or lowered spear – the warriors were resolute and uncompromising. A few hours passed before their prison warden, so to speak, returned as miraculously as he had left earlier – popping up from nowhere – again quite strangely, just when attention was not being given to his arrival location.

'Just like Mr Benn,' Brody mused to everyone, but obviously only he got the reference.

'Where is Cash when you need him? Typical. I only wanted to take the piss out of a midget magician and nobody is here to appreciate it.' No response came from either the group or the butt of the joke. It was frustrating but also quite useful as it indicated he could still hope to communicate to the children in relative secrecy. It appeared that Mr Benn or Tyrion did not or could not detect their unspoken dialogue. Then the small man made an announcement of his own:

"The elders have made a review of the evidence and feel you, the eight, are potentially dangerous to the village and that you might try to deceive us to your own ends. They wish to keep you here a little longer and observe you to ascertain *their* potential safety, *if* and *when* you are to be released." This was not what Brody had hoped would happen at all. Things then went from bad to worse.

"According to our laws it is necessary to hold you for a statutory period before the issue of your release can be reconsidered." A buzz went around the group but before any decision was made, Brody stepped forward and asked,

"What is your statutory period?" His jaw dropped when he heard the answer.

"One year, only." Without any communication required, they all knew that Evet could not be allowed to be free for that length of time, especially in possession of the *Necronomicon* and with triclipse day fast approaching. Just as the eight of them huddled together to discuss the damning decision and just as quickly as he had reappeared, the small man had once again… gone. This really bothered Brody. He knew in his own mind he should be concentrating on thinking of ways out, but was now preoccupied with the little guy's way in.

Just like Brody's testing of the Saxon guards, at another location Evet had been intermittently but carefully monitoring the comings and goings within the captive group. Brody's predilection for irrelevance and preoccupation with his captor had intrigued him to the point of not being able to resist interjection, hence the statutory period suggestion he had so carefully planted in the minds of the little man's elders.

As a result and whilst unable to do much else, Brody stirred up a silent conversation about what to call the elusive little jailor. It was fun for him and if nothing else, a harmless form of minor distraction from the seemingly insurmountable issues at hand. As usual, bigger boats floated around in *his* head. He relayed some amusing anecdotes to encourage them to lean towards choosing one of his more comical suggestions as a name for their tiny dungeon master. The favourite was Tattoo but, after seven, individually short but complex thought transference discussions about the differences between someone called Tattoo and an actual tattoo (which then led to Brody having to show the seven children his extensive tattoo work and further needing to re-explain the name relevant to its origin in his mental TV history files) he finally decided Hervé would be better and quickly declined to even attempt to explain what a midget actor was. Perhaps Tyrion would have sufficed but after all that, his mind couldn't even comprehend explaining such broad and complex issues as dragons, dire wolves and ice kings.

Brody was frustrated and annoyed at not being able to inspect the ground directly behind the monstrous six foot seven warrior where their newly named diminutive captor, Hervé, kept disappearing and reappearing from. He paced up and down hoping for some movement from the big guy to reveal something that they had missed, pre-gas episode. No movement from the giant gave

Brody little option but to be patient, as he certainly did not want to encounter this six foot eight man mountain in battle – he knew who the winner would be…

This innocuous thought suddenly resonated with him and made him think again of Cash and likewise, Charley, who used to moan at him regularly when he would recount stories of his underground fight matches. They knew he embellished the details to make his achievements grander but Brody was a relatively tough guy for a smallish man of nearly forty. He considered, however, that if pitted against a six foot nine giant with a sword, he didn't fancy his chances too much. After all, six foot ten was enough for anyone to fear. Then another old but comfortable thought occurred to him; he always used to say the same thing to Cash and he quoted it verbally to himself now, just to feel what his own voice felt like again.

"You don't have to be tough to make money fighting, you just need to be quick and know who is going to win. Blah, blah, blah… Backing the right guy is the skill. Yadda, yadda… You have to learn to know how and when to lose safely." A chord was well and truly struck and its reverberation stayed with him. The next time the little warden appeared, Brody beckoned him over and suggested that he could defeat all his mighty warriors in battle. He suggested a fight and would gamble the freedom of the other seven against permanent servitude for himself, to be able to take them all on, one at a time, outside on the grass.

The diminutive prison warden now christened Hervé, declined the wager and smiled at how Brody had been so blatantly obvious in trying to work such a transparent escape plan.

The seven had only been able to agree in principle on the final naming of the little guy, as Brody was the only person who knew the full relevance of any of the chosen names he had bounced around the group. By now everyone had agreed he looked like and should be called Hervé. After its repetitious usage and Brody's continual derogatory non-verbal impressions, the name started to make the others laugh out loud. This in itself was a massive moral victory, as Brody couldn't remember having heard them communicate verbally in any way and had not heard laughter at all, not even within their thought streaming. They were genuinely amused at his mimicry and projected funny voices when Hervé was not present.

'Boss, Boss, De Plane, De Plane... Deep-Rain.' They did not fully understand the references but laughed, at first partly out of politeness but eventually more infectiously because they were so amused and entertained at how completely titillated Brody himself got. *He* was amused at how much better his mentally transmitted voice impersonations were compared to the verbal versions that he was so accustomed to doing his best to amuse with, back home. He was, however, still annoyed with the little guy for not taking his bait but, more importantly, wanted the group to remain upbeat.

'A good comic should never laugh at his own jokes,' Brody smiled, but it took the edge off the seriousness of the current dilemma. He had only wanted the opportunity to get outside, then fighting would most definitely not have been his objective. Moreover, flight would have been the priority. Even at this pivotal moment Brody still drifted to humour – the idea of *flight* reminded him of a t-shirt he once owned and the comparison between 'fight club' and the 'weird fishes' comically named 'flight club' raised an internal smile.

More seriously, and back in *this* reality it now seemed that a plan B was definitely required and Brody used the amusement created about Hervé and his stature to keep the others' and his own spirits from dropping whilst he set about coming up with a new angle of approach.

The windows above were beginning to darken again and Brody

knew time was of the essence. He decided to try a radically more dangerous tactic and ran headlong towards the entrance. With no chance to get through the solid locked doors, his purpose was to once again test the reactions of his guards and, more riskily, their willingness of causing his potential injury in stopping him. They were predictably lightning fast and comfortingly, only seemed interested in containment with no apparent intention to injure or kill him. On this occasion, the two nearest swinging spears came across the entrance directly level with his chest as he skidded to a safe distanced halt. Frustrated but heartened, he returned to the middle ground and began silently communicating to John and a couple more of the seven.

He recounted a story from an old sci-fi movie where one of the main characters was stuck in a complete no-win situation and cleverly managed to change the test parameters to enable a victorious outcome. The debate on it being cheating or innovative thinking spread to the other children and soon votes came in with a resounding five to two victory for a similar solution being implemented if possible. Brody was unable to fully explain the complexities of the Kobayashi Maru but recounted another similar case that they understood far better.

'*Why do you mention it in this way?*' asked John's thoughts, individually transmitted but together with the inquisitive stares of the other six.

'*Well, these warriors look pretty tough, but I doubt they are blessed with our scientific knowledge and our friend Hervé and his unseen elders are pretty much an unknown quantity, so what about a game of poker or, better still, three-card brag?*' Brody silently suggested. It then took nearly another hour for him to mentally transmit an explanation of the ins and outs of card gambling and what bragging was, just to get the seven to the point of being able to understand his new plan. When they all stopped frowning and started to smile broadly, he knew they understood.

'Do you think your currently reduced individual powers can act like a chorus and resonate enough to rattle this place a bit?' Glancing over his shoulder he looked to see if any movement of the guards might give away a clue to their ability to covertly listen into their thought transmissions. Again, all was silent and un-moving so he felt sure that the potential ruse was so far undiscovered.

'And can you still manage to show a flame eye here and there?' he asked hopefully with an added thought and was heartened further at the silent but positive smiling response:

'Let's give it a go, then.'

Hervé soon returned as strangely and unexpectedly as before when, now deliberately, nobody was paying attention. He asked if they had any requests before the daylight went. Brody sprang up to the normal twitch of blades and chains as the warriors reacted to his rapid forward motion. As they relaxed back to guard position, Hervé strolled confidently forward and asked if Brody's sudden movement indicated he had a specific request.

"Yes, actually I do and it's extremely important," he replied contritely.

CHAPTER 10

Back on the Trail.

"I need you to release us before morning as the Fesarius plasma build-up within the individual bodies of the other seven cannot be properly regulated in this confined environment." Brody started the proposed surreptitious card school by feigning fear and anxiousness in his voice to add to the subterfuge.

"The stress of this forced captivity is starting to cause their internal plasma glands to over generate, which makes them get very agitated." Right on cue, one of the seven, very coincidentally, walked passed and flashed her flame eyes in the direction of Hervé. A second passed in the opposite direction and he too glared brightly, looking directly at Hervé, straight into his eyes and then suddenly without warning screeched out, "**Brody!** Our Fesarius plasma is becoming over-stimulated, please **HELP US!**" Hervé was completely startled at this, but Brody was even more shocked. Keeping a straight face became an added issue for him. Neither he nor Hervé had ever heard proper vocalisation from any of the seven before. Its generation of such true surprise created the perfect con. Hervé recoiled and started mentally questioning himself about what this all meant. Brody's genuine aghast facial expression at the outburst was the perfect finishing touch. Unbeknown to him, it had been added by the children's full understanding of what he had planned and wanted. Then Hervé made the perfect mistake of asking…

Brody was obviously only too happy to explain to him all about how, deep within the seven were glands that exuded a chemical called Fesarius plasma which, in humanoid terms, he explained was a hormone equivalent of TNT explosive. He went on to elaborate in great detail how, if they were confined in small areas for long periods, the Fesarius glands would go into overdrive and the bodies of the seven would naturally produce excess plasma. This could not be re-absorbed into their systems and would have to be released as pure energy through the eyes, hence the flame effects.

Hervé was baffled but the passing by of three more children all with eyes aglow soon made him start sweating. When all seven began to make low groaning noises he really started to become perturbed. The dull noise of moaning, combined with the final semi-circular standing positions that the seven had now taken up – all hand holding and eyes glowing in unison – had the desired effect and Hervé asked desperately,

"What will happen if they are not released?" Knowing his hand was heavily weighted with seven boss tricks, Brody laid it on thick.

"All I can say to you is, you don't want to be within two hundred and fifty metres of them when it reaches a critical point as the mental energy displaced from them will be damaging to your neural receptors. It will lead to blindness and deafness, as well as mental and physical injury. If you were in the room with them at the time it occurred… death! So, please, whatever you do, do not leave me in here." He waivered his voice attempting to sound scared for his own safety when he was actually close to laughter.

"Regardless of what you think of me, do not expect there to be much left of this lovely building or anything of these warriors. No matter how physically strong they may be, the power surge will tear them apart at this range."

"How long before it becomes critical?" Hervé's nervous question gave Brody the chance to press home his advantage and he took a punt for freedom.

"Less than one hour, I would say, but you will know it's close when the windows start to vibrate or shatter." Hervé disappeared in his usual inexplicable manner as soon as Brody conveniently looked away, but returned not long after with a suggestion.

"If you can convince them to stop this occurring, we will let you go," was his very weak ultimatum. Brody saw the tenuous ace high call on his adversary's face and could hear the 'I hope he thinks I have more', in his voice and so, raised again immediately,

"You don't seem to understand; if we stay here *we* will all die, you and your warriors along with me, there is no off button. They need open space to release their energy build-up safely. Trust me, they are not built for captivity. As hostages they are useless, but if you release us all we can help you in many more ways than Evet will have mentioned." He felt sure he had already won the pot and to rub salt deep into the wound, he pushed all in with his next and very impudent meretricious poker reference,

"It's obviously your *'call'*, but I don't want to die… Think about it; if you keep us here you seem to have everything to lose, but what have you got to gain?" With perfect timing at that very moment, the children ramped up their pre-organised mental harmonising and created a resonance, the equivalent of a very high-pitched but inaudible noise which had the desired effect of starting to rattle the stained glass windows above.

"The previous visitor, who you call Evet, promised many things for keeping you captive but did not mention this possibility." Hervé shouted over the jangling of glass above. To help the cards hit the table face up, Brody finessed his hand even further by laying on the details and exaggerations good and thick.

"What you need to know about the previous one, as you call him, is that he is inherently evil. He is on the run; he would kill you or us, just to eat. He left us starving, dead on our feet. He is trying to go all the way to becoming nature's beast. Please, do as we wish; do as we ask, please. He runs now while we fight to breathe. He makes it tough." A glance at Hervé's slowly greying face let him know to press on.

"You should see us for what we are, but even if you cannot the children will still break these walls; they are coming out one way or another. They cannot be your prisoners, we are all free beings and our blood is our own. I don't care too much for where your past dealings with Evet were leading but we know *we* must be going and… NOW! Please, save all this destruction and let us out." Brody was enjoying the game and the desire to escape was by now secondary.

"He, Evet, the one you insist on calling the previous one is completely evil. He is a habitual liar and has totally deceived you. He will not give you anything and only seeks to hurt all of us. Have you checked to see if he has delivered upon ANY of his promises?" Feeling a little sorry for his opponent but knowing for certain that Hervé was about to finally fold his very weak hand, Brody pressed again and deliberately gave his opponent an escape opportunity, looking upwards nervously and cringing as dust drifted down from the beams within the roof substructure. With Brody's eye taken deliberately off the ball, so to speak, Hervé was once again able to do his disappearing trick.

'Keep it at this level, please; we might finally have him,' he thought quickly to the group via John. They all continued to moan and glow their eyes eerily in their semi-circle. The glass and beams were now resonating nicely along with their subsonic emissions.

When Hervé reappeared, his despondent face made it obvious that whatever the keen to deceive Evet had promised him had not been delivered and Brody knew his own fake prial of threes was completely boss. He indicated to the others with a disguised wink. Their mental reverberation increased causing the first fragment of glass to fall to the ground. It smashed right by Hervé's foot. He instantly folded and ran to the doors gesticulating to the warriors to open them promptly.

"Quickly get out of our sacred building! We do not feel that the benefits of holding you any longer are worth the potential consequences." The panicked call of the one they had named Hervé was exactly what Brody had hoped for all along. The current events by their very nature were a kind of fantasy and, with the stretched assumption that the location they were currently in was, nearly, well… island-like, similar in many ways to Brody's England in his other phase, he now felt the previously jocular naming of this person had been even more apt than he had originally intended.

He smiled smugly at the thought and transmitted his pleasure to the seven who instantly understood. The successful and fun game of brag that had extricated them to freedom was finally over.

'Let's get off this fantasy island and get after Evet as soon as possible,' Brody sent to the rapidly re-linking children. They didn't fully understand the TV reference but totally got the implication of leaving quickly. Once outside, Hervé immediately approached Brody in a resigned and humble fashion. He looked directly up at him stern-faced.

"You were bluffing, weren't you? I see no great energy release. Was it all just some magic trick? It was, wasn't it?" He was agitated, pushing, hoping for a confirmation but disappointingly knew the true answer…

"Sorry, my small friend, I have to admit it was all a ruse but we meant no harm and, to be honest, they could have brought down the glass if they had wanted to but perhaps not the walls – whilst in your room their powers were severely hampered. So, what is *your* magic? How did you shield the building and keep getting in and out without us seeing an access door?" Brody countered and inwardly congratulated himself on his very own Corbomite Manoeuvre. Hervé explained his own trick more fully:

"Simple, really, there is a secret access hatch in the floor directly behind where my head warrior stood, which is why he stood there. It is only small and disguised as stones; it works remotely on a spring-loaded lever buried in the floor nearby. All I needed to do was distract your attention and merely step in the right place to drop down the hole and allow the hatch to cover me over. Once down there a tunnel leads out here." Mutually respectful smiles spread across their faces as they realised how very much alike they were in their thinking, if not stature.

"About five hundred years ago the building was originally our church until it was deemed by the elders that all religions were corrupt and not fact-based. Now it is very rarely used and generally only as a meeting place or a pretty decent prison cell," said the now much more genial man stroking his beard thoughtfully.

"The reason why your friend's powers were affected in there; it was not the previous one's doing or intention. The building carries this natural ability in its foundation stone. It is linked directly to a charging station that is boosted every triclipse. It always retains this property but we are unaffected by it, not having your abilities. Evet did not like this place but wanted us to keep you here. He was a convincing liar but thankfully we have learnt much from you." Brody smiled, as being atheist himself he thought that it seemed this phase had at least got something going for it and perhaps much more now. Hervé's use of Evet's name more casually now, added to Brody's comfortable feeling.

"Evet is no friend of ours, in fact, he is a wanted criminal. The ancestors of these seven have been pursuing him for hundreds of years. I am only assisting them as he has stolen an item I need to help me get home." Brody did not want to divulge too much detail as this unusual and intriguing little man had initially sided with Evet against them. Knowing the crafty nature of the criminal that they sought, he also remembered how he, too, was similarly taken in by his various acts and lies and so was guarded but very hopeful of his new small friend's truthfulness and probity.

He was interested to find that the fleeing Evet had concocted a story that made Hervé think that the children were murderous criminals themselves and had promised that, if he could successfully incarcerate them, he would return with gold and silver as a reward. *Lies and more lies* just as the children had warned were apparently all that this strange being seemed to use to attempt to get his own ends satisfied in what Brody briefly considered to be a very Pat Phelan sort of way. There had been many nights passed with opportunity for him to utilise the *Necronomicon*, so why was he still staying in this phase? Brody mulled this thought for the rest of the evening whilst they were being entertained by Hervé and the elders in the altogether more social atmosphere of the real village meeting rooms.

The night brought with it a powerful dust storm and the group of new acquaintances sheltered warm and out of danger with the elders playing host. They supplied food and drink to all who coveted it. Brody fairly filled his boots having not had what he considered a proper meal for months on end.

Hervé and the elders wanted to know all about what had been going on with their guests and the one they had the misfortune to have trusted before their arrival. Brody, by now feeling much safer and at ease, explained much more of Evet's history and how, according to the children, his past was seemingly littered with murder and mayhem.

Evet's historic claims of self-defence and vengeance, etc, were always a spit in the eye for any and every legal system that had ever attempted to defy him or bring him to justice. Brody described how the children had communicated his power and that most who had ever had the misfortune to have experienced him and survived were left feeling afraid whenever his name was called out in public.

Running, fighting, catching his breath and running again seemed to be his life. It must have been tough, but Evet had chosen a path and lived his life where he wanted to, making the rules up as he went along. There was always hell to pay for anyone who tried to stand in his way. Brody's lament finished on an advisory note by suggesting, "Scratch him from your record books. Try to forget him – he runs rings round most and usually brings destruction. You are better off not having anything to do with him." Hervé nodded in agreement and took it all on board; he hoped never to meet Evet again and, although embarrassed at being twice conned, was pleased and relieved to have even survived the first encounter, but merely embarrassed about the second.

Amongst many other less intense things discussed that night it transpired that little Hervé's true name was actually (and in quite bizarre coincidence) Baylok. This fact was initially only amusing to Brody as he was the only one aware that the name Hervé was taken from a diminutive actor's real name. Balok, however, although spelt differently, was a character's name from the very show that had inspired Brody and the children's successfully bragged escape. He laughed uncontrollably for many minutes and was forced to recount the whole story of the TV series episode he had taken his inspiration from – quite a task – and as he was telling the tale he started to feel as if the coincidence was too great, but the amusement took hold when halfway through the conversation Baylok himself said,

"OK, I get it so far but what is a television again?" After much more laughter and drinks had been downed, Brody dismissed his earlier misgivings as paranoia. Hours later, he, his small drinking buddy and the slightly larger elders, all realised that the storm had lasted the whole evening, most of the night and that morning was nearly here, yet again. This fact reminded and sobered Brody to action and, noticing there were no longer any guards present, he apologetically suggested that it was time for him and the children to go.

"We must leave and try to find our nemesis before he can do any further damage or escape us completely – thank you for your understanding and patient hospitality. We are sorry you were dragged into this but remember, if ever you catch sight of him again, light a beacon immediately to warn us and we will come to assist you." The elders and Baylok rose, escorted the eight out of the meeting room and waved them off on the same path that they had arrived on. The formally fearsome Saxon warriors that held them prisoner earlier now lined the street to see them go; a new group of allies had been made but the journey still seemed without end. Picking up Evet's trail after the storm would not be easy, even with, or possibly because of Brody's tracking skills. As they climbed the steep hill out of the village, Baylok hailed them one last time.

"I think he was heading to Langgnād which is about twenty miles south. Take the right fork at the end of the second rise. If you do have to ask for directions try to pronounce it 'Lang-gnawed' like a rat would gnaw but without the second g, or the locals will look at you funny and hey, be careful who you ask. Good luck, my friends." His sarcasm was lost on the seven children of others but Brody and Baylok laughed loudly and understood each other's previous mistakes.

They quickly got back on the trail they had left a few days before and started to head toward the place referred to as Langgnãd. As no other signs of Evet's trail remained and with the dust storm having erased any possibility of tracking by his size eleven footprints, only occasional animal markings were visible. Brody did consider it unusual that such a long and powerful storm had brought no rain at all. The tracks were all bone dry.

As they settled into a steady pace the sun rose high in the sky and large black birds were seen whirling in the distance as if over a dead or dying animal. On the horizon, a lone horseman's silhouette could clearly be seen – the same one Brody had seen before, he felt sure. It was now five or six times he had spotted this same single outrider but this time he could see a more defined headdress that resembled an Earth-bound native American or Indian chief.

The seven children passed a few cerebral comments between themselves about the elusive nature of the stranger on the horizon, but Brody was intrigued by the regularity of the sightings of him.

As if he realised he had been spotted, the lone figure reined in his horse and turned away, disappearing into the dusty horizon.

'Who is this strange watcher from afar? Will he, or she for that matter, end up being a friend or foe?' Brody thought long and hard on this as they pressed on into the unknown and towards the town that Baylok had cryptically called Langgnãd, but pronounced just as if it was spelt 'Long Nord'.

Speech now not being necessary, the journey that lay ahead became a silent one and they all took time to reflect upon the last few days' events. They now had new friends that they had accidentally made, ironically because of Evet's attempts to delay them. Now free, they were strangely pleased to have been delayed in that way and had learnt valuable lessons about themselves and each other.

Just as Brody and the seven children left Baylok, Evet was

preparing to leave Langgnād, having put into place the next stage of his complex and convoluted plan to generally interrupt and delay the progress of Brody and *the others*, as he still referred to them. Preventing them from recapturing him had become his life's job. He was dedicated and methodical and, at that moment, remained a few steps ahead of the game.

After six or more hours of moderate walking, the eight travellers had not caught sight of the lone horseman again and saw the increased circling of raven-like birds as they approached the depressing outskirts of Langgnād. Smaller than vultures but still quite disconcerting, the circling birds increased in number the closer they got to the town. They were all drawn to the feeling of deep foreboding that the dark and dismal-looking place that lay ahead exuded. It looked somehow seedy and was unusually surrounded on three sides by large cemeteries, with many broken and overgrown headstones. Closer to the road were countless freshly dug, open and abandoned-looking burial plots. To the fourth side there was what looked like a large prison, with twin gallows blotting the horizon above its walls.

It all gave the feeling that death would be the most likely result of a visit. Not particularly a welcoming sight in the slightest. Well before their arrival and from a vantage point undetectable from the main approach road, Evet watched enraged as the group made their way slowly towards Langgnād. He was not perturbed at the fact as much as annoyed by the timing. He would now have to change his timeline plans and bring forward his next objective, as Baylok had failed to delay the group for as long as he had wanted. This changed things and it angered the fraudulent king. Even as annoyed as he was, things he had been working on in secret for months in Langgnād should, he thought, be sufficiently intriguing and complex enough to compensate. He skirted around the town in the opposite direction to the approaching group to avoid detection. Heading back towards Baylok's settlement to formally discuss his failure, he left Brody and the children of others behind, confident his work would keep them entertained whilst he rectified previous errors.

As the eight approached the town gates and with further fresh headstones and older broken memorials on both sides of the track, it became obvious that in comparison to the quieter settings they had so far experienced, this was or had once been a far more populated town and could potentially be a much more dangerous place. This was especially true if Evet was running the show, which they all agreed was highly likely, given his known form. The assumption that he would not know they had managed to get out of Baylok's recent confinement was thought to be potentially their only saving grace at this point. How wrong they were but intrepidly and with indefatigable perseverance, Brody and the children headed into the unknown once again.

As they passed street signs leading down various avenues left and right, there was a definite arterial pattern developing. They noticed all roads seemed to lead back to the main high street, which would be the symbolic heart of the town. It gave access to all areas and would be easy to keep under control for whoever might need to police such an area. Strange names adorned the road signs like Manton, Tiller, Goldthorn, Bhylls, Acacia, Forton and many other such similar and peculiar sounding places, but all listed as either an avenue or lane – no street or road in sight. As they passed them the sights were all very similar and nothing much stirred.

'Where is everyone? Evet has been here for sure; this is not normal,' Brody thought his concerns to the group. The sun was high in the sky but the town's main high street (which was peculiar by its lack of name plate) stretched ahead and seemed very dark. The eight

travellers felt as if they were being observed and scrutinized rather like bugs crawling into a jar trap. Their overriding desire to find and recapture the elusive Evet was the only thing making it worth continuing – everything else screamed 'keep out!'

Brody was mildly perturbed by the simple fact that *he* was not even surprised to find bodies lying here and there face down in the gutters or propped up in doorways; they looked tired or drunk and paid little or no attention to the approach of eight strangers, which in itself was an unusual thing. Some twitched occasionally, which was only reassuring that they were not yet dead. However, based on the number of open graves surrounding the built-up area of the town, it appeared to be only a matter of time. As they walked down the main thoroughfare, it seemed that the place was a sort of dead town; every side street was proliferated by similar deathly-looking layabouts. As the day wore on while they searched the deserted avenues, they were approached by no one, but still felt uneasy as if they were being watched.

Brody decided to try and get some clues or information from one of the street sleepers. He walked over to what looked to be a slightly more mobile character who had managed to prop himself up against a balustrade outside a small bar, giving the distinct impression of an alcoholic on his way home. As Brody approached, the wretch looked up and caught his glance. Both his eyes were bloodshot and his pallor was greyish white as if he was nearly dead or, as Brody considered, thinking of the open graves, possibly risen from the dead.

Being a horror film fan and something of a connoisseur of all things deathly with his music tastes and tattoo representations adorning his body, Brody knew that it was, in reality, a complete impossibility. Nevertheless, he had seen stranger things recently and was prepared to consider anything.

"Are you OK?" he enquired of the bedraggled character.

"Down, depressed... lonely," he drawled back.

"Hey, man, I know a place where we can go, just a few streets away, twenty-two on the Ac..., you know..., the... gzzzzz... Goddamned Avenue... meet someone I know," he continued, slurring badly as if being restricted from giving information – not so much by his condition but perhaps by some other controlling force. Brody started wondering if Evet was nearby.

He wasn't, but he still had a strong influence over much. His interventions in Langgnãd would very soon become more apparent but, for now, he was well on the way to wreak more havoc elsewhere.

"Which one, maaaan? They are all Avenues or Lanes." Brody played along, hippy-like in tone searching for more details. He listened intently as the man mumbled and lamented, hoping to get some small piece of worthwhile information. He was looking for anything that might solve the riddle of what was happening in this town and whether it related to the fugitive Evet.

"Hey, maaaaaan, if you're looking for a gooooood time, are you prepared to pay the ultimate price? Fifteen quick minutes is all is asked of you. Everyone's got a vice, man, you know where I'm at, yeah?" His ramblings made little sense but resonated inside Brody as if he had been warned rather than invited. It was more than déjà vu but less than a memory. Somehow in the recesses of his mind he knew what this drunken soul alluded to but at this moment it meant nothing.

"Don't wait for too much of a long time, man; just go, tell them I sent you – you might be seeing these stars too. Go soon, man, and heeeeeeey, it's free," he continued, getting more agitated as if his message needed to be delivered before a deadline. His ability to speak coherently seemed to mirror his need to finish what he was saying. The feeling of a gun to his temple was apparent and Brody feared for his sanity as well as chances of his long-term survival.

"Don't waste time, man, don't you hesitate. Just go; you can take my honest word for it, shhhhhheeeee..." His sentence trailed away as if an unseen hand had choked his silence and, when he spoke again, the rest was indecipherable in its tone, meaning and language. It was more of a garbled version of backward speech or some sort of speaking in tongues.

"Whthosed detingwiddetreebonce, donmedlwidtingsyudun understand." This was followed immediately by a huge, belched spray of blood-filled vomit and the complete collapse of the individual. The stench that rose from the body and the blood-infused regurgitated matter was unbelievable and Brody quickly recoiled, nearly heaving. The others watched in a characteristically calm way and thought-said to him,

'There was something about not messing with the three-headed and to not get involved in things you do not understand. We could feel it in his thought patterns, but what does it mean?' John was bemused at this condition that seemed to afflict all who were around them.

'What is going on here? They all seem to be dead or close to death. Surely this cannot all *be Evet's doing, even if he* is *here, how could he have done all this so quickly? And if he has, why and to what gain?'*

'All good questions,' but Brody couldn't answer any of them yet. He was still reeling from the contrary ramblings of the recently deceased mess lying near his feet.

'Let's try to find someone a bit more alive, before nightfall. I am concerned that what they have might just be catching.' Brody projected this to the collective mind; the effects of their village captivity having long since worn off.

They searched most of the side alleys that branched off the main street but only found more seemingly zombified dying specimens. They were just about to give up and leave the deathly place when Brody saw, down one particularly dark avenue, a door being closed. Knowing it likely didn't close itself he set off at pace to investigate.

CHAPTER 11

The Horrors of Pleasure – Part 1.

As he approached the door a sharply dressed individual stepped out from the growing evening shadows and barred his path, holding what looked like an old-fashioned Tommy gun across his chest. Brody noticed that quite uncharacteristically for his modern attire, this individual also had what looked like a Viking sword belt slung around his waist.

"What do you want here?" was the stern opener from the supposed gangster.

"Errrr, just trying to find out what is going on round here. Can you tell me who lives here? We haven't found anyone who can actually communicate," he replied hurriedly.

"We," was the even sterner questioning response,

"I see only YOU!"

"Errrr, yes, that's right. Sorry I meant me, I mean, I, you know… just scared, I suppose. What's going on?" he swiftly blagged.

'Help me,' Brody silently projected back to the children. The apparent doorman levelled his weapon towards him looking, to all intents and purposes, as if to execute him right there on the spot. A red light flashed in the window above him and the well-dressed sentry promptly raised the weapon to chest height again. Without any other form of communication seeming to be received by him,

the guard motioned to him with the barrel of the large weapon to pass into the building. Brody carefully squeezed past the bulging henchman through the narrow gateway he was guarding. No attempt was made to move out of the way to ease his passage.

"You can go in; she is expecting you," was his strange back-handed invitation after Brody had already breathed in and gone through; it gave him the distinct feeling that the man was acting out of blind loyalty, based on fear and was not confident enough to take charge without instruction. This intrigued him greatly, but he felt that whoever was actually in charge did not fit Evet's profile.

'Hold back, I'm OK and I think I have found something or someone,' Brody quickly informed his seven friends who were by now almost in visual range of his position. They stopped and surrounded the house which had two, large, distinct ornate swan-like number '2's on the wall, one of which had fallen crooked. The large red beacon in the upper window glowed ominously for a moment and then went out. They were ready to assist but, as of yet, knew nothing of what was going on; this was only fractionally less than Brody himself knew as he blindly entered the house and climbed the stairs towards a meeting with the unknown occupant.

It was rapidly getting darker outside now and characteristically, the two moons began to rise. Shafts of blue and pink light flooded into the open windows on each landing area allowing him to find his way tentatively up the staircases. A blank space on the wall of the first floor landing gave away a missing picture; Brody wondered if it were aging well in some loft somewhere.

As he reached the second floor, two more guards, both carrying similar firearms and mismatched sword belts met him. It was at this point that he started to consider the difference in historic evolutionary development between these people and those of the previous two settlements he had experienced. Only twenty miles apart or less he had seen ancient Anglo-Saxon and Viking warriors and now what looked like nineteen thirties-style gang members protecting some yet to be revealed big boss. The cross-over in equipment was confusing enough as well as the form of plague in the streets and an elusive lone native-looking American Indian chief who appeared to be following his every move.

'How much more bizarre can the occupant of the next room be?' he mused and, for a fraction of a second, considered turning around and just jumping straight out of the open moonlit window behind him to see if he could fly. It would certainly confirm this to be some crazy nightmare, or end it either way. He decided against it and knocked uncomfortably between the two unflinching guards. The door had a brass number nine on it. With only one screw loosely holding it in place, Brody, for no particular reason felt that it should have been a six.

"Come on in, Brody," was the softly spoken invitation that enticed him from within. He was only slightly surprised by the pre-knowledge of his identity and slowly eased the door open and attempted to enter. The two guards were rigid and didn't give way. As he tried to squirm between them, he felt them tense up as if a twinge of pain had afflicted them both at that exact moment. Immediately they relaxed and turned sideways to allow his easier entry.

"Close it behind you," the voice requested in a slightly firmer tone. Brody felt he recognised this voice, but he couldn't place a name to it. It was coming from the other side of a classic, high-backed spy thriller-type chair behind a grand desk. The chair was facing the opposite direction, hiding its occupant.

He gently closed the door and it clicked shut crisply behind him as the chair began to rotate. His initial fascination with a huge red coloured, apple shaped logo on the far wall and the room's overall dour décor, was soon distracted as his attention was caught by a six inch, red, stiletto heel that protruded over the top of the left arm of the chair. Its occupant was more lying in the chair than sitting and Brody's eyes followed the shoe as it moved from left to right like a stage curtain drawing back to reveal the first act of a drama. From heel tip to ankle, fishnets started revealing a slim, long leg that disappeared back into the still rotating chair.

He assumed the other leg was in there tucked away somewhere and was proven correct as the rest of the owner came fully into view. As the chair swivelled one hundred and eighty degrees, a vision of crimson, red sexual arousal sat semi-cross-legged. One leg draped suggestively over the arm of the chair and the other crossed under the knee revealing an ultra-tight, very high-cut pencil style dress that left absolutely nothing to his imagination. The full extent of the athletic leg was revealed to well past the stocking and garter line as Brody's gaze drifted, passing the suspender top to...

He quickly averted his gaze to higher and drier ground to take in the vision of a tiny waist squeezed into an even tinier dress that looked as if it had been sprayed on. The complexity of how this garment had even been put on, rapidly gave way to the concentration breaker of the most amazingly displayed cleavage he had seen for a long time. Charley's wry smile entered his subconscious and a pang of guilt swept over him as he continued to enjoy the semi-pornographic display in front of him.

This girl, to a very large degree both physically and facially, looked much like Charley. He felt his cheeks flush and knees tremble; she was as close to his secretly held idea of female perfection that he could possibly ever have imagined. He had privately dreamt about her all his adult life and now she was sitting directly in front of him. He knew full well that most men secretly liked the idea of casual promiscuity and like most, his fantasy had been with him as long as he could remember, but he had never known why and had never sought to do anything about it. Charley was his complete perfection in his real life, but this was something different altogether and transcended emotion.

Like a favourite number or colour it had just remained harmless and unimportant in the recesses of his imagination. Brody had never dared to try to chase down such persons, act upon the thoughts or explore them in any form in real life, but the ideas had proliferated his dreams on a regular basis. How completely strange and unlikely was it that now, here of all places, a version of Charley who was also his secret idea of 'unreal' perfection was now sitting in front of him, somehow hybridising the two worlds. His pure and honest innocent true love from his real life somehow joined with his one and only sexual fantasy in this unusual alternate existence.

As his rising gaze reached her face, he was well aware that, without choice, he had already become physically very stimulated. This was embarrassingly confirmed by her coy smile and she gleefully teased him with the erotic and flirtatious biting of her lower lip. She had quite obviously fully appreciated watching the arousal occur in real time slow motion right in front of her.

Her long, blonde tousled hair fell about, complementing her perfectly proportioned neck and shoulders. His stare was momentarily distracted back to that oh so hypnotic bust that was virtually fighting to escape its red, low-cut captor of a dress.

The whole ensemble was crisp and perfect with a certain firmness that he couldn't fail to notice was accentuating his own. His eyes flicked impolitely back to her face and he saw that she was obviously checking him out in a similar manner. Brody was a serial flirt but felt, by now, if anyone else were watching, this staring and fixation would merely make him appear as some sort of pervert.

This bothered him greatly and his self-esteem was driven painfully low, but he couldn't resist and continued to gaze.

Fleetingly, he considered she would have only seen a slim-looking older guy with an embarrassing bulge in his chinos, the obligatory budgie being very poorly smuggled! He was blushing and awkward but unable to move. He wanted to run but couldn't turn away.

Her brilliant crystal blue eyes caught his; their mutually appreciative stares locked onto each other. In the silence, the tension between them was palpable. Who would speak first was unknown? He was confused, aroused and scared. He sincerely started to worry that he may not be able to contain himself for a prolonged period if required to take this situation any further – not a feeling he had ever experienced before. Deep in his consciousness he knew it was a ridiculous thought to have under the circumstances. It was as if he was being primed to react this way.

He attempted to break the ice with a pressure-releasing cheesy one-liner. Physical movement seemed virtually impossible and mental concentration was not easy, but his speech was apparently not impaired. Talking a lot and not saying much was a skill that he owned, so the utterance of,

"Do you come here often?" was a semi-serious attempt to soften the situation, but not his finest chat up moment.

He realised this vision of sexuality and forbidden fantasy was not just a *little* bit like, but actually pretty much the spitting image of his ever-elusive love, Charley. If it weren't for the blonde hair and blue eyes and perhaps the much sluttier look (which he absolutely appreciated) it could easily have been her twin sister. It was a look not dissimilar to one of his own visualisations conceived when regularly daydreaming about Charley, usually when bored and at home… alone.

Somewhere in his head he tried to fight his sexually-orientated response and could not understand why he was so uncontrollably moved in this way – he had literally gone from scared stiff to just stiff within seconds and it didn't make any sense.

'Master, he is here!' The girl sitting so sexily before him did not outwardly speak and was herself unaware of how or why she had made the mental transmission or even why she addressed the recipient of it as Master. She had damningly and silently communicated on a totally different level but Brody, now fully able to intercept such communication thanks to the children's teachings, was completely aware of it, but he could not intercept the reply. In almost synchronised response to the shielded and unheard mental reply from her unseen master, her eyes sparkled, her glistening lips parted, and she whispered,

"Come closer, Brody, we need to talk. My name is Charlotte. The Master told me you would come and I am not disappointed by his description." Her invitation was impossible to refuse and by now, thoughts of Evet and getting home were almost completely blocked out, as his primordial instincts kicked in. He was involuntarily being drawn to her, but in his mind, he felt in complete command as if he was making all the plays. He did not at this point realise that she was, via Evet's endowed powers, fully in control and using him for her and her devious master's own ends.

"Sit down, Brody, make yourself comfortable and take off your T-shirt." Her request was so smooth, confident and sexily phrased that he was unable to refuse and virtually tore his T-shirt over his head and sat down in front of her chair like a lapdog.

"The Master has endowed me with special gifts for you and promised to return and reward me if I use them well and keep you busy. He told me you would come with the others; where are they?"

Even this provocative and cryptic request did not break his semi-hypnotic trance.

"Out there," he replied vaguely, pointing randomly out the window behind her, whilst staring fixatedly at her fully revealed crotch area, which she had put so deliberately but casually on display. She had athletically swung the previously tucked leg out, up and over his head on to the other arm of the chair. She spread her legs wider now directly in front of his face, enticing him to approach with a forward thrust of her hips, he failed to notice that, in the distance behind her (clearly visible to him if he had just been able to look up) was the glow in the sky of an orange-flamed beacon fire, likely to have been set by Baylok back at the village as a distress call. Also unbeknown to him at this point was the fact that the children *had* spotted it and had responded after feeling that Brody was now safe from danger.

'I want him alive – two months and I will make you my queen.' Charlotte was not fully aware of receiving the transmissions but deep inside she responded instinctively, partly in fear, partly in anticipation. Brody, eyes now glazed, salivated and moved forward in anticipation of what lay ahead. His mouth watered, he was on autopilot and his tongue started to protrude from his slack-jawed gawk, a soft but firm hand on his forehead pushed him back.

"Not so fast – no sweets between meals – we must get better acquainted," was the heart-stopping statement he heard next. Such was his excitement, his veins were now throbbing throughout his body and he felt like there was electricity running through them. She slipped off the chair and sat with legs spread wide either side of him.

"Take off your trousers, Brody, and kneel for me." Like an obedient schoolchild being told he was top of the class, he obliged and not being a lover of undergarments, soon knelt naked in front of her. Still not fully aware of the absurdity and unlikeliness of the situation, his mind was now a mess of conflicting sexual information floating in and out of a hypnotic semi-conscious state. He was seeing Charley, then Charlotte, Charley, then Charlotte

– red hair then blonde hair, green eyes then blue – it was all a complete erotic blur.

Although *he* was kneeling, everything else about his body was completely standing to attention. His tense torso twitched periodically as she held his mind in hers, delaying, for her own satisfaction, what she had been instructed and encouraged to achieve. He just stared fixated at her teetering breasts as they hypnotised him and seemed to struggle to be released from their captivity within her spray-fit attire. He fought the primitive desire to hold them in both hands and the urge to suckle, but was unable to look away; something in the back of his mind nagged that she was not real and may not even be there at all. These thoughts were rinsed away as he felt her mouth slowly and warmly kissing his inner thighs.

The feeling had made him flinch; she was no longer at eye level and as he looked down, the top of her golden-haired head rose from between his knees and moved slowly upward towards his lower midriff. He felt the dizzy rush of testosterone within himself as she glanced up. She opened her bright red mouth, slowly and very suggestively licked her top lip and looked deep into his glazed eyes. For a fraction of a second a sly grin rippled her lips and, as her hair fell over her descending eyes, she… All went blank.

When he awoke, he was re-dressed and lying on a bed in another room. He felt completely shattered and was drained of energy. He was dizzy and took about an hour to get up. He was obviously still at Charlotte's house but could not see her anywhere. He didn't remember much of what had gone on the previous night which was very disconcerting for him – he normally had great recall and liked to use such memories for fantasy motivation on days when he was not able to fulfil his own needs, which over the past few years, had become all too often the norm. Weirdly, he remembered her body in every glorious detail but could not remember what happened a minute after the chair spun round.

The sun shone in through the undraped window and as the consideration as to whether blinds would be better than curtains drifted across his confused state, he finally saw the wisps of smoke from the remnants of the beacon fire at Baylok's. Set alight to attract him and his companions' attention yesterday it now smouldered weakly. He jumped up and ran to the window, immediately regretting the action when he collapsed in a heap. A few minutes later he managed to haul himself up and looked out. Finding the streets deserted below, except for the dead or occasionally crawling bodies of the mystery plague victims, he realised the on-guard children of others *had* obviously responded to Baylok's call.

'Have they caught Evet, or were they too late, even to save Baylok?' He pondered, whilst trying to gather enough strength to get up. He needed to get back to the children of others, to regroup, to find out what happened last night. As he glanced out the window on his way back to the bed, he noticed the sun was moving lower in the sky and tried to remember more.

'How have I been asleep for more than twelve hours? Is it nearly night time again?' He opened what he had previously assumed was Charlotte's bathroom door but found himself back in the office that he had vaguely remembered from the previous night when the two had met. Looking across the room to the grand chair Charlotte had been sitting in, he saw the stiletto heels crossed, resting over the left arm. A feeling of déjà vu hit but he silently laughed at the idea as it was surely only yesterday and it wasn't that he felt he had been here before, he HAD been here before!

"Hello, Miss Charlotte," he introduced himself carefully and enquired, "Have I slept all day? I do apologise for being so rude, but I must leave now and go to my friends, I fear they may be in some danger." His question and statement went unanswered so, after a brief wait, he started towards the door that he had entered by yesterday. As the door creaked open it revealed one of the henchmen – the aggressive, gun-in-hand stance gave him enough clues that this was not his best exit strategy.

Turning back towards the desk expecting a slow sexy reveal, he was shocked to find Charlotte just inches away from him. The door he had thought to exit through slammed behind him and he stumbled back against it, taken aback by the speed and silence that Charlotte had apparently moved with.

Her attire was even more erotic than yesterday, all silk and virtually transparent, her very firm bust being the only visible form of support for the whole outfit. She locked him with a diamond blue stare and undressed herself in an instant by the mere pull of a single small tie on the left side of the skimpy silk negligée. It slipped with intent, leaving her completely naked except only for those red stilettos! The whole outfit had been perfect and seemed to take an age to hit the floor, stopping its slide momentarily, delayed by the interference of her extremely erect nipples.

Gravity eventually winning over drag coefficients, the garment floated to the ground revealing her full captivating excellence and Brody was once again spellbound. His mind blurred images of this seemingly completely liberated temptress with those of the hard-to-please, far more demure Charley back home. Somewhere deep in his mind he felt the pangs of guilt again. Was he just about to involuntarily betray his true love once more?

The confusion and comparison of wanting to be true to the one he had no real relationship with but loved with all his heart and the desire to just take that which was so flagrantly being offered, made his head spin.

'What of the others: Baylok and Evet and what about getting

home to see Charley again, let alone getting that elusive date?' It all wheeled around his head like some crazy thrill ride with no off switch. Like a slap in the face, his attention was re-centred by Charlotte who silently and, with amazing speed, had closed in to millimetres away from him and was now standing naked, pressing him to the door with only the firmness of her beautiful body. As usual, her lips glowed with shimmering red lipstick. His mouth fell open and she kissed his tongue, probing his open mouth with hers.

His mind was alert and active, but his limbs were somehow useless. He could not resist her – sexually he understood the urge and needed no encouragement as he was ready for action, but his hands and body were unable to move – he didn't understand this confusion. He wanted her, he was erect and ready to take her, but he didn't want to do anything. He was scared and wanted to flee, but he *must* have her right now. He wanted to fight her off and run, yet felt compelled to stay; of course he should just do it and… of course he shouldn't give in to her... Should… shouldn't… do it… don't. He wanted to… oh how he wanted to… Above all the buts, maybes and contradictions, he simply just couldn't move a muscle.

The feelings of complete turmoil continued as she slowly lifted his T-shirt over his head and unbuttoned his chinos one button at a time as if in slow motion. A tear escaped the corner of his eye and inside he screamed out,

'HELP!' The children were otherwise engaged and couldn't respond even if they had heard his cry. His trousers slid down his unmoving legs and he desperately tried to move his hands. One part of his brain was begging for the opportunity to caress the amazing naked body of this strange girl who completely controlled him, the other wanted to brutally grip her throat. Neither was successful and his limp hands only managed to rest uselessly on his thighs as he made a desperate and futile attempt to stop her. She

slowly slid down his torso, her firm but soft bust brushing briefly against his already alert penis. She crouched and took him fully into her soft, wet, red pouting mouth.

Brody awoke and took a while to focus his eyes. He was once again on the bed, dishevelled but this time only half-dressed; it was the same bed but he was inexplicably poorly attired with different clothes. It was dark, so he assumed he had not slept as long this time. With no way of calculating he tried to get up but fell straight to the floor like a stone. He lay there, one leg in the bed, the other out, as if completely paralyzed for at least the next ten minutes or more before feeling some form of strength returning. Eventually he dragged himself up onto his elbow and started to massage his legs to encourage circulation and get himself going. It was perhaps half an hour later when he finally managed to sit on the edge of the bed and gather his thoughts.

'What the hell is happening here? Am I slowly getting killed with sex? What a way to go, but I wish I could remember more of it, and I wish it didn't hurt so much.' On any other day the idea would not only have amused but would probably have aroused him. Not today, he was too scared and tried again to get up. Failing once more he slumped back and continued to rest, drifting quickly back to sleep. When he awoke again, he felt slightly stronger but not great.

Making his way to the only other door and, what this time he guessed *must* be the bathroom, he stumbled not fully in control of himself, pushed the door open and fell into the room. As he steadied himself on a handrail, he caught sight of his own face in the mirror opposite. Now he was truly frightened – he looked drawn, haggard and unnaturally white with bloodshot eyes just like the unfortunates he had encountered in the street however many days ago.

'I can't believe I've contracted the disease that seems to have

infected this whole town, merely by close conversation. I doubt it could have been so virulent and airborne.' Then it dawned on him that far more recently relevant…

'Could it be venereal?' The thought of this and the sight of his terrible appearance in the mirror repulsed him and he vomited uncontrollably into the sink; the stench from this was unbearable just as it had been before and his fears were instantaneously confirmed – he guessed he must be ailing in the same way that the dying person he had seen previously had done. A minor panic set in and momentarily he considered the window again, but his desire to escape overrode his feeling of capitulation.

Cleaning himself up, he washed his sick-stained T-shirt and then emptied the half-full basin of its vomitus contents, squeezing the excess water and puke out of the T-shirt as best as possible before hanging it up to dry in the breeze by the window. He looked again in the mirror and was heartened to see slightly more colour in his face and the bloodshot look in his eyes was possibly fading, perhaps he had been overreacting. He went back to bed and slept another few hours.

Later as he pulled on his, not so super, but semi-dry T-shirt and moved towards the door that he knew led back to Charlotte's office, he paused and considered the possibility of escape. If he could quickly grab one of the goon's guns and make it to the stairwell, he thought he could make a break for it. He knew that somehow, when he looked at Charlotte, she was a siren and he might be unable to fight her draw.

'Where are those magnificent seven dwarfs when you need them?' The semi Freudian slip did not amuse him but the analogy was interesting. Could he be Snow White and if so, had he already eaten too much of the apple? The thought of apples being in some way sinister and the unusual logo he had seen in Charlotte's office

refocused his mind, but his original excitement at seeing her had long since given way to the horrors of that particular pleasure and he knew it was way past time to do something about it. Hoping for a rescue by the magnificent seven may well have been wishful thinking, but he desperately needed the seven children.

CHAPTER 12

Death Stalks Close.

'I suppose they might have bigger fish to fry if they have caught up with Evet, though.' He brushed aside thoughts that were beyond his control and mentally planned to rush the door as soon as he was in the room, without even looking in Charlotte's direction. He barged the first door open and raced instinctively towards the other side of the room, not even looking over at the desk or chair, fully expecting a scrap with a burly, armed doorman to be his next obstacle. As his hand approached the handle of the second door, Charlotte grabbed his wrist completely from nowhere, spun him one hundred and eighty degrees to face her and locked her steel blue gaze on him.

He froze as before but was less intimidated this time. Feeling warmer and contented, strange resignation and euphoria were the emotions that flowed over him.

"Where do you think you are you going, Brody?" she purred in that sultry tone he could not resist answering,

"Charlotte..." He fought to get words out that he wanted rather than some dumb love-struck moan and submission.

"Please, listen for just one minute; can't you release me from all this madness? Can't you see the horror and sadness it brings me? It feels like you are slowly killing me with your pleasures... Ii-iss this wh-what you-u really ww-w-want?" He stuttered the last few words and syllables, regained a semblance of control and pleaded his case again.

"Is that the power he bestowed upon you? You might be getting something from the other men you entertain like this but for those that I assume you have released, it seems to be spreading like a disease." He gulped for air to try to get all the information he wanted to give, out in time before she took control again.

"Don't you know the risks? We might all die!" The effort of forcing the statements out of himself against her will as she held him in her power, was enough to buckle his resolve and he fell faint to the floor. How much time passed, he could not tell but as he awoke at her feet, he guessed it to be only seconds. He could though, not understand why he seemed now to be wearing different clothes, again. Was this a dream, more déjà vu, or was he remembering? Had he passed out at her feet like this before? It was all becoming one blur of pain and confusion.

She lifted him to standing with apparent ease just by grabbing his shoulders and from within his questioning haze, he started to realise the futility of any future physical fight he might have with her. Her gaze once again gripped his brain. He tried to look away but couldn't. As she teased his clothes off and threw them aside, she smiled and looked deep within him.

"I know you are trying to fight me, but *you* want this, you have always wanted this and, believe me, I can teach you more than you can know." Her words defeated his resistance and, with a feeling akin to wetting the bed (apart from the three bits that were useful to her) he completely relaxed and was hers to do with as she pleased, once again.

She carried him into the next room with ease and laid him on the bed. The attire she was wearing on this occasion had passed him by, but she made attempts to rekindle his attention by stripping slowly, releasing her ample qualities in a visual crescendo that even he in his dizzy state could not ignore. Blood flow was not an issue and she would have got what she wanted anyway, but now his attention was re-centred it would be with a slightly firmer but still unwilling partner.

"Brody, just think about it. These days, now that you are over the age of thirty, I bet you regret your younger days when you were not getting laid like this, with me. Soon your youthful beauty will fade and nobody will want you, but for now you can come in me; I am warm inside, my fire burns bright for you tonight." Her cryptic chanting seemed somehow soothing in his head and he focused his bleary eyes as she climbed on top of his weakened body and thrust down with an intensity he had never before experienced.

If it had been Charley, he might have cried and worried that she would have been disappointed at his lack of restraint but the emission that resulted from her first and second thrusts was like the bursting of an over-full water balloon and somehow, although the sensations were intense, he was glad it was all over.

But it wasn't and she was savage in her sexual voracity. Pounded him up and down repeatedly, grinding down and squeezing herself internally, gripping him and forcing him to copiously respond again, two, three or more times in relatively close succession – he couldn't remember how many. The last occasion that he was fully conscious for felt like having barbed wire pulled through his veins.

It seemed like hours before she fell off him, exhausted herself – no wonder he had been so shattered on the other occasions if this was what had happened. He rolled on his side and cried himself to sleep as blood oozed from his now red and extremely sore foreskin.

Seconds, minutes, hours or even days later (he had no idea which by now) from below the bed a hand reached up and gently grabbed his testicles in a tender cupping motion followed by a slender finger of the other hand worming between his legs and being inserted deep into his rectum. He couldn't respond in opposition and felt every movement of her probing finger as it gently massaged his prostate and, without the ability to do anything about it he was immediately readied once more, ready to satisfy her insatiable lust yet again. Ready, yes, but willing and under his own control no more.

His head was completely fried; old and new tears were mixed, stained and streaming down his face as the raping he had jokingly feared from the Viking warriors months ago was now being visited upon him again and again by the one he would have been happier taking out on a dinner date.

"OH, CHARLEY! Pleeeease stop this, I can't take any more!" He screamed her name in pain and pleaded in desperation.

"My name is CHARLOTTE, you… heathen dog; you would be well advised to remember it. The locals get but one chance to please me and rarely come close; I am only keeping you for the sake of my agreement with the Master." As he began to pass out again, she ranted on as if to further add insult to injury:

"He promised many things if I kept you from leaving this place; your body issues good volume and you stay firm well for an older one." She gazed deep into him as she spoke, rose to her feet, dripping profusely from between her legs, moved around to the end of the bed and climbed back on, astride his unmoving form.

"Cum again NOW and let's finish this!" she seemed to shout and whisper simultaneously, her still fully erect nipples grazing against his legs as she moved slowly and very deliberately up the bed towards her goal. The weight of her breasts rested on his knees for a split second and then, using her tongue like a thirsty dog with a bowl of water, she took him into her drool-laden, salivating mouth and as before, everything went blank.

Once again, he awoke in the now badly smelling room. Unable to move he lay thinking of how he could possibly escape this seemingly eternal torment. By now he had no idea how many times he had been taken advantage of but it was painful to even sit up. After an hour of resting to gradually gain his strength he dragged himself across the floor to the bathroom and stripped his unrecognisable and ragged clothes off to wash himself and them once again. It was, by now, his only remaining form of self-respect, to at least be clean in readiness for the next terrifying encounter. Time blurred and when the metaphorical bell for each next sexually torturous round was rung, he had no desire to go on. He was physically and mentally wrecked to the point of being completely unable to help her or resist.

A fleeting film-related memory flashed his brain and he dejectedly quoted it to himself without the ability to even smile at its irony or his poor Austrian accent.

"Wash day tomorrow? Nothing clean!" Finally, he managed to stand and looked dejectedly into the mirror. There was another similar mirror opposite, and the double reflection showed his tattoos that were normally not visible to him. They were his pride and joy and depicted his personal interpretation of the songs from his favourite group's greatest albums. It seemed centuries ago since he had listened to their music but now, as the tattoos caught his eye, he started to feel a connection between them and his current predicament.

His mind fought to focus and as he gazed at the image of a boat on his back, it brought him to thinking of his recent escapades with warriors who wouldn't look too far out of place on that very ship.

Then, like a flash from the blue, his focus was drawn back to the closer mirror and he saw blood dripping from small puncture wounds that formed a uniform set of double tracks on his lower abdomen leading down either side of the base of his now flaccid penis. He blacked out with the realisation of what else had been happening to him and fell limply to the floor.

When he awoke he washed himself yet again and dressed as best as he could with what remained of his variously stained but unfamiliar clothes. He didn't recognise them and knew that he smelt bad, but nobody was here to care – deodorant was not a priority. What *was* important was not allowing Charlotte to do as she had been doing. Draining his body, not so much of semen, but more importantly:

Blood!

He couldn't have imagined before that he would ever have been thinking these thoughts. The puncture wounds he had found were starting to heal varyingly and the further up towards his naval they were the fresher they seemed. He could guess and calculate that he had been physically taken advantage of and drained of blood to a near critical level at least ten times. He started to formulate a theory of how the other events fitted in to this.

It seemed a given, logically, that the Master who Charlotte referred to was certainly Evet in one of his many guises. It also now seemed sensible to assume that if she was not already vampiric before meeting him that she had more than likely become so after his influence had taken its course. Either way, the disease he had witnessed with the poor souls in the town streets was definitely spreading. It was probably being transmitted from person to person now as a viral infection and was apparently unchecked; being passed from Charlotte's other victims who, by her own testimony, she had only drained once.

'Why did she refer to Evet as the Master?'

The numbers of gravestones compared to unfulfilled burial

plots seemed to indicate to him that her blood lust was growing but could only realistically have started relatively recently. It coincided with Evet's arrival in this phase and he must have visited this place well before ever meeting him. He *must* have been here before, planning.

The sheer mathematics of the disease's progression indicated an unabated spreading process which was apparently deliberate. The possibility that Evet had visited this place before meeting him and set the wheels in motion in readiness of this now very painful meeting of Charlotte and himself, loomed large.

'All part of the plan,' he considered.

'So, how had he infected her with this taste for blood? Simply by accident or design?' Either way he had nearly destroyed the town, ensnared Brody in a trap full of sexual abuse and bloodletting and managed to escape scot-free again. Could Brody ever undo the damage which Evet had created and save Charlotte as well as the town itself from further horrors?

Instinctively he got up and headed towards the office and the probability of more of the same carnal battery. He was met by his captor; as usual, waiting for him to come to her. It was like cat and mouse with the cat regurgitating the mouse on a string daily, only to gobble him up again each day and start all over again.

His mind was blank to time and his only way of gauging its progression was the ever-increasing number of twin incisions on various parts of his body. As he passed the mirrors on one occasion he paused... Thinking that he looked less human now and more like a zombie, perhaps even a bit like his good old Bruce and not anything anyone would particularly desire, he stood dejected. Still, Charlotte drained him daily of most of the bodily fluids that he had managed to regenerate in his unconscious time off from his horrific new job that he was rapidly becoming a slave to. The irony of his real work stopping his sex life for years was not lost. He desperately needed Cash to intercede now. He had been trying to stop Brody becoming a slave to work by introducing him to a woman – how apt now that he desperately needed someone to stop him being a slave to a virtual carbon copy of the same woman.

The sun streamed through the window of his dingy back room and warmed his punctured skin on one of many similar mornings. He dragged himself along the floor and up the doorframe inch by inch, collapsing twice before fully standing. As he opened the door, Charlotte was standing in the middle of the room in nothing more than her red stilettos; as usual, more than ready for her normal feeding frenzy.

His captivity continued in this similar perverse sexually-led bloodletting manner for weeks, Charlotte just keeping him weak enough to be of no danger to her and barely strong enough to fulfil her sexual desires and need for fresh blood – it was far more torture than sex. By now he cried a lot and dreaded waking. Each day or every other day, he could no longer tell which, he once again pushed the door open and entered the office knowing what awaited him.

He had already attempted escape from every angle possible on many previous occasions and now virtually resigned himself to merely surviving if possible, hoping against hope that Evet's deceitfulness and lack of promised return might influence Charlotte at some point to release him. The only small redeeming factor was that he seemed to be a carrier but not to have developed the disease that her other victims perished from. This tiny redemption felt more like further punishment and he regularly fell asleep hoping for death to take him before morning.

On the next occasion that he could remember, as he entered, she was again, hardly dressed. He paused at the door knowing that he was seconds away from being held in her visual spell; those steely blue eyes already flaring and seeking his glance, but he kept his head down and defiantly asked,

"Charlotte, isn't it time you stopped this mad life? Surely you know the difference between good and pure evil; why do you force me to live this way? Am I that good? Or does Evet offer you pay, just to keep me here? It surely can't just be the sex, or the blood."

"You please me," she replied, thoughtfully cocking her head to one side like a dog, then she hesitantly conceded,

"Nobody has ever done that before and you don't seem to hate me either." Regaining herself with a shake of her head she reverted to the less mellow.

"The Master said to keep you subdued as long as you were of worth and then he would return in time and reward me with a better gift." Brody listened and countered, head still down, avoiding eye contact for as long as possible.

"Surely, when you walk down the avenue and everyone stops to stare, you know they are all secretly dreaming of having you themselves. Couldn't you just be more humane and control your carnal desires?" He tried desperately to break through the mental barriers Evet had put in place. Thinking to her instead of speaking,

'Could you not live in harmony with the townsfolk? Many would probably pay good money to service your sexual needs and then, given time, the blood thing could be somehow arranged. Surely you could compromise?' Trying to confuse he switched back to speech.

"Please, Charlotte, you beat me, you mistreat me, you even make me get down on my knees and you bite me; I know you need the blood, but it definitely doesn't excite me to be continually abused and misused in this way. You have taken all that I have got and, so far, not once amongst all the perverted caresses and internal molestations have you ever told me WHY." He paused to compose himself as his body and voice were shaking like an infirm octogenarian.

He had learnt by now that he only had seconds each time to try to get through, so he hurriedly continued his plea, this time direct to her mind, again using the children's teachings to try to hold her concentration on to him.

'Even though I do everything you want and please you to the best of my ability, you are completely ruining my life now; you know exactly what you are doing so surely you know I am close to being completely spent – I can give you no more. You are taking my life and throwing it away; isn't there something inside you that I can appeal to? Surely you couldn't have always been this way.' Without answer to his desperate cerebral transmissions, she shook her head to break his link and, without further acknowledgment or any more pleasantry, lifted his chin, fixed his eyes with her own, pushed him back into the bedroom, tore his clothes off and continued with more of her normal sexual ravishment and perversion. With no more than a cursory glance at his tear-stained face she brutally raped him again and again.

As was only too often as she finished him, she threw her head back with pleasure and laughed with a blood-curdling primordial screech. Brody's unwillingly supplied bodily fluids spilt from her soft lips that curled back to reveal her razor-sharp vampiric incisors. Pearls of semen ran down her chin and neck, down over her left breast onto her thigh and would no doubt in another lifetime have been a source of great visual pleasure to him, but at this moment he was unaware of anything. She continued to pleasure herself long after he had passed out. When he was comatose and ready to be drained of blood, she did not rush but was completely efficient in all departments, wanting only to please herself and the master.

'Well done, but DO NOT let him die or you will join him.' She

quivered from the stimulation that Brody's unconscious but still firm body was providing. He supplied her pleasure, but a secondary shiver caused by fear and created by the remote and distant mentally-transmitted warning, rippled through her naked form.

Brody had awoken mid-session and blacked out again moments later from lack of blood, as was the usual end to his daily punishment. When he awoke back in the bedroom he felt more excruciating pain than ever before. On inspection via the mirror he saw thirty or more pairs of incisions leading right the way up to his waist. He was, by now, looking more like the personification of a junkie's arm.

'Where has that month gone?' He had no real memory of it save that of blurred sex and violence, but realised he could not go on much longer.

Days or weeks later, Brody stumbled and crawled once again into her office. As was now normal, he fell in front of his mistress ready for what he feared and actually hoped would be his last visit. He was so weakened he felt sure he could not survive another session. Most of his torso was marked with telltale incisions where Charlotte's insatiable appetite for blood was regularly stemmed. He looked up as if to some heavenly reprisal and spoke his last delirious words:

"Charlotte, I no longer want to live or die, I just need you to stop this horror. As Charley in another life, I truly do love you so much; please forgive me? End me now… please?" As usual, all went blank.

He awoke with seven smiling faces around him and in a less familiar but far sweeter-smelling room. He saw no beards but smiled back thankful of the fairy tale ending that had apparently whisked him magnificently from danger.

"Where am I? What happened?"

CHAPTER 13

Stolen Ideas.

"What the hell happened?" Brody verbally repeated his enquiry to his seven friends who were surrounding his bed and staring down intently at his gradually reviving form. He had got out of the habit of regularly using transmitted thought, speech or any other saner forms of communication. Not much had been said at all recently for that matter – sex and violence having been all he had experienced for the past few months.

'We fell for Evet's trap and left you to go to assist Baylok when we saw his beacon fire but when we arrived we found him – all the elders and even the warrior guards were nearly all slaughtered. We are unsure who did all the killing, but it was certainly Evet who instigated it and he who had set the beacon to distract us from you so that Charlotte could, as he had apparently pre-arranged, keep you busy, if you pardon the term of phrase.' They thought the information back to him, this and the further details of how Evet had once again trapped them in the damping chamber by creating a visual illusion of another building.

He had transmitted a false façade mentally to disguise the building that they had previously been held captive within. His fakery removed the risk of encountering Baylok's damping field and caused the seven of them to fully believe that they were re-entering the friendly surroundings of Baylok's council rooms. In their haste to assist their small friend they were as easily captured there for a second time and, on this occasion, without the need for any nightlight cheese. Evet subsequently locked them in, blocked Baylok's secret hatch and left them to rot, eventually making good his escape with the aid of some new allies who had apparently rode into the village on horseback earlier that day. Whoever these new people where they had obviously also been taken in by more of his lies and deceit. It was looking likely that they were now assisting him and would probably end up being his next unfortunate victims. Brody's head was still spinning from the rescue let alone the details of the latest episode in Evet's complex web of deception.

'What is he up to? Surely if he understands more about the Necronomicon *now, he could just escape and leave us trapped; why stay?'* he thought disjointedly to the children. The now all too uncomfortable and repetitive question that none of them had yet come close to answering, remained. It didn't get an answer this time either but the convoluted conversations that followed certainly aided him getting re-acquainted with his ability to communicate on their level. The seven appraised him of the fact that Evet had probably lied and deceived the newcomers as he did with everyone else he came across and it seemed most likely that he had killed at least one of them. They had been informed that three horses with riders had arrived in the village and when they left there were still only three riders, but he was one of them. All this and much more the others had ascertained from the only remaining survivor of Baylok's village; one of the big Saxon warrior guards who had uncharacteristically but quite sensibly gone into hiding after being badly injured in the initial skirmish when Evet had returned.

Brody listened to mental transmission after transmission, learning that nearly three weeks later when things had cooled down a little and after the evil perpetrator of the violence had left, the injured guard was able to come out of hiding and release the seven from their prison home. Unfortunately, the warrior who was by then nearly completely emaciated, having clung on all that time sustained only by lapping the moisture from the morning dew and chewing on grass to survive his ordeal, later sadly died of the wounds that had been inflicted during Evet's nice little visit.

The children tried but were unable to save him without medical supplies that were ironically freely available in the derelict and abandoned clinic in Langgnãd. He had survived long enough though to not only free the children by unlocking the chamber door but also to pass on this and other information about the details of Evet's next potential destination. It seemed, from the dying testimony of this brave survivor, very much like Evet had made a run for the hills with his new comrades and was aiming to take refuge amongst the native American Indian tribes that resided in that area.

Brody thought back to the lone silhouetted figure that had appeared to have been following them and wondered whether he or she for that matter would be next on Evet's hit list or if they could be their next unfortunate ally. Baylok had not enjoyed that status for long and it was a worry to Brody that whoever they befriended may eventually meet the same fate.

As he strengthened and healed over the next few days and weeks, the eight discussed at length their next moves and decided that a completely new tactic must be decided upon. Evet's ability to deceive others, turn them to his own advantage and against his enemies, was very much more powerful than the children had originally accounted for. Brody refrained from any 'I told you so'-type comments as he hadn't actually told them, but he did feel somewhat vindicated personally for his suspicions and negative thoughts on the subject of their naïvety. It was of some small personal comfort to him as he had initially felt quite embarrassed of himself, to have even thought that he knew better.

Evet's true intentions with the *Necronomicon* were still unclear and his ability to survive without linking to them was now a moot point. Amongst the information the children were able to impart back to Brody were the impressions that they had drawn from the memory engrams of his recent encounter with Charlotte.

'*We clearly see now that Evet deliberately created Charlotte in the image of someone from your memories. She may in reality have been no more than a local prostitute, but he bestowed her with a near perfect look to attract you. At the same time, we think he used the blood from your injury with the shovel that was on the rags to wean her to you. It gave her the desperate need for not only just blood, but specifically YOUR blood to keep her alive, thus keeping you and her there indefinitely unless you died. Realistically, only we could release you and we were conveniently similarly trapped.*' Evet's plan had so nearly worked and Brody swallowed hard as he mentally digested all the missing pieces that the children now put into place.

'*Lucky for us all, that the big warrior at least, temporarily survived and was able to free us or it might now all be over,*' they explained further – more bad news.

'*We were not fully aware of these advanced abilities within him.*' Brody gave thought to the idea of biting his own tongue, to avoid the 'I could have told you that weeks ago' feeling, slipping inappropriately into his transmitted thought patterns.

'*It seems he has scoured our civilisation and many others collecting and developing all sorts of powers and information over the centuries. Many have considered him to actually be an incarnation of whatever god or devil their respective religion accepts. We should have been more open-minded and have been foolish to assume we were in control. Ironically, the rejection of religion by the high council of our phase allowed him a less hindered start on his original quest for power.'* Brody felt a pang of guilt now for refraining and felt he possibly should have done what he would normally have done, which was just to speak out and bugger the consequences. Momentarily, he considered that this was not the first thing since arriving here that appeared to have mellowed in his demeanour.

Back on track, gaining confidence in his mental abilities and not wanting to repeat the same mistake twice, Brody finally intervened.

'Do you think this is perhaps the reason he returned and destroyed Baylok and the elders? Remember how he told us that his people had rejected religion as dangerous. How right they were as Evet is ultimately dangerous and we still don't know his full intention or end game.' The children agreed. It was then unanimously decided, seven to one, to return to Langgnăd to attempt to forcibly communicate with Charlotte to get answers about why Evet, or the Master as she called him, had used her to trap Brody in such a despicable way rather than just destroying them both as he had done with so many others. It was difficult to imagine which fate either would have found worse, but Brody was understandably the nah voter and did not relish ever seeing her again, let alone so soon. He had been completely captivated by her contrived beauty, fully controlled by her hypnotic nymphomaniac-vampire persona, but the thought of being continually brutally raped and used as a food source was not his idea of fun. He had profusely thanked the seven for saving him from more of this barbaric treatment but was not happy at all about their choice of the next course of action or even destination.

Having decided that as soon as Brody was recovered sufficiently they would all set about their next crusade, Brody rested and planned. If he were to admit it, it was a couple of days longer than it could have been before he reported fit for duty. He was mentally and physically afraid of meeting Charlotte again and delayed the departure for as long as he felt he could get away with it. In the back of his mind he knew full well that, like any fear, it had to be faced head on, sooner or later.

Not having overly far to travel they decided to wait until a morning to do so as arrival and travel in daylight was deemed safer than at night. They knew that the diseased inhabitants that Charlotte's carnal lust had infected in her search for the purity of blood (that only Brody could provide) were far less active in sunlight than at night. At sundown, for ninety minutes or so of twilight, they seemed to roam more and were potentially far more likely to further spread the disease by any bodily contact. As it seemed that the infection was in most cases deadly, even though Brody exhibited an apparent immunity, it was not worth taking any risks. The secondary diseased may carry a different strain to that which Charlotte and Brody were the carriers of. So, daytime travel was agreed.

Evet's plans to thwart Brody and the others had been deviously conceived to the finest detail over time and, in hindsight, had been virtually infallible in complexity which made Brody realise how lucky he was that the single warrior had survived long enough to release the others.

As they approached the town gates and passed the now all too commonplace strewn bodies and open graves, Charlotte was already organising a welcoming committee.

"They are here, I smell his musk. He has washed and got new clothes, but I sense his freshly regenerated blood." Charlotte's varyingly armed henchmen moved and got into position, readying themselves for the arrival of their mistress' potential next fix.

The eight entered the town as before, but on seeing a much less plague-ridden individual scurrying for cover and distinctly heading in the direction of Charlotte's place, this time they went straight to the avenue and looked for the crooked numbers on the wall where her house was easily found again. On approach, three henchmen stepped out to bar the way, guns outstretched menacingly. The children had dealt with this before when rescuing Brody from Charlotte's clutches weeks ago. Luckily they were well prepared and by quickly linking hands and minds they sent conflicting imagery to the guard's individual cerebrums and were allowed safe passage as if invisible.

They entered and went straight to the office to confront Charlotte to try to get to the bottom of the mystery of what the so-called Master was trying to achieve.

"Good, you have done well." The satisfied voice softly praised the work that so far had successfully enticed the quarry back to the lair.

John led the seven and pushed the office door open. They entered and surrounded the rear side of the room already linked and ready to countermand the power Charlotte had previously exerted on Brody if it surfaced. Brody timidly stepped into the room, scanned all corners and waited for the secret agent chair to rotate. As it did, they were all completely surprised to see sitting in it…

Evet himself.

"I have tired of the cat and mouse chase game and want to negotiate a deal," he announced. Nothing Evet said or did should realistically have shocked at this point, but Brody was speechless and even the children took moments to respond.

'Link with us again, allow us to control your actions and we can all attempt to use the Necronomicon *to return to our respective phases. Justice can then be done fair and square – no negotiation is required as no other choice can be made.'* Their initial ultimatum was met with silence, so they probed further.

'You have nowhere to run now and must accept that after all these years your time is nigh.' Their extension to the well-considered and firmly delivered first thought transmission was rebuffed immediately.

"I cannot do that, I have evolved further than you can possibly imagine and my powers are far more than you realise. You no longer have control and cannot contain me, however, we are in many ways kindred and I do not want to hurt you without good cause. I would like to offer a compromise," he replied verbally for the benefit of Brody and the now recovered guards who had arrived behind the eight. They stood listening with trepidation.

Evet was apparently unaware that Brody had been taught the methods of mind linking to the children, so he deliberately thought blankly to himself to try to avoid giving this skill away as it might be a sleeved card to keep for a while. The seven replied mentally, instinctively understanding Brody's initial silence,

'What do you propose? We cannot compromise but for sheer interest's sake will listen to your offer.' Evet paused and then opened his can of worms mentally and verbally at the same time in a show of raw power.

"Let me leave, do not pursue me and I will allow you all to live! When I am safe, I will supply the information of how you, Brody, can get home; I wish you no further ill. This is an offer that, if refused, you will certainly all regret having not accepted. Sentiment makes me want to be more benevolent, but time constrains my patience. Triclipse approaches soon and I WILL find a home once and for all." His voice and mental transmission boomed out simultaneously to all within the building and beyond.

The guards were understandably completely baffled. The intrepid visitors, including Brody, listened and considered the finality of this rather uncompromising compromise, realising that even if he was not lying (which was highly unlikely) that if actioned, his proposal left seven of their number completely stranded. It seemed obvious that this was exactly what he wanted – no pursuit. He probably felt Brody would not want to chase him to the ends of the cosmos but knew full well that the tenacious children would most certainly do just that. This way they would be stuck out of phase forever. This was definitely not an acceptable plan and Brody was not convinced that the offer to help him to get home had ever been anything more than a shallow bluff to soften him up anyway.

As the reality of the standoff was starting to sink in, Charlotte came through the bedroom link door. She took up an expectedly sultry position behind the big chair by lifting a stockinged leg over its arm and placing her stiletto heel provocatively into Evet's lap, slowly rubbing him in a very sensual manner. She looked to tease Brody who was already starting to come under her optical control. Evet quickly brushed her aside casting a stare into her eyes that seemed to physically hurt. She backed away as if whipped and stood at the back of the room with a pained expression on her face and cowered. Brody was, for once, indebted to his evil adversary and shook his head to regain mental control of himself. He had, until then, been unaware that she had even entered the room; such was her power over his mind.

'We realise now that you have developed many more new abilities over the years and although we have always known you have tried to hide things from us, we obviously severely underestimated you. However, even though we have been yet unsuccessful in returning you to face justice we have still always had some control over you and we feel your overstatement is unbecoming and inaccurate.' The seven replied and silently delivered a firm and appropriate confirmation of their original ultimatum. Brody, feeling that he knew better (again), thought they were overplaying a weak hand.

'Release Charlotte from the bloodlust that you have chained her

with, come of your own choice and when we find a way home, we will even plead for clemency on your historic charges. This is our best and only possible offer. If this is not acceptable we will have to reconsider your destruction – you know we are capable of it.' This thought echoed round all the linked minds, Brody's included, and definitely strengthened the play.

Evet did not even flinch. He sat silently in contemplation for a minute; a sly smile spread slowly across his lips and he rose to his feet, everyone braced for action. Charlotte's guards stepped back in fear, Charlotte herself cowered lower as if she was a dog being scolded by its owner.

'So, you have finally learned to understand the art of lying and how to try to get your own way by deceit,' he thought to them whilst slowly moving towards Charlotte. She recoiled even further, crouching under the window as if awaiting a beating.

'Well, you must understand then that I cannot agree to your terms and must leave this place. All these years I chose to let you be in control but now the secrets I sought are better understood and I still have the Necronomicon. *It is hidden with allies far from here and, now that I fully understand its usage, when the time comes I will leave you ALL here forever!'* He mentally screamed the last part of his threatening response.

Even though she was still cowering from Evet, Charlotte was now salivating and squirming. She had fully re-scented Brody and was lusting after his blood, as was all part of Evet's original plan that he had initiated months ago; keep everyone busy or near death whilst he learned from the *Necronomicon*, develop his plans and, when the time was right, leave them all to die.

A nice man he was certainly not and the offer to help Brody get home having now been revoked, only confirmed it more. It had always been a mere hollow and useless gesture in the first place.

Nevertheless, Brody was now starting to think that Evet had no real reason to return to Langgnãd at all. He could have merely waited and by biding his time have just simply left at his leisure. There must be something more to it. He and the seven children knew instinctively that Evet was once again plotting some new ulterior and self-motivated evil plan. As usual there was no doubt of yet another hidden agenda to uncover.

Charlotte sensed Evet allowing her to rise and stood up, pushing her chest out through her virtually see-through silk blouse, provocatively posing peacock-like and attempting to fix Brody's gaze again. The children had pre-planned against this and easily blocked her with a mind barrier that protected Brody from falling once again under her sexually charged influence.

Still, even whilst protected from her he was subconsciously attracted to her visually and found it extremely difficult not to gaze at her so obviously proffered bust, which was accentuated by erotic piercings. Brody had never even noticed this before but as her nipples showed clearly through the skimpy blouse he saw that she was adorned with subtle circular barbells on each and he became unable to detract his stare from them.

His mind drifted and he recollected a painful six-hour sitting with his tattooist where the most pain was the last thirty minutes. In that time Giles (his award winning tattooist friend) had, at Brody's own request, over-inked barbell nipple rings onto the already see-through blouse-wearing girl that he had previously chosen to portray his accentuated sexy female caricature. The idea of this girl was taken directly from Brody's interpretation of the lyrics of one of his favourite songs and, mixed with his own fantasies, had been carefully tattooed on his lower left shoulder blade. In the song that inspired this session the girl was a prostitute… Things started to spin in his mind.

As if falling asleep or being hypnotised by this new vision he started to sway but, helped by the children's protective mind screen, managed to steady himself. Brody didn't fully understand why, but he felt as if he needed and wanted to help her and was soon unable to refrain. He broke the tension and spoke out.

"Charlotte," he asked; confused and desperate, "do you believe that while you are earning his trust your life is good? Don't you know you are not only hurting me but all the people who might otherwise have loved you? Don't cast them all aside. I'm just a man, but look at yourself, drooling; this is no life for you just continually screwing me and drinking my blood. My friends might be able to help you. Why not pack a bag and come with us?" he pleaded in a genuine and desperate attempt to break Evet's control over her.

She stared back at him silently, animalistic, and then with a sly smile and a simple shimmy of her silken shoulders, dropped her blouse to the floor in a raw attempt to reassert herself on his mind. The block from the children was too powerful and she merely stood there naked, quivering, shaking, fully aroused and ready to sexually strike but unable to move against him. Singularly, to Brody she was an amazing sight to behold. He was physically moved by her plight and, although she had nearly killed him on multiple occasions, kept him as a virtual blood bank and raped him continually, her resemblance to Charley was compelling. He wanted to help her and his surreptitious need to submit to her sexual desires again resurfaced.

His subconscious excitement was now becoming visible and in fleeting moments of clear thought he felt very uncomfortable standing so out of control of himself. Mentally he was alone in this crowded room. The seven sensed his growing discomfort, altered the resonance of their transmission and Charlotte immediately slumped to the floor as if shot by a sniper. Once again Evet did not even flinch but spoke aloud, "Well, here is my vow to you then... You will soon see that I have come with wrath. My time here in this phase is short. You must understand the numbers at least; the human numbers of triclipse are six months, six days and six hours from today... I WILL leave alone!"

Brody's mind went blank, he needed time to think, to get the horrific memories of Charlotte's treatment of him from his mind. As he got a grip of himself, he looked again at Evet – what did he see? Could he believe that what he saw as night drew closer was real or just some sexually-charged weird fantasy? Was what he was seeing just old dreams or was Evet warping his mind by staring back at him? He knew that in his real dreams back in his own phase that Charlotte as Charley, was always there, not some evil being twisting his mind and bringing him to complete despair.

It was daylight outside but in Brody's mind things were confused now. As he fought to regain his own sanity, he didn't realise that at this point, Evet himself was now controlling his inner conflict; he was actively trying to undermine and break the protection that the children had been able to silently offer. In his mind it was night and oh so black! Paranoia was kicking in and he felt as if someone other than those in the room was watching him. In the mist of his tormented mind, dark figures moved and twisted, provocatively dancing and cavorting naked in front of a fire. Sticks or spears were waving and poking at him and suddenly he was upside down, falling into the heat.

'*How is this happening?*' He thought it might be madness taking over or perhaps it was just Evet forcing these images upon him. It confused and tired him even more.

'*What does it all mean?*'

Was this real? Was it a dream, a controlled mind state, or just some kind of mental hell? Questions, questions and more constantly swirling unanswered questions.

He felt like a puppet on strings being pulled in all directions and a stray thought of Bruce entered his mind but quickly faded as he tried to make sense of all his other inner conflicts and confusions.

'This thing, Bruce, is such an irony, I must find a way of using this affinity he has with such a worthless and inanimate object – it may hold strength that even Charlotte does not.' Even as he mentally battled the seven for control, still Evet probed and plotted further.

It was now virtually impossible for anyone to second guess Evet's next move. Strangely, these ideas of mental puppetry now scared Brody more than the thought of being the target for physical destruction. He had faced injury and death many times before in various forms. The underground fights, the loss of loved ones to cancer, accidents and many other horrors of day-to-day existence on his Earth, not to mention the raw nerve that was Charlotte. The thought of being manipulated by some super being whose motives seemed evil in intent was far more terrifying to him than any harmless memory.

It reminded him of a night terror he used to have as a child after watching a particularly graphic horror film where an alien species had hibernated within human hosts and wreaked havoc and destruction upon their gruesome and violent pupation and how they acted so indiscriminately to such devastating effect thereafter.

'Eureka, ha, ha! He provides so well, so easily, so detailed in his thoughts, he can never escape me. It is what he wants. I need only play the tune and he will dance the dance without encouragement. This is truly too easy...' Ideas could be stolen like loose change and Evet was growing rich on his successful theft from within Brody's confusion.

CHAPTER 14

Realisation and the Pain of Separation.

He awoke back in Baylok's meeting room with the seven children standing over him again, just as he remembered having awoken a few weeks earlier.

'We have to stop meeting like this,' was his first hazy thought to them and they smiled in response, all now having become accustomed to Brody's ability to find humour in desperate situations. Asking verbally now and shaking his head to loosen thoughts that were stuck out of focus, he said,

"What the hell went down? I remember Charlotte looking like she was about to jump me again and Evet ranting, not making much sense, but then it all went weird." Initially he was agitated but soon settled and listened intently as the seven explained:

'We had to beat a hasty retreat as, whilst we were mentally protecting you and ourselves from Charlotte's attentions, Evet was trying to infiltrate our minds and twist us to hurt you. He also attempted to subvert your memories and turn you against us whilst simultaneously controlling the guards to herd us to some more unwanted captivity. We chose to stand and fight, old-school as you might call it, and we managed to get you out while we could.'

"What happened?" Brody interrupted, woozily shaking his head again. He felt dizzy and nauseous.

'He was not exaggerating when he told of his increased capacity and we were imminently going to lose one or other mental battle so, as a last resort, we released our protection on you momentarily and took control of the guards making them fire their weapons randomly into the ceiling.' Brody conjured images of the O.K. Corral.

'It got very messy very quick but was just enough to distract Evet and Charlotte long enough and, whilst they ducked for cover, we grabbed you and got out quick,' was the conclusion to the exciting explanation.

'Wow, I wish I had been there,' he thought jokingly, his eyes gradually closing.

'I am actually feeling really tired and a bit sickly. I think we are going to need a bigger boat next time.' His dry analogy of an insurmountable task was initially not fully understood but, over the next few minutes as sleep picked at his head, he slowly explained it away to the satisfaction of the children save a couple of questions along the lines of,

'But what is a shark?' He started to feel dizzy again, his eyes wouldn't focus, strange music swirled around his mind and he just really wanted to sleep.

'Don't worry, be happy,' he thought to them in a singing tone as he drifted back to a fitful and very deep slumber.

When he awoke next it was about midday and the sunlight was blazing in through the un-shuttered window of Baylok's room. It seemed hotter than normal and the sun seemed brighter – the rays entered the room at a different angle to normal. No one seemed to be around so he got up to find out what was happening. As he opened the front door, he was greeted by just two of the seven.

'Where is everyone?' he had more instinctively asked mentally and it felt different. He hesitated and became aware that he was only thinking to two as compared to the whole group and then

realised they were no longer all linked.

"Where is everyone?" he asked out loud in a semi-panic-stricken tone as they entered.

'No need to worry, we have split into three groups whilst we have been attempting to find where Evet has gone. He is not at Langgnăd and Charlotte is also missing; the town seems virtually dead now. Everyone is hiding, too scared to venture out. Only a few disorientated guards and some zombified close-to-death specimens remain out in the open,' the two explained.

'Well, for all the fire, brimstone and pornographic treatment he released upon me via Charlotte, mentally and physically, I actually feel great; what did you lot do?' Brody enquired, stretching out and feeling better than he had for ages.

'We have done very little for the past three months whilst you slept.'

"THREE MONTHS!" Brody exclaimed out loud. They ignored his tone and continued, *'We monitored you, but it seemed your mind and body put itself into some sort of self-induced coma. We think the mental stress of us protecting you combined with Evet and Charlotte trying to mentally tear you away from us pretty much short-circuited your cerebral cortex and you, in effect,* closed down. *For the first week we worried for your recovery, but we soon realised you were in no real danger, so we turned our attention to finding the beast that caused all this.'* They explained the reasons for his current state, calmly.

'So, have you tracked him down yet?' he thought back to the two a lot quieter and in apologetic tones, as he knew the high volume of his exclamation would have affected them.

'YES!' They attempted to jokingly shout back their cerebral response, fully understanding his communication and sentiment of apology. They went on to explain how they had managed to discover that Evet was, as suspected but for unknown reasons,

currently living with a tribe of native American Indians in the mountainous region to the east. Brody vaguely remembered having considered it before, but now started to further question the validity of his previous assumptions about this place.

The phase they were trapped in was like a mixed-up version of many of Earth's own historic periods. To find native American Indians, Saxons, Vikings and 1930s gangsters all within a few short miles of each other in a terrain that varied from green olde England to barren 'way out west' tundra did not add up. He now started to realise more clearly that although the theories and extrapolations that he had been working on *could* be bang on with respect to prospective avenues of rapid travel-through phases. It sadly also seemed likely that they might be wholly *inaccurate* with regards to what existed within these alternate phases; ironically, this may have been one of the only truths Evet had given him since their first meeting over eighteen months ago.

All these thoughts were very reminiscent and he felt he had experienced these very same revelatory feelings more than once before.

Brody drifted and remembered how back on Earth it had always (apparently naïvely), been assumed that any life within these alternate planes and phases would be a diversification from future or past evolutionary patterns of development and could only be an image or reflected representation, not actual life.

No real hard evidence had ever been uncovered to confirm the existence of other true sentient life in the galaxy and he knew that no wider theoretical proposals had ever been proven. It seemed more and more likely that one of the suggestions Evet had made months earlier had in fact been true. His race, the *human* race, was simply not ready for what they might find if they opened these rifts in time and space.

Somehow, replication more than diversification was the theme here. Surely travel of any type or speed could not be worth the incalculable consequences he was now apparently realising because of it. This thought chilled him to the bone.

He tried to force it to the back of his mind. If it was true, his whole existence seemed to now hinge, not only just upon miraculously learning how to control some mythical book and the runes held within it, but in also, at all costs, stopping the apparently all-powerful character that seemed hellbent on doing the exact same thing before him.

It felt to him most unlikely that a being as powerful and with such potential longevity as Evet would be overly concerned on just returning home, especially when if legend was to be believed, he would be hated by most of those who were waiting there to receive him. Everything pointed to there being a lot more to it and, pretty much everything that Brody had experienced, could quite easily now be part of some other complexity put in his mind by Evet to throw him off the truth of the situation.

Again, he knew he had experienced these ideas on more than one occasion – had Evet managed to forcefully wipe his memory? Or had all these passing out events and dizzy spells been symptoms of something else lying dormant within him? The only thing he was now comfortable with and confident of was the fact that the others, the children, were genuine. He mulled all the facts as he understood them and now realised why there had always seemed to be odd discrepancies in the various tales he had been told; it was all leading to one scary but strangely comforting conclusion which he also felt certain he had already known before.

Evet apparently did not want him dead. Not yet at least.

He possibly needed him in some more far reaching consequential way to complete whatever dastardly plan he had been pursuing all along. Had every single occurrence, apparently successful or not, been calculated to bring him to the right place at the right time? There seemed little chance that it was mere coincidence and more and more likely as time went on that Evet, really had just planned everything so deviously and in such meticulous detail.

Brody didn't want to be part of whatever Evet was planning but was beginning to realise that he and the self-proclaimed Master were intrinsically entwined in some strange mutual destiny.

He snapped back to reality and thought it best to try to deal with what he could see, hear and touch rather than driving himself even further towards total insanity, trying to unravel the complexities of what *might* be. As he glanced at his two comrades, he noticed tears in their eyes and realised they had felt and understood all he had been feeling and fretting over in the last few moments and realistically the last few months too.

"Sorry," he apologised verbally without need of any real explanation.

'So... what's the plan then, guys? Who's on first base?' He transmitted a weak and far too complex concept to try to lighten the mood, although not understanding the nuance, the two realised it was meant as a humorous statement and smiled politely and silently answered:

'We feel for your sadness and confusion but must now wait for our brothers and sisters to return and then we can re-link with each other for your safety and strength in numbers in case we too soon encounter Evet again.' They were sincere and solemn, sounding as if they already knew a problem lay ahead but were holding back the details.

'We must find him before the triclipse day as, we believe his intent is, not only to use the book of Necronomicon *to travel out of this phase but possibly to collapse a rift behind him, bringing a complete*

end to this reality.' Brody was shocked and silently stood staring out of the window in disbelief.

'If he has found a way to harness the energy of the triclipse, that might be his method of destroying things as he leaves.' Shuddering at hearing this idea rattle around his head, Brody's immediate thought was that if Evet was successful as suggested, it could leave this manic individual free to travel to any other phase with relative ease. If so, he would be completely incognito and free to do as he pleased. Even if he visited a place that he had been to before and was recognised, with care and deception, along with his non-too-shabby set of other skills, suspicion would probably take years to find him out by which time he would have potentially succeeded in doing the same things time and again. Brody had one of those pangs of forward thinking memory that occasionally troubled him and the turn of phrase he had used in his thoughts was 'time and again', which stood out in his mind like a bushfire. It was soon extinguished by the tsunami of confusion that it caused and the thought drifted away as he tried to fathom what it meant.

The two others confirmed his fears and suppositions even though he hadn't deliberately transmitted them.

'We believe his greater aim is to destroy all the other realities that hold humanoid life one by one until only one remains, then he can reign supreme as a type of god over whatever is left of the universe.' Brody listened intently to their thoughts as they unfolded this bleak scenario.

'To the best of our knowledge there are only six humanoid inhabited reality phases. This one is yet still unnamed and was either created by accident from the collision of our two respective phases when in flux, possibly a direct result of Evet's transport experimentation down the years or equally as possible, a deliberate act by him, done as a test for his own abilities and powers. His ego is

such that he may have risked capture just to try to destroy something that he himself created and when you arrived it just made the game more intriguing for him.' They knew their revelations were not pleasing Brody but they had no choice but to lay the bare bones out for him. The suggestion of sitting down before they expanded their theory further had been extrapolated from Brody's own memory and was well used in this instance by the two, who didn't even fully understand the concept. Unfortunately, by the time he re-entered Baylok's quarters and found a suitable chair it had only served to create more trepidation.

'This is where we believe the nexus between you lies; we think that you and Evet are linked by your experiments in travel and, although he may have inadvertently or deliberately created this phase, YOUR *arrival and continued interaction with it, seems to have changed its substance and now you both affect each other's destinies.'* This was a hard pill for Brody to swallow. He didn't like the idea of potentially being even *partially* responsible for the creation of this horrendous situation and temporarily he deliberately blocked the thought. He desperately wanted to continue listening but without having to consider the possible reality of his own culpability.

'Then there is our phase, which is called Ainran. Yours is what your scientists refer to as Laniakea, which contains the Milky Way and all your other alien life form inhabited planets and solar systems.' This fact pinged a bell and intrigued Brody; he listened intently as the thoughts wafted through his mind.

'And there are three others which we refer to as Asgardia, Kandaria and Orbertah-ein-lein.' On receiving this he struggled even with the pronunciation of the last example but, somewhere in his consciousness, he recognised these names. The bold but casually thrown out statement of other alien life forms seemed to have been mentioned in such a casual matter-of-fact way, that he

was momentarily inwardly ashamed of his own race's overriding disbelief in such a concept.

'We believe that it is Evet's goal to rule supreme over Kandaria and all that dwells there, destroying all human or other life and as many phases of reality on his way, that he can...'

With no real time for Brody to start wandering off on the massiveness of the alien life subject, he tried to concentrate on more pressing concerns. Chasing the prospect of other life forms and planning a future of convincing the rest of the Earth (if he ever saw it again) that they *do* exist now seemed trivial in comparison to the imminence of the potential obliteration of all known life. Complete destruction in five separate phases of reality or possibly even more was way more than his mind could take in. Even as the children were transmitting to him he started to drift but suddenly snapped back to it as he remembered...

Meanwhile, Evet's mind absorbed everything from his distant position. He used, abused, twisted and plotted.

'Oh, how clever you children of others think you are, but you can have no comprehension of the pain I will bring you, pay-back for the centuries of your persecution and the constant pursuance your kind have reigned upon me – it will be my pleasure indeed.' His monitoring was exciting and inspiring him. If he hadn't been planning what the children had suggested before he was certainly considering it closely now. If Brody had known this, he may have quoted Murphy's law, but equally, because of the lengthy explanation it would have led to, he might not have bothered.

....His drift halted, as memory of the passage in the *Necronomicon* rushed forward and spat cerebrally towards the two children.

'*...KANDARIAN DEMONS!'* Brody's thought was like a shout and he jumped to his feet interrupting the flow of the two and Evet simultaneously. *He* stopped and thought more… *They* hesitated but quickly continued...

'Yes, alien life forms, like us! They do exist and yes you are right, although we have never seen one. We believe the mythical creatures mentioned in the Necronomicon *do actually exist as well.'* The information was by Brody's normal rationale, quite unbelievable but here, now, after the happenings of the past year or so, it all seemed so logical and obvious.

'Since, to our knowledge, Evet is the only being to have ever travelled to all six of these phases, it is possible that he has chosen Kandaria as his favourite and wants to destroy the rest in some mad omnicidal apocalypse.' A shiver squirmed its way up his spine at the mention of this term. As the two continued he shook nervously and felt a dull pain starting to throb deep within his core.

"You have no idea… Kandarian Demons. Oh, yes! And meet them you shall." There was nobody in the Wi-kiya-pi to hear him, so Evet spoke aloud to himself, with glee, and waited.

'He could potentially succeed if the legends within the Necronomicon *are even close to being accurate and possibly hold more clues.'* Brody slumped back to his chair as if this world had already ended.

'We can only yet surmise where you truly fit in to his plans as he has had ample opportunity to dispose of you on more than one occasion and has not only refrained from doing so but actively seems to want to hide his real intent to keep you alive.' Brody was glad of this hidden intent, but could not be certain to what ends and lengths this was to be temporary.

'We think you are, as he said to you when you first met…the key.' Brody started to feel dizzy and sick to the stomach again and hoped another self-induced coma wasn't about to strike. After a short while it seemed to settle and he realised it was no

more than hunger pangs. He had not eaten properly in months, surviving only on the water and broth that the children had been passing through his lips whilst he slept, blissfully unaware of the devastating revelations that were being uncovered around him by the intellectual probing of his seven companions.

And elsewhere…

"I am indebted to you my false brethren, your attempts to probe my inner intentions and the summary of information you gained was not as completely accurate as you thought it was, but it has certainly given me some new things to consider now," Evet whispered to nobody again as he waited impatiently for Cu-bér to return from a tribal meeting. His triumphant whisper slurred slightly as he drifted to an unexpected and unusually deep sleep.

Back at Baylok's Brody rose, went out and collected some wild grass and leaves and made some weak stew to abate his growing hunger. Whilst boiling the concoction on the stove in Baylok's kitchen, he realised with more clarity that when he had met Evet on the beach all those months ago and for every moment since, the probability was that it had actually all been a well-orchestrated game that he had been dragged into. At every turn Evet had been using, testing, probing and gaining information for his own ends, only giving out pertinent snippets where the gain back exceeded the loss. He surmised that based upon this premise, there was a fair chance that his pod was not his pod at all, and it, whatever it may be, could still be on that beach only having virtually disappeared due to an illusion created by the devious master of deception himself.

Bizarre as it seemed, it was even possible that Evet had his own transportation device and had infiltrated Brody's thoughts from the start to make him think it was his. Had it simply vanished purely to create the need for immediate confusion and to generate trust in the unlikely King's sudden appearance? Or vice versa, Evet had no device and just wanted control of his? All this and more screamed inside his skull like two washerwomen arguing over the soap and Brody had no time for the new physical pains growing within him.

He was slowly realising what an evil beast this Evet really was – lying, deceiving and even murdering at absolutely every turn.

He finished his cooking, quickly drank the not-so-tasty brew and returned to the children who were back outside, standing on the veranda waiting for their siblings' return. He transmitted his deeper feelings about the whole long-term deception and the other two agreed. Their thoughts felt as if they were embarrassed when imparting more back to him. The admission that whilst they were linked to Evet and attempting to take him home, that they were, in truth, only able to retain that link by the slimmest of margins seemed near painful to them now. The mental connection at that time was obviously nowhere near as strong as they had wished. They feared that he had been holding back and that his recent claim to have been able to escape at any time had probably always been true. If so, he had been using them as much, if not more, than they thought they were containing him. More pertinently and the reason for the embarrassment was that they now fully believed that he had been waiting for the right moment to act all along. That moment had apparently always been Brody's arrival.

'*We were stupid and innocent.*' Now it was Brody's turn to say it.

"Don't blame yourselves, the fault was not yours." It seemed to carry more feeling when spoken aloud. Their tears were enough to make him realise that he had not only been understood but had touched a nerve.

As he watched the two children cry, in the back of his mind he saw peculiar visions and felt a memory kick in, or was it a premonition forming? He saw flames and people dancing; he was upside down again. He shook his head and re-connected to the here and now.

The three fell silent and stood watching the sun disappear and the twin moons start to rise from opposite horizons. After about five minutes' silence the children wandered down the steps, started to look around, picked up some broken tree branches and constructed crude torches. By wrapping old pieces of cloth that they found hanging on a nearby fence, around the top of the twiggy ends of the branches and dipping them into what Brody thought was just muddy water, they created torches. When lit Brody realised the water was actually some form of crude, surface lying oil.

Getting a flame to light the cleverly constructed flambeau, from their own fingers was quite disconcerting for Brody to experience but it reminded him of Stan Laurel and he smiled broadly, knowing this thought must be kept to himself – the potential explanation would be mind-blowingly complex. After all, it was certainly an efficient method of lighting the newly manufactured torches, which now gave aid to their vision in the twilight time before sunrise. The two now sensed the return of the other children and indicated to Brody that they would arrive within minutes. At this point they started to quietly sing their inner thoughts in a sort of mentally whispered rhyme. Whilst their torches blazed, they silently phrased more sacred chants and praised the return of their kin. It was unnerving and Brody instinctively felt it was a negative sign rather than good cheer.

They lifted the torches and verbally exulted, a cry which contradicted his gut reaction and momentarily heartened him to hear. It was as if they were now suddenly expectant of good news arriving. As their hands were held towards the skies, they both openly started to scream, tears rolling down their cheeks. Suddenly, Brody's feelings of hope were re-dashed and he felt the total dismay in their thoughts.

'*What has happened?*' He dreaded to find out but did not have to wait long to do so. As the first of the other children arrived back and the night drew in, they all stood holding torches burning bright to light the last few yards of their remaining brothers' and sisters' return journey. Brody waited anxiously to hear the news of what they had all found, but only three returned, two were still missing and it was obvious the other five by now had all shared their absent kindred's fate – they were all weeping and wailing as if chanting to some unseen deity. To his amazement, all five then spoke aloud together.

"No longer can we be patient and try to take him to justice, now justice must be meted out here. A ritual must begin; we must completely end him. Unfortunately and undeniably our evil work must be done before his." The tone was firm and resolute without much emotional waver, even though tears flowed freely as they continued their unified decree of retribution. They gave a minor pause for thought and then continued,

"Perhaps not tonight, but we *will* spawn hell and fire upon him; he will never be released, we will sacrifice him to prove his evil is defeated." Beyond the tears, no further outward emotions showed – their faces calm and serene – not giving a clue to the truth of their inner suppressed angst. There was certainly anger in the tone of their voices and it seemed that they had chosen a definitive path to destroy Evet and nothing was going to change that decision or weaken their resolve.

However, to Brody this held issues of its own as it seemed for the moment at least that Evet was possibly his only ticket home as well as being his potential damnation.

He learned from John during later thought transmissions that Evet had taken the other two children as hostages. He was apparently torturing them mentally and physically to impress his new allies in a show of unbridled power and strength, possibly to gain loyalty, fear or perhaps just for the hell of it.

Two of the children had seen some of the tribesmen dancing around a fire chanting and poking sticks at the bodies of their kin that hung upside down above the flames, just low enough to be excruciatingly painful but just high enough not to be fatal. Although he could not sense it himself, the others informed him that, even at this distance, they could still hear and feel the silent thought-laden screams. All of a sudden, Brody had a flash of the true horror of what they had witnessed and realised just what the images he had seen earlier were about.

Back in Langgnād, he felt as if he remembered then but now knew that it had been a thought planted in his head by Evet before it had even happened. Back then it had seemed like just an obvious but horrific ploy to draw Brody and the others in for further negotiations. Now with the reality of its truth, it only served to further revile them all against him. It was this thought that had been haunting Brody periodically since, not a memory, but a precognition implanted by Evet.

'He will eventually kill them both for sure, regardless of whether we go to him or not. He is preparing as triclipse draws nearer and his plans are obviously nearly complete – but for some reason he needs you, *Brody… As much as we want to save our own, we cannot relinquish others to his evil plans.'* The thought reached Brody and gave him hope but it also disturbed him as their predicament seemed relatively hopeless. It was obvious now that Evet's method of torture mirrored that which the children had described as their chosen method of his own possible execution months ago; he

realised how cruel this was even to those who were not physically being tortured.

Evet was playing with them all mentally and physically like that old cat with the mouse, relentlessly poking and picking at the scab of pain and suffering that would not heal within the minds of Brody and the children.

'What lower depths can this being stoop to?' he thought to himself, holding back his own compassion-laden tears.

CHAPTER 15

Meeting Cu-bér.

For well over two years the seven had tenuously held Evet captive to facilitate taking him to justice in their own phase, such was their resolve and compassion for any life form. If they had just executed him years ago then perhaps all this might not have occurred, but apparently, he could have broken away at any time and now, temporarily at least, they were only five.

With knowledge and experience from the other phases and the information gleaned from the *Necronomicon*, Evet seemed to be growing stronger day by day. The six of them hoped to overcome him and get themselves back to their own respective phases. However, there was the added worry of what repercussions their actions here would have back in their own realities. It all seemed somehow belittled by the immediacy of their own current dilemma.

Brody's earthly known super cluster of *Laniakea* and the other four naturally occurring phases seemed now completely dependent on his next decisions, choices and actions, along with the completely unpredictable interventions of an apparent evil madman – a madman so dedicated to his cause he was even wreaking havoc here in this unnamed and unnatural, accidentally manufactured place.

Brody *time and again* sat and churned the infinite possibilities and outcomes of this complex mess he found himself in. It was certainly another mess, but it certainly wasn't a fine one. His latest jocular mental dig in his own ribs really annoyed him, as he was convinced that if he had been at home, he would be saying it glibly to himself with a very poor Oliver Hardy impression. Could nothing evade his own stupidity and lack of seriousness? No wonder Charlotte punished him and Charley just ignored his foolishness. He didn't deserve either of them. He wallowed in this pathetic pit of inaccurate self-pity for a few moments before berating himself out loud.

"Brody! Just get a grip; it's not appropriate. The time and place for this stupidity and self-recrimination is not here and definitely NOT NOW!" He shouted at himself in frustration at his own relentless need for humour to cover the cracks of reality and the foolishness of feeling sorry for himself. He knew on these accounts there was only one person to blame.

The last eighteen months or more seemed to now blur into one. Since his arrival on the beach and the unlikely chance meeting with Evet, everything had happened so fast. He could not fully comprehend or believe the chances of Evet and himself both experimenting in the same way, at the same time, in separate phases and ending up in the same alternate reality together. He just could not open his mind that far to accept it. And rightly so…

Temporarily, he decided to try to block these thoughts because the more he considered them the more he started to believe there was no coincidence at all and that this whole adventure was part of some bigger, more complex plan, and that scared him even more. The fact that random thoughts and silly parodies continually interspersed his normal thought process concerned him greatly as he felt that 'serious' should be the only sensible choice. However, by accident or deep-routed habit it still happened oh so regularly. Like a hidden alarm clock, the old saying:

'Truth is often stranger than fiction' was pinging and twirling repeatedly round his confused head. An untapped part of his brain now continually sent him the same worries and the same inane jocular methods to try to ignore the information? Perhaps it was sending him these ideas to warn him of some other, yet to be revealed, future horror. Not realising; perhaps he had somehow set the alarm clock himself in the past or even in the future and these repetitive episodes were that very clock attempting to awaken him to the impending apocalypse of what Evet might be planning. Or worse, what he may already have achieved.

He drifted from scenario to scenario – daydreaming. An episode of a sci-fi drama involving an android who wanted to be human welled round his brain. Data had been caught in a temporal loop trying to warn his crew of… the exact same sort of worries.

Concerns, doubts, misgivings and stupid parodies kept coming back *time and again…*

'Perhaps I really do have a brain injury?' he questioned himself and answered the question with an even more inappropriate film analogy.

"Now, that might be a real 'phenomenon'." He was even talking to himself now. Very ironically, this was initially completely unnoticed by him, a real sign of the possibility of a correct assumption… or not… depending on your own true state of mind.

"Oh! Please! Stop with the plagiaristic bullshit and get a grip of yourself. You are acting like you're having a complete meltdown; let's not actually have one." He chatted to his other self and mentally kicked it in the arse to re-concentrate.

"Talking to yourself to tell yourself to stop talking to yourself… Shit!" Suddenly he realised he was now even frustrating, to the frustrated.

'This can't go on; it must be the final straw. Evet is still real; he is

like a devil incarnate and no longer some crazy dream I thought I had experienced as an innocent young boy. I have felt drawn towards his chanting hordes more than once. I can see the missing children and their thoughts now and they seem to mesmerise me like Charlotte did but, in my control, not hers. I can't avoid their eyes.' He shook himself to get rid of the horrendous visions he had of the mental torture the remaining five of his friends were experiencing. And the other two? Well, he didn't want to even consider their painful reality any further.

It was too late, the memories of his own thoughts were now etched and he hated it. Every time he closed his eyes, he saw their terror.

'Our number may only be six in total now, but this beast is only one – surely we can overcome him.' Brody, having tired of his self-inflicted solitude, re-joined the five and pleaded with the children who had quietened and were resting now.

'We may soon be seven,' John transmitted cryptically, yet in a hopeful tone.

'Whilst searching for Evet we managed to make contact with the chief of the tribe that we think Evet has coerced; he is their medicine man and is of great influence within their community. He is the one who was watching us from his distant vantage points those many times before.' Brody's mood lightened a little. He was heartened but also concerned, as this unknown watcher might be a new danger or worse, might be himself in danger because of them. *Or* even because of Evet's evil desires to influence him to help capture them.

John continued:

'He is not fully committed to helping Evet and may be swayed to help us if he can be convinced it will ultimately save his people.' This revelation was the best thing Brody had heard for ages. Comforted, he returned to the warmth of the building and later

managed to fall into a light slumber, but whilst sleeping his mind continued spinning and planning possible ways to utilise this new information. Pre-occupied, his yet hardly noticed physical pain was much like his anxiety. Growing!

Evet thought to himself and then spoke aloud to his newest unwilling collaborator.

"So, Cu-bér, stoke the fires, please, I think at least the other five are in need of encouragement even if Brody is not."

With everything that had occurred over the past months every time Brody slept, he was plagued by horrific dreams and, when he awoke next in a now customary cold sweat, the five were preparing to leave.

'We think it best that you stay behind, Brody, it is obvious now that it is you he wants and for us to bring you to him on a plate would seem foolhardy.' The transmitted thought initially struck him as over-protective but as he considered it closer, he decided to agree – true, he could not risk falling into either Evet's or Charlotte's control again. If they were to succeed in getting their two missing friends back and stopping whatever evil plans that were being contrived against them, a cunning plan would be needed. Brody had such a Baldrick-type event hatching in his mind but revealed nothing to the children for fear of contradiction.

"What is the chief's name?" he asked out loud, feigning tiredness. The thought response was in unison:

'They call him Cu-bér...'

Cu-bér timed his visit to see Evet carefully so as to maximise on time spent unmonitored.

"Drink, Evet, it is our custom. We are an old and very traditional tribe and even after your powerful displays, most of my people will only follow my words and do not like outsiders. Drink to gain their confidence and my trust." Cu-bér proffered a huge jug of foaming liquid towards his newly acquired house guest. Evet smiled a conceited and confident smile as he took the refreshment from his latest potentially unlucky and seemingly unaware confidant…

'What, like the country, Cuba?' Brody's unspoken reply was lost on the children as they obviously had little knowledge of Earth's geography and he realised it even before the sentence had left his brain. He quickly apologised with his eyes alone and thought better of such flippancy – he should have spelt his interpretation.

'No, Cu-bér, like a person who makes cubes,' was the surprisingly comical response. Their empathic qualities had extrapolated his look and feelings of apology and helped their reply, but on this occasion the humour was not deliberate.

'We believe it is actually spelt and pronounced Cu-bér like a long line of people chasing a large carnivorous mammal, as you might say, Brody.' Brody smiled at this genuine attempt at humour and laid back down feigning more tiredness.

"Mmmmm, Cu-bér, eh?"

"Queue Bear… Aaaarghaawwwww, good luck, my friends." He spoke aloud and had yawned even louder.

"Cu-bérrrrrr…" He yawned the word out and faked drifting back off to sleep as they quietly and solemnly left. They did not rush and looked visibly nervous to be embarking on possibly their most dangerous or even very last journey; a quest to save the two who were missing and perhaps the Universe as well whilst they were at it! Brody lay still and whilst contemplating their bravery, he let only his body drift…

He did not allow himself to mentally stray far but did spend a few moments thinking about the repetitious nature of his own recent thought patterns; it seemed as though he was continually reminding himself of the same issues and thus subconsciously further undermining his own ability to solve the issues themselves.

It epitomised something Cash had once said to him on a drunken night out. "Brody, your biggest trouble is you think far too deeply; the answers are quite often right in front of you. Stop confusing the issues with the minutiae and OCD detailing and just LOOK! You are your own worst enemy sometimes." The words of his friend resonated, so he resolved to try and be more logical in his approach.

He realised that this drunk but profound statement slurred out whilst in a bar back in 2023 meant more, now than ever, and he mentally promised himself to try and look past his own paranoia and try to see the bigger picture.

He was not tired and only kept his eyes shut for as long as his reminiscences lasted. He felt it necessary to convince the children that he had accepted their plan to leave him behind and, once he was sure he felt no further thought patterns infiltrating his mind from them, he opened his eyes and got up. He sneaked to the window to peer out and could just make out the five small figures disappearing into the glare of the rising sun to the east. They would turn to head north-east on the track towards the settlement in that mountainous region. It had been months since his ordeal with Charlotte and the scars from the puncture wounds where she had drained his blood to sustain her own fraught existence were all but healed, but the internal and mental scars still plagued his every hour.

He had long since figured out that Evet could have easily killed him and Charlotte on many occasions but wanted either or both of them alive for some ulterior plan. Keeping him near death and Charlotte dependent on him for sustenance was an intriguing way of, not killing two birds with any stones. What worried him to some degree was, what would happen to Charlotte without his bodily assistance to keep her alive? More immediately pertinent, was whatever Evet had planned for him that could necessitate the cruel torture of the two children now held so brutally captive in the tribal town tucked away in the hills. Even at the risk of a complete loss, he just had to find out the answers to these troubling questions and his desire to assist the children against their common enemy was overriding. He planned to follow and knew he had to follow unseen.

The idea he had so far formulated was to try to scout well ahead of the group, keeping them in distant visual range but not close enough that they would detect his presence. Ironically, by blanking his mind, which they had taught him how to do, he was hoping to mentally hide from them. He would thus try to reach the settlement first and have a chance to speak to this so-called chief Cu-bér before they arrived. He considered that a direct approach to a sympathetic third party might be the best way forward but did not know much about this man. He tried to build a mental picture of him as he left and began to run amongst the trees to keep out of sight of his five more slowly travelling friends. If it worked, he knew he'd soon catch them up and hoped to pass unnoticed.

In fact, he was very quickly and easily able to overtake them, as their shorter legs and apparent reluctant pace was no match for his excited, long striding urgency. As the day wore on, he regretted rushing and not having provisioned better as his one and only canteen of water was soon dry.

It was about an hour or so until the rise of the twin moons when he sighted the settlement, and decided to rest and wait for the ninety-minute window of twilight. Knowing he had to risk detection from the children and fully concentrate on blanking himself against Evet's potential cerebral monitoring of the area, he thought the dusk gave the best chance for him to make his final approach undetected.

Brody had needed to hide a couple of times whilst en route. On one occasion he had heard galloping noises and the whinny of a horse in the distance followed by muffled whispers, but never saw anyone – friends or foe. At this point, discretion seemed prudent so he moved on without further inspection. If he had gone looking, he would certainly have been surprised at what and who he would have found lurking in the higher tree line only metres away. Had he have given it longer consideration it is pretty certain that he would have burst into song with a popular children's ditty about going down to the woods today.

However, he was pre-occupied and at that very moment, much better than *his* singing, but possibly worse than meeting locals, was the thought of bumping into Evet himself; Brody also surmised, that it could even be a chance meeting with Charlotte that truly threatened his mission, if Evet had taken her along – Brody assumed that he would. She would logically serve much better as an unwilling helper or guard in fair comparison to becoming a wasted corpse back at Langgnãd.

'Could she have survived without me to feed her craving for my particular strain of her very sustenance?' He thought about this as he approached but realised of course, that the hunger was likely manufactured for her by Evet anyway. Her self-proclaimed 'Master', so it seemed, was just as likely to prolong the condition as to abate or remove it – he hoped for the latter, for Charlotte's sake. As the sun dropped slowly behind him and the moons started to appear at either side, darkness fell, gradually giving way to the strange, pinkie-blue half dusk of this phase's night-time.

'He is approaching the rendezvous point as arranged, very brave but naïve in many ways,' John communicated silently to his four kin.

'Hell apparently holds no fear for him.' They were waiting back in the high tree line, observing with admiration Brody's progress towards their recent, secretly pre-arranged meeting, that unbeknown to him, he was just about to have.

The half-light nights had been very disconcerting for a long time but now seemed normal and, as his eyes adjusted quickly, he started his panther-like approach to the tented settlement below, making as little sound as he possibly could.

He was concentrating hard on blocking any stray emotions and thought patterns as he had been taught to do by his friends, the strangely named children of others. He paused by a tree to decide which way to approach the largest of the tall tents which he presumed to be the chiefs and where he hoped to find his potential new ally. Catching his breath, he leaned against the trunk of a huge redwood.

To try to convince this Cu-bér to reject Evet's plans in favour of 'the truth according to Brody', which he now hoped to get the opportunity to fully explain, he would need to not only find Cu-bér but also ideally find him alone.

He was immediately successful on both counts as a razor-sharp knife rested firmly against his throat, restricting him from calling out, but not breaking the skin. He froze in fear that his next movement might cause his own serious injury. He waited a ten-year-long three seconds as the knife's owner stepped from behind the tree that he had so regrettably and casually rested against. His assailant spun Brody around, quickly holstering the weapon and twisting him into a firm wrist lock in a very Rambo-esque way.

"Who are you? Why do you stalk us like a thief?" the knifeman asked, pressing finger to thumb to firm up his wrist hold further. Brody dipped forward to alleviate the pain but knew from experience, the further he went the harder it would be to extricate himself later. He took a chance and spoke freely and honestly:

"You are Cu-bér, the great chief and medicine man, I presume. I am Brody, leader and friend of the few that follow and your two captives; I believe my other companions have asked you to honour me with your friendship – I mean no harm." His gamble paid dividends; the released wrist lock was a welcome feeling. He straightened and turned to face his stealthy captor with a smile and proffered a hopeful hand of greeting.

The man was only a few inches taller than him but was standing on higher ground and towered over him, increasing the impact of this height difference. He was naked down to the midriff, wearing tight leather trousers and some form of soft moccasins on his feet. A single feather adorned his long braided hair that hung below his waist. He was not a big man but was built like a steel girder; every muscle toned and rigid as if made from some supple stone. Brody thought it unusual to see someone so obviously tribal without a single tattoo or painted mark on his skin. He was quite used to people being taller than him so was not intimidated but was secretly impressed by the physique he now beheld. It reminded him of many a gym session with Cash where he would experience that same non-erotic man envy.

Cu-bér grabbed Brody's outstretched hand, wrist and forearm in a ritualistic shake; Brody returned the grip and the two held each other tight, staring deep into each other's eyes as if searching for a truthful soul. Respect being a two-way street, Brody knew he mustn't release first, so gripped as hard as this new man without trying to seem competitive and he locked his gaze, trying not to blink. The tension appeared to last days for the next few seconds, then a smile cracked on the darker skinned man's face and he relaxed his grip.

"The small ones were right, you do not back down. I am a chief, a medicine man and was once a brave but you are truly brave; I have killed men for less than your transgressional arrival here tonight." Returning the smile he had received, he relaxed his arm back to his side. Once again, as was becoming a regular occurrence here in this phase, his first meeting with someone new resulted in them apparently knowing much more about him than he about them.

"Welcome, friend, come down into my wi-kiya-pi and we shall speak. I know of what you hope for and, having seen some of the things the big man does, I lean your way already. He has powers we do not fully comprehend and I can only temporarily control him with my medicines." The strong but softly spoken man showed Brody to his abode and flipped the door flap open to allow him in. They sat inside and Brody scanned the large, round and very warm interior. He had never been in such a structure and was impressed that it didn't feel basic even though it was simply furnished. He felt comforted and safe here.

"You say you control him. I am surprised and impressed. How do you manage such a feat? I cannot imagine it as he tends to control others," Brody asked with genuine surprise and deep-rooted interest in how anyone could so quickly get such impressive results, based upon his own failed experiences of Evet.

"Originally, when the big white man came, as you have seen, he brought with him pain and misery. He killed a tribe and then decreed himself as our friend. The tribe he killed were our enemies, but we had been at peace for some years so did not want this violence. Having witnessed his power we decided to be cautious and not openly oppose him." He continued to explain to Brody all that had occurred since Evet's arrival a month or so ago.

"I can only control his ability to read our thoughts temporarily and mostly at night. I have secretly been giving him my medicines hidden in his food and drink. We need our privacy and have quickly realised he only wishes to be in control to get us to help him to capture you and your friends." Cu-bér explained further how he thought Evet only actually ate the food he was given as a physical hokum, so as not to seem strange or out of place. He added that it was his opinion that Evet didn't even seem to require the food at all. This was interesting to Brody and corresponded with thoughts he had previously blocked or perhaps had blocked for him. It all matched up and they both found amusement in the giveaway fact that, no matter what he ate, nobody ever saw him urinate or disappear for the purposes of defecation. They laughed at Brody's phrasing of it:

"You can't trust a man who never farts – well, I'd been thinking that he was full of shite for quite some time, but that explains it now." Cu-bér laughed again and continued,

"So, we work mostly at night, which is as you know, not long. I'm sure he looks at his daily control of us as a game, played for his own need."

The children also did not seem to eat, but they were always the same and did not hide the issue.

Brody was now considering, as some of the children had long suspected, that Evet might not actually be of their race at all. Time might tell…

He listened intently as Cu-bér explained that nearly half his tribe had immediately fallen under Evet's spell and were now loyal to him, but the others were playing along and were still loyal to the chief himself. Together they were looking for ways to overthrow their new unwanted guest.

"We cannot fight him hard, physically, like a normal human. If we tried, it is plain to see we would just end up fighting him in hell. Although he is only one, he has the power of many and if we lose, we wonder if we would ever be set free." A nod of appreciation masked Brody's surprise at how insightful this young chief was. He was a definite leader and potentially a great ally to have, especially if he was to be successful in stopping Evet from opening a rift and destroying this and other phases.

To that end, he described what might be his way home via this possible rift and how he hated needing Evet, but until other options presented themselves, he saw no other safe course of action available.

They chatted about this and many other recent events for quite a while and Brody soon learned that the tribe Evet had decimated to curry favour with the chief had apparently been called the Redback. They were so-named, not for their skin pigmentation but their skills at using the venom extracted from an indigenous snake to make a poison to tip their arrows. Cu-bér explained how Evet had ridden into the area, watched both tribes for a few days and then randomly chose to destroy one of them for no apparent reason.

"It was horrific to watch and, even though these were our enemies, we wept for them as we saw it happen. They looked confused, killing each other as he stood watching, arms aloft, with no remorse..." Horrific memories flooded back to Brody and he cringed remembering the headless Viking corpses and worse.

"...It was as if he was testing himself to see if he could – well, he could and then some. He rode through the dust clouds and out onto the barren wastelands, galloping hard towards the plain." Brody was taken aback at the stark realisation that alone, Evet was fully capable of the same or possibly more than the horrors that he had experienced first-hand with the Viking slaughter. Back on day two of his weird adventure it had seemed like justified salvation, but now all his doubts rolled into one and the result was the belief that the Vikings, had, as with the Redbacks, just been brutally murdered.

"After the slaughter, only one young brave remained and he chased this final Redback into a hole, fighting him one-on-one just for a game. He even taunted the child, offering freedom before murdering him with a single stab in the back." Cu-bér was near to tears as he recounted the fate of the last survivor of this once proud ancient tribe.

"He was such a completely devious coward killing women and even a child in his personal attack," he continued.

"Many of our tribe exulted as our long-standing enemy had been defeated, but more ran to the hills running for their lives to hide and we have not seen them since."

"How have you managed to remain here, and for him not to be alerted to your dissention?" Brody asked.

"Those who remain hide in full view with the help of our medicine's after-effects; they rely upon my skills to keep him occupied and stop him from probing their thoughts. At least at night we get some respite and I hide them as much as I can manage so that they can fight to resist without arousing his suspicions for the rest of the day."

"It must be difficult."

"Yes, we… They are not all soldiers. Blue skies in the mornings that we used to enjoy are now barren – what a waste – hunting and killing should not be a game."

"I understand your pain, my newest friend and potential brother in arms; your sufferance is greater than mine but born of the same root, I feel." Brody empathised with his new comrade and tried to tailor his words and tone to suit and please his new companion. In the back of his mind he was starting to consider that, as bad as things had become and as tenuous as his new acquaintances were, at least he seemed to have eight friends to rely upon even if two were currently estranged. Weirdly, that was six more than he had in real life back home and this fact was unnervingly upsetting to him.

Was this wild adventure teaching him to be more tolerant? If so, he needed to survive the events to be able to potentially give a second chance to many relationships he had previously dismissed as unworthy of his efforts or unlikely to be successful. He needed to be less judgemental and more accessible. But NOT now.

Cu-bér continued:

"We only wait for the arrival of darkness to be temporarily free of his mental hold." Brody found himself moved by the powerful nature of his new ally's story.

After all the revelations Brody further strengthened their growing bond by opening up and explaining how Evet had used Charlotte to control *him*. He relayed the story of him being raped *by* a woman and the feeling of being wasted *as* a man – just for blood. It was difficult for him to recount but it had the desired effect and a pact was soon made between the two to try to finally rid themselves of the evil that was Evet. After breaking the ice and overcoming his own ego, Brody began to draw the comparison between Charley and Charlotte and admitted for the first time to anyone other than Cash that he was madly in love with Charley in his own phase. He was half ashamed and embarrassed to admit that he was very attracted to the hidden inner being that was captive within the beautiful but very violent Charlotte.

Cu-bér similarly opened up to Brody about his recent past, specifically events leading up to their meeting. It was heartening to know that, even after the horrors of the Redback, not all Cu-bér's tribe had been tamed and the two men ended the evening in relative comfort. Brody told Cu-bér all this and more over many glasses of a home-made whiskey-type brew. He even started talking about some of his youth and other golden old times.

A few hours passed and Brody, feeling exhausted, asked if it would be safe for him to sleep for a while. They laughed about being middle-aged and that things tired them out quicker these days. Also, about how funny it was to see men like them trying not to look or sound old.

Cu-bér assured him that, even though Evet was far too powerful for them to control in the day, his medicine was very effective at night. It turned out to be a concoction of the whiskey brew Brody had been drinking and large quantities of something very similar to old-fashioned hashish but in liquid form.

"No wonder he couldn't probe their thoughts at night," Brody complimented Cu-bér as he settled down to rest.

CHAPTER 16

Do Not Grieve Us.

As morning was only ever minutes away, when he finally dropped off, Brody slept deeply and was still dreaming after sunrise, well into the morning. Awakening with a crowd around him was by now nothing new. However, on this occasion it pleasantly surprised him when he awoke to find the five others *and* Cu-bér standing over him. He smiled back up at their friendly faces and asked how they had found him so quickly.

'*We were already outside before you arrived; it was us that arranged the meeting you had and pointed you out to Cu-bér. You were sneaking about around the wrong wi-kiya-pi and it looked as if any minute you were likely to bound in on Evet who was sleeping in the larger one next door.*' All five transmitted to Brody who flushed, humiliated at the revelation of his poor attempt at a secret approach, but he glanced accusingly at Cu-bér as his stealth was now also being called into question by the apparent tip-off. Cu-bér had understood the transmission and was not himself embarrassed but smiled down at Brody and handed him a steaming cup of tea – at least Brody hoped it was tea, based upon the dull throbbing in his head.

The children explained that they knew full well that Brody was tracking them all along but did nothing about it as they thought any attempt to stop him would have been futile – the results would have ended the same but perhaps noisier. Their ability to feign lack of knowledge had rivalled his own and they were all amused at the friendly nature of the mutual con that had occurred. The children had mentally probed ahead. Although initially it might have been confusing to Cu-bér, the chances were that their subconscious suggestion of a meeting would most likely be accepted based upon their prior observation of his disgust at the treatment of their two siblings *'in his care'*, as they put it. They had preyed upon his good nature and integrity to successful ends. Having then re-contacted Cu-bér to alert him to Brody's progress en route, if nothing else to act as an insurance to avoid further bloodshed. His accidental trespass on a nearby sacred burial site might not have gone down too well in current circumstances elsewise. Brody smiled broadly when he was asked, '*Who is Baldrick?*' He didn't try to explain and glossed over the enquiry with a smile and a question of his own:

"What of the other two?" He spoke aloud for Cu-bér's benefit, not realising he was also able to communicate on their level.

"I have constantly tended to them as best as possible when Evet was either sleeping or away at Langgnãd on a couple of occasions. I raised them slightly higher up, further away from the flames to try to alleviate the pain." He hesitated, knowing that his next sentence was expected but still likely to be devastating.

"Normal mortals would have died days ago but they are, I'm sad to say, still very close to that same death. It seems their sheer willpower and desire to see their kin one last time is all that is keeping them alive." This revelation hit Brody hard and he lay back onto the bed staring up at John who was ashen-faced with tears falling.

"I am *so* sorry, I couldn't release them; I feared that if I did, his fury with us might equal his previous nonchalant disregard for the lives of the Redback. I couldn't risk them *and* my whole tribe with the same fury that so decimated our neighbours. I am truly sorry to you, my new-found friends." John and the remaining children of others held no ill will against Cu-bér but they all looked at him hopefully as if in desperation, to plead for the survival of their two estranged family members. Even without telepathy, Cu-bér understood the look and replied gravely,

"I wish I could help you on that score, but I think they are far beyond our help." John glanced around the group as if to silently communicate the news. Brody was certain the other four already knew before confirmation of their thoughts and understanding reached him.

"Unless you know of any other ways of controlling him, we'd better get moving; he doesn't stay still for long once awake. If you are intending anything I would advise speed is of the essence; his plot is thickening and coming to a head – I think it all centres around you, Brody, and definitely the next triclipse which is only weeks away now." A bitter but understanding smile was flashed between the six who knew Evet better. Cu-bér had certainly caught on fast.

"What do you want to do next?" Cu-bér asked of the group. "Some of my loyal followers are brave warriors but only number about twenty. Some are old and frail and all the rest are dead, dying or have sided with Evet from fear or stupidity." He explained *his* plight to them and they sat discussing it for the next few minutes.

"He will soon awaken from the medicine I slipped in his water earlier and as soon as he does *you* cannot be here," Cu-bér warned, nodding in the general direction of his guests.

"Time has come then... Gather the loyal braves, we must make a break for it. If we are quick we can release the other two from further suffering and between us, if nothing else, we can carry them to a more dignified resting place. Then we can re-group and plan a better alternate strategy – but as you say… we cannot stay here…" He hesitated, hoping his next question would meet with approval…

"Or should we just steal in to his tent and murder him as he sleeps?" Brody spoke with a decisive air but his compromising suggestion was in reality more of a hopeful request.

The children had difficulty with the reference to a 'tent' but soon translated it between themselves. His idea was rebuffed by a grammatical correction and Brody, with Cu-bér's verbal help, phonetically pronounced it slowly to get himself used to the difficult word.

"Wi…kiya…pi," repeated Brody, slightly distracted. He re-centred his thoughts and *so* wished the latter murderous option he had tabled moments ago had been agreed upon, but had his hopes further dashed by Cu-bér's next reply.

"He is guarded by my two loyal pet wolves. When aroused they are vicious animals and could easily tear you apart. He took their minds as soon as he arrived here before any of us had even spoken. It started as an amusement to us that he was unafraid and that they followed him, until we realised his powers. Now only *I* can get near him or them without being bitten; any rushed attempt on him physically will fail, I fear." The medicine man shrugged his shoulders in resignation and looked dejected.

Without warning, the five children grouped close together and joined hands.

'We will create a diversion for you. The animals will not be harmed by us but please get our kin fast and let us be gone – back to Baylok's seems prudent.' The thought transmission of the five was fully understood by Brody and Cu-bér and they all sprang into action. Cu-bér led and Brody followed out of the chief's modest wi-kiya-pi. Brody even managed a smile as they went past Evet's grander *tent*, but then he locked his mind back onto the serious

business of escape and quickly followed Cu-bér directly to the camp fire. The fire was still burning, if only now a low flickering glow. Pungent smoke was drifting straight up into the severely burnt faces of the two who were still hanging upside down. Had they been human they certainly would have perished days before.

"Let's get them down quick and be gone from this place," Brody exclaimed urgently. The strong chieftain climbed nimbly up the gallows-like structure that was usually used for roasting animals for the tribe's sustenance. It had been so cruelly commandeered and modified for Evet's torturous endeavour. As he reached across to cut the ropes holding the two captives' ankles, he was disturbed by a screeching and yelping of pained animals; it was very evident that the children's diversion was struggling to contain the now awakened Evet.

Cu-bér tried to ignore the painful howls of displeasure and cut through the ropes with his serrated knife and the first hanging, now completely singed bald child, was lowered whilst Brody carefully supported her below to avoid her falling into the red-hot embers.

Brody laid the twitching body of his nearly unrecognisable friend to one side of the fire and promptly prepared to help the other. The smell of burnt hair and skin was acrid and Brody winced as he lowered the brother of the first released child next to his horribly disfigured sister.

The snarling noises they had heard moments ago had obviously emanated from the chief's pet wolves. The children were trying to mentally control them in a desperate attempt to contain Evet within the second wi-kiya-pi, whilst Brody and Cu-bér worked to free their injured siblings. The growls were the wolves being turned on Evet, but the yelping was the wolves in sudden searing pain from Evet's strong mental counter control. The noise suddenly changed and became louder; the door flap of the larger structure flew open and the two wolves burst out in a massive rolling mêlée. Now battling, they sprang at each other, lips curled and teeth snapping wildly. From experience, Brody knew it was Evet alone now that powerfully controlled them both and he had, out of spite, turned them against each other.

The savage fight that ensued was like watching a whirling dervish or a sandstorm in the desert. Saliva flew in all directions as teeth gnashed and jaws snapped together. The male, slightly smaller of the two, showed the forced anger set deep in his eyes as he attempted to flip his bigger sister and end the pain they were currently experiencing. The larger of the two beautiful but savage beasts squirmed free and recovered her footing. She sprang sideways to avoid a secondary lunge aimed at her throat. As her brother overshot and attempted to correct his trajectory, momentum overtook and he slid to an unceremonious stop in a complex pile of teeth and claws. His sister turned, pounced and sank her fangs into the back leg of her smaller male sibling. A heart-breaking yelp was screeched out accentuated by the crunching of bone and sinew. The leg was obviously broken above the hock and blood poured from the wound staining his still beautiful but ruffled grey fur. The pained animal tried to retreat, scrabbling desperately for the futile safety of the wi-kiya-pi, but its sister was relentless this time, striking towards the head of her younger brother, tearing his throat out and shaking the helpless dying animal like a great white shark with a seal in a feeding frenzy.

The male wolf yelped no more and sank limp to the dusty floor, blood spurting up out of its open neck wound. Steam was rising from the hot corpse as the body twitched its last. Cu-bér let out an anguished howl and the victorious she-wolf turned to face him with her snout dripping and blood-stained. Its hackles were up, lips curled, teeth shining pearl white and gums stained blood red.

It snarled and slathered and part of her brother dangled from her mouth. Her normally immaculate deep, black coat was covered in dust and debris, but she ignored it and stared deep into Cu-bér's unflinching eyes. It was, without fear, ready to leap at its own master's throat. It looked long and hard at him with the rust orange irises of its steely eyes that were nearly blotted out by its heavily dilating pupils, giving away its malicious and externally controlled resolve.

She continued to regard him intently staring piercingly deep, as if directly into Cu-bér's very soul. The brave chief merely stared back, half-smiling with tears rolling down both cheeks. His once faithful companion cocked her huge head to one side and then the other as if in distant recognition and desperate apology for its previous and subsequent actions.

Reminded of the task at hand by the painful mental stimulus coming from Evet who was now emerging from the larger wi-kiya-pi, she tensed, ready for attack. Evet stood triumphantly over the still body of the male wolf, raised a hand and flicked his fingers towards Cu-bér. The female wolf breathed a sigh of resignation and then lunged forward to strike at her lifelong, beloved friend, the chief.

The power of the lunge took Cu-bér off his feet. Animal and man rolled head over heels towards the glowing fire. A blood-curdling yowl and a small whimper was the last noise the graceful beast made. Cu-bér had un-holstered his hunting knife and manoeuvred its sharp blade in front of his chest. As his beloved pet had attacked, the knife had punctured the underside of the animal's lower jaw. His punched upper-cut thrust had embedded it directly through the mouth and into the she-wolf's spinal column, killing her instantly. They both lay motionless and, at this point, no one knew if the chief was also killed.

Dust billowed near his face as Cu-bér exhaled and Brody

realised he was alive. Cu- bér began to heave the huge wolf from his chest as Brody finished helping the previously hanging captives by releasing their bound limbs. He worked feverishly whilst he had the chance. Evet was calm and was stoically standing by the other wolf's corpse. He was, in fact, recovering from the mental exertion of controlling the five children and the two wolves. As Brody managed to haul the bodies of the two children further away from the fire, the five appeared from their previously concealed vantage point within the smaller wi-kiya-pi. They quickly started to help Brody tend to their two horrifically injured siblings.

"We must go NOW!" Brody shouted.

"NO, HE DIES HERE!" screamed Cu-bér, wriggling from under the carcass of the dead she-wolf. Picking up his knife he ran towards the semi-prone Evet who had dropped to his knees and looked like a punch-drunk boxer trying to recover between rounds. His eyes glazed with sorrow, muscles tensed and bulging, Cu-bér re-focused as he ran. He leapt at Evet, knife above his head and brought the large blade down with both hands like an axe towards his adversary. The blade stopped dead as if hitting a tree, millimetres from Evet's chest.

The bigger man slowly looked up and casually cocked his head in a primitive, inquisitive but scornful way, as if to mimic the animalistic confusion displayed earlier. He looked at the figure of the Indian chieftain, now frozen in full flight above him and then, with a swift wave of his arm, mentally flung him away. Cu-bér flew up and back, landing two metres from Brody and the children. His knife sent spinning out of his hand, landed point down impaled into the warm dust by the fire next to Brody's foot. Like a Mexican stand-off, they all glared at each other for a second – no words needed to be said. It was now or never – kill or be killed.

Surprisingly, Cu-bér was the first to react. From lying flat out he lifted his knees to his chest, rolled back, slightly compressed his spine and neck and flicked both feet forward with immense power, leaping onto his feet. He whistled twice like a bird and slapped both thighs simultaneously. Within seconds he was surrounded by the remainder of his loyal subjects who then positioned themselves between him and the lone Evet who stood and dusted himself off. He casually observed the situation and raised his arms to shoulder height, closed his eyes and lowered his head as if to pray.

Brody, Cu-bér and the children had all seen this before but the five knew better than any, having been the tools of war in use against many attacks in the past. At least, back then, it felt as if they were contributing to their own salvation. Stubborn or not, they could never have realised how powerful and distorted their willing captive had become. This time was going to be different though because, instead of channelling his power, they were now to face it full on. The five children reasserted their mental link and joined hands; eyes flaming bright in readiness for his mental attack in whatever form it came.

Evet's arms held steady in a semi-crucifix position with palms down; he looked up and his eyes too flowed red. He turned his hands palms up as if to call something from above and his mentally-controlled tribal followers appeared as swiftly as Cu-bér's men had done – the stand-off was complete. If it had been a straight fight, a betting man would have backed Cu-bér with superior numbers and undying loyalty, versus blind recently converted cannon fodder. Brody thought to himself,

'It can't be this easy,' and he was right!

As if a starting pistol had signalled the commencement of a one-hundred metre sprint race, the fight began. The Indian braves clashed between the opposing leaders, but it soon became evident that the braves, being controlled by Evet's willpower, were unable to feel pain or were at least being protected from it. Whilst it was still possible for them to be killed, they fought on whilst mortally injured, in comparison to Cu-bér's men who writhed in agony like any normal mortal man would when badly injured.

At one point an arm, having been severed by a tomahawk of one of Cu-bér's braves, was picked up and its knife-holding hand was used as a weapon by one of Evet's pain-free fighting clan. It was a blood bath and Brody, although used to a good scrap, was now carefully picking his opponents based upon his tribal allies, having half-killed them first. He found his previously concealed knife that he'd smuggled without Evet's knowledge months ago and despatched four or five injured opponents with it. He started to become the clean-up guy as the battered kept getting back up zombie-like and would only cease their attacks when actually killed. One such re-animated opponent took four attempts to go down; Brody finally burying his knife into his eye socket but then being unable to retrieve the handy implement after the corpse landed face down and the blade became wedged into the back of his skull.

The blood and guts battle continued hand to hand for fifteen minutes or more with any method possible being used to dispatch the relentless Evet-driven super braves until only the children, Cu-bér, Brody, Evet and one extremely large opponent remained. Brody stepped in front of Cu-bér who was gasping for breath after recovering from a strangle hold from his last skirmish. He took up a fighting position to protect the chief but, on seeing the size of the giant warrior ahead of him, soon wished that he hadn't. He was instantly reminded of his own advice about knowing how to lose safely when a piledriving right hook caught him unawares from such a long distance – he couldn't believe it was possible. The blow knocked him clean off his feet and he landed, winded on his back, at Cu-bér's feet.

Brody shook his head and scrambled back up. Losing safely was not an option here so he pretended to be groggier than he was and waited for the massive brave to step in for the kill. As he did so, his huge body loomed overhead; Brody dipped his left shoulder and delivered an uppercut directly to the breechclout-covered crotch area. It felled his opponent like the Canadian redwood he had so casually leant against the night before.

Grabbing the downed fighter's dropped tomahawk, Brody made a swing to finish the task with one final blow but found that his arm was held back solidly and he looked instinctively up towards Evet. He was surprised to see him still standing in concentration trying to control all his fighting party whether dead, dying or dismembered. Brody turned and realised he was being held not by Evet, or any superpowered opponent, but mystifyingly by Cu-bér.

"LET GO!" he shouted desperately, wanting to finish his bloody task.

"NO. Let me, my friend. The blood of my brother should stain my hands, not yours." He took the axe from Brody and brutally removed the huge brave's head in one almighty two-handed backhand, tennis-style strike.

Picking up the severed head and holding it aloft, he screamed in exultation and anger. His own torso was cut in multiple places but most of the blood staining his clothes and body was not his own. His tears streaked the blood on his face as he hurled the severed head at Evet to the effect of claiming the victory. Evet merely glanced at it and redoubled his efforts of concentration, his eyes glowing white as if they were about to explode.

The five children who had, throughout the battle, been trying to break Evet's concentration to reduce the effects of his control over the braves empowered against them, started to waiver. With Evet having no braves left to control they became the target of his vengeful psychokinetic rage. One by one they fell as limp bodies, eyes losing the flamed effect, tumbling to the ground in disarray. Some lay in slumped positions looking as if all their bones had been somehow internally disconnected. No outward damage was evident, but Brody knew instinctively that his worst fears would soon be realised as fact. Even his own unusual and optimistically warped, humour-searching mind could not conjure a comment to truly explain the feeling of complete despair that seeing his friends in this way now caused him.

Brody did not know the extent of their injuries but he and Cu-bér were not able to get to Evet to stop his non-physical attack on the suffering children, let alone reach the children themselves to offer any, possibly futile, help or comfort. Both were virtually held fast as if trying to push against a locked door; they couldn't unlock it no matter how hard they pushed and three of the children were now lying unmoving at their siblings' feet. It was agonisingly slow and visibly distressing to see them fall silently one by one knowing they were not likely to ever rise again. Brody screamed in a futile attempt to catch Evet's attention, but he was steadfast, concentrating all his power on the destruction of his ex-, if ever, kinsmen.

Once again, the thought of knowing how to lose safely hit Brody but his desire to assist the two remaining children overrode it. As another fell, he buckled and turned away to flee the horrors that burnt at his eyes.

As he turned, an instantaneous realisation hit; Evet was only *resisting.*

'One direction?... Forwards!' It gave him an idea and he stepped back and re-lunged towards Evet. His backward step was unhindered, but he was unable to move forwards again; his theory was proven and, in an instant, he decided to try another.

He turned again, sprang away from Cu-bér and headed for

the fire. Quickly grabbing the soil-embedded knife, he whirled around and threw it, handle first towards Evet. It flipped end over end twice and travelled arrow-like to its target. Such was Evet's concentration on the destruction of the children and the holding back of his other opponents that he didn't even see it coming.

His mental control was at that time only centred on the living potential attackers present and had no effect on the inanimate blade as it hurtled towards him, as was the crux of Brody's last-ditch theory.

'*Quod erat demonstrandum,*' Brody projected out to Evet in defiance but then fell to the floor dazed, not having previously realised that the right hook of earlier was not from a fist but the blunt end of the tomahawk his big opponent had been wielding. Testosterone and adrenalin had been keeping him up, but his head fizzed now and his legs had buckled.

'*That explains the extra reach!*' he thought groggily, trying to right himself for the next round, blood now dripping from his gashed chin. He began to black out as the knife hit home, square into Evet's right chest area. As Brody fell, his last conscious thought was that the knife he had thrown so well and which had struck Evet so accurately, had, for grief's sake, actually pierced his *own* heart.

'*Do not grieve us, it was not him; we released ourselves for your sake.*' The children weakly transmitted their thoughts to him and it rang around his rapidly fading consciousness as he fell and, like the pause button being pressed on an old tape deck, everything stopped. Brody collapsed back to the floor, Cu-bér fell onto his backside from the release of Evet's mental push and the seven briefly reunited siblings were all left lying, unmoving. Cu-bér looked at Evet holding the knife now sticking out of his chest. He seemed to watch in slow motion as the big man stumbled to his knees, pulled the blade from himself, blood sprayed profusely onto the floor – a big vein had obviously been ruptured.

Cu-bér started to smile feeling victory was at last his, but as he watched, a mirage effect occurred and, like a wavering palm oasis in an empty desert, Evet's falling body disappeared and Cu-bér dropped back to the floor deflated and dejected, as well as completely exhausted.

When he recovered enough to focus, he sat and watched the spot where Evet had fallen in total disbelief for hours, waiting for him to return or re-appear so that he could hopefully finish the job that Brody had started with his inspirational knife-throwing. As night started to draw in, his full attention was reasserted and given more to Brody who was unconscious but obviously still breathing and alive – less could possibly be said for the children.

Brody awoke the next morning and was relatively comfortable, with a blanket covering him. He was still positioned where he had fallen. Blood was all around but no bodies were to be seen – the fire was cold, and he was alone. He struggled to his feet and immediately wished he had stayed down longer; his head was pounding and, although the blood flow had coagulated, his chin now felt four sizes too big. A thought of a cartoon character of large chin fame sprung to mind but did not amuse him much, only serving to distract him briefly as he, at that moment, felt more desperate than his imagined comic character was named.

He went back up the path to the smaller wi-kiya-pi and entered. Cu-bér was sleeping, completely covered in blood as if he had bathed in it. Brody curled up and joined the slumber party; his head on fire and his thoughts not coherent enough to even question who was where or what had happened to who – he desperately needed sleep. His last waking thoughts of being stabbed in the heart and the children's pleas started to squirm their way back into his mind but, as he pulled a large bearskin over himself for comfort and drifted off, it quickly slipped away again.

Cu-bér awoke first and left Brody to sleep again whilst going to clean up and change his blood-stained attire. He set about re-stoking the fire and threw on some fresh logs to get it burning well. The morning air was fresh, the weather had started to change and Cu-bér would soon explain to Brody that this was a sure sign that the triclipse was approaching. It was now only about three weeks to a month away.

By the time Brody awoke it was nearly night again and the fire Cu-bér had been tending all day was ablaze one side more than the other. Brody realised immediately that he was cooking; the spit support rack that had so cruelly been used to torture his friends was now in proper use with what looked like a boar rotating in front of the leaping flames, the red-hot coals cooking from below. The smell of the cooking flesh of some unusually shaped animal was glorious, but the sight of the fire took Brody's mind to his friends' plight.

"How are the children?" he asked with a hopeful air.

"No!" was the solemn one-word answer from Cu-bér's bowed head. Brody understood but was hit hard by the revelation and, although he had no need for the details, he asked anyway.

"How… I mean, ALL of them? No, surely… What about Evet?"

"Your throw was a great ploy and I'm certain if it had missed we would not be having this conversation. You certainly injured him quite badly; he was bleeding a lot but somehow tricked my vision and made good an escape with some sort of vanishing act. The others were all but dead by the time I could get to them." Brody's head dropped in dejection and sorrow as what he had sensed inside was confirmed.

"Only the one you called John has survived and, Brody…

before you rush, you won't be able to save him and he wouldn't thank you if you could. Be prepared, my friend, it is not a sight for the squeamish. He is by the lake where he asked me to place his siblings." Brody listened to more details of his friend's injuries and directions to his resting place, before jumping up. He ran to the edge of the camp area passing the bodies of the two huge wolves which Cu-bér had laid ceremoniously tail to nose near a readied shallow grave. He hesitated out of respect to the fallen as he passed the battle site but saw no bodies. Cu-bér had been very busy as Brody had slept. He dropped down the steep bank to the lakeside where he found the twisted and terminally damaged body of the one he had affectionately called John.

Cu-bér's last words of warning about the injuries were still ringing in his ears as his tear-filled eyes tried to focus on the devastation he now beheld. "Blood had been seeping profusely from their ears, noses and mouths before they even hit the ground; I think their minds were literally fried as if they had all experienced the heat of the torturous flames. They saved us both by delaying Evet with Selene and Corvin." Brody replayed Cu-bér's last few words in his head and realised what the names were, he had been talking about his two gallant pets. Brody knew that *his* loss was in many ways far heavier than his own. The remaining tribe, even including his own brother and his two pet wolves had all been destroyed. The pent up hatred and suppressed grief bubbled inside and Brody couldn't help himself, he dropped to his knees and screamed out in anguish.

As he sat near the seven devastated bodies it looked as if their skulls had imploded and most were completely unrecognisable. Even their distinctive blond hair was in most cases gone or burnt black. There was a completely stark contrast to the sight he had beheld when they first met compared to now. He arched his back and stared up at the rising sun to try and make sense of this outrageous waste of life. As he calmed himself, he felt a pull on his trouser leg and glanced down to see John's outstretched hand touching his knee. He quickly leant down, putting his arm around his small friend's crumpled form and turned his head gently to face him.

"Please forgive me for the hurt I have brought to you and your family," Brody pleaded, holding John's body and hand delicately to support him upright in a seated position. John opened his left eye; the right being swollen shut.

"Do not grieve us, Brody; it was for you that we capitulated and we thank you for your trust in us..." Brody was unused to hearing his voice and it started to trail, he leaned in closer to listen.

"My name is David of Zellaby, by the way, but..." He gasped for breath; it sounded to Brody as if he was drawing directly from the last reserves of his previously improvised Fesarius plasma.

"The brag was amazing and being John was such fun... Oh... My... " His eye closed and the last breath drifted from his lips. His body spasmed briefly and then lay relaxed in Brody's arms. A sort of smile on what was left of his previously beautiful childlike face comforted Brody slightly. He lay his friend back to the floor with his brothers and sisters and turned to re-climb the hill back to the camp fire and Cu-bér.

CHAPTER 17

Langgnãd Revisited.

Nothing stirred and nobody was about; perhaps some were still alive or in hiding. The bigger picture portrayed them, if indeed they were there, as possibly having been the sensible ones. If they chose to flee when Evet first arrived it would in hindsight have been their best option.

The strong and the brave who had stayed and even those swayed to the wrong path – all were dead. Brody felt tears welling again as this thought stuck in his mind and jabbed at his conscience. He fought them back and felt guilty for doing so.

Returning to Cu-bér at the fireside, the two silently embraced in a comforting man-hug that lasted but a few seconds but spoke a thousand words about the respect and compassion they had for each other's losses.

Brody could hold his emotions back no longer, he was devastated and wept openly for his seven small childlike friends – 'the others' as Evet had referred to them or the 'children of others' as they had proudly preferred themselves to be known. Since arriving here, they had been his saviours on more than a few occasions. What would he do now without them?

As they sat and consoled each other, Brody began to re-live the last few moments of battle.

"When it was all in the mix back there, the children sent thoughts to me telling me not to grieve and that they were releasing themselves for me. Why do think they would they do that? Now I feel as if it is *my* fault – they died for *me*." He was sniffing hard against his dripping nose.

"And just as David passed away, he said it again – do not grieve, we capitulated for you."

"Can I take it David was John? Perhaps they knew something you didn't?" Cu-bér comforted him with this positive but questioning statement and Brody was still baffled as to what could possibly have been worth that sort of self-sacrifice.

"Yes, David of Zellaby was apparently his name… We must find Evet and destroy him before he can do this again, or worse, destroy everything." Brody regretted cutting the mourning process short but realised they had little time and no idea where Evet had gone or what he might do next. This was especially true with him now having had a piece of revenge motivation stuck deep in his chest pocket at heart's height. He might do anything or everything. Either way it was certain to be, if nothing else, malicious and destructive in its intent.

"I have already said my token words over my people and we can bury your friends alongside them in our tribe's sacred place if you would like to. They will be honoured there in all eternity, no matter if we succeed or fail."

"Yes, that sounds very fitting, thank you. I would like that."

"Let's do it now then, because I think you are right, we must go and soon, but where?" Cu-bér wiped away a stray tear. Brody straightened himself, puffing out his chest like a bodybuilder about to pose off but he couldn't speak to answer as grief grabbed him again and silenced his attempt.

In a slow but determined manner they walked back to the lake together in silence, Brody had not yet even thought of a suitable eulogy to say at the grave of these small but immensely influential beings. Friends who had been killed or sacrificed themselves in battle to save him.

They systematically moved the seven small bodies to Cu-bér's sacred burial site beneath the orange grove at the opposite side of the settlement. The graves were already prepared as had been Corvin and Selene's that he had noticed earlier. The burial process was quick and they delayed no more than respect allowed. Brody dropped to his knees and, after a few moments of silent contemplation, uttered two softly spoken and sorrowful final words.

"Thank you."

After an hour or so they were ready to press on and leave this site of horror, carnage and death. It was no longer home to Cu-bér but a terrifying reminder of his losses and, to Brody, just another nail in an imaginary coffin he envisaged himself being slowly incarcerated in.

"Let's go, I think he will have gone back to Langgnãd," Brody suggested.

"It's not too far but there is a lot to discuss on the way." Brody started walking towards the ridge where he had crept in to meet Cu-bér originally but Cu-bér waited and called him back.

"Do you ride?" he asked.

"Not for a long time, but I have ridden. Years ago, I worked for a short while on a stud farm breaking in colts and fillies." Cu-bér led him round to the stables at the very farthest north end of the settlement.

"Take your pick, they are all prime stock, hand reared and broken by me. Most are only good for meat now as there are no braves left to ride them. Those who ran may come back for some, but I think I may just let them all go free."

It had been a very long time and, as with many of Brody's previous jobs, the experience gained had not quite been as extensive as he might have let on. He took the reins of a beautiful, big, brown and white piebald pony and flicked himself into the saddle like an old pro.

The two allowed their horses to walk at their own pace back the short distance to the fireside with Cu-bér sitting bareback aboard his enormous grey-black stallion. They dismounted and ate a quick but hearty meal of what Cu-bér described as a shoat hog, packing the rest for waste's sake in a large leather satchel just in case they did not manage another cooking opportunity.

Brody had enjoyed the taste and was gratified by the hunger-reducing meal, but the thought of the fire haunted him even with his eyes open. He could only see burning flesh and hear children screaming inside his head. He apologised for leaving the last few morsels and tipped them back into the fire as if to feed and appease the monster that had devoured his friends.

"Give me your hand, Brody," Cu-bér asked firmly. Brody offered his right hand as if to shake without question. Cu-bér took it in his left, spun it palm up and quickly reached across himself to pull out his knife. Brody didn't feel it but flinched as Cu-bér flashed the extremely sharp blade across the thenar eminence of his right thumb. Blood slowly oozed out as Brody stared at his hand in disbelief. Cu-bér then proceeded to repeat the process. Releasing Brody's palm, he flipped the knife to his left and swiftly cut a similar small incision on his own right palm. He then grabbed Brody's hand again and forced the two together in an arm wrestle-style hold. His newly split thumb stung as the blood mingled between their two palms.

"Blood brothers!" proclaimed Cu-bér, smiling.

Brody was, after the initial shock of the action, very honoured to have been held in such high regard by this man he had come to like and respect. Now he could call him brother without feeling it was only for effect or to win his trust. This action spoke louder than any words could ever have done and it reminded him of Cash as they had done similarly, aged ten. Over thirty years ago it had been a lot more painful, less ceremonious and done with a drawing pin on the tip of the index finger of the left hand. He glanced at the tiny scar that was still visible all these years later. He smiled.

After another half an hour in silent contemplation they paid their last respects to the freshly laid to rest and left quietly. With full stomachs, they tried to relax whilst trotting the horses steadily towards Langgnād where Brody had surmised Evet would go, probably to re-enlist the help of Charlotte and her henchmen and, no doubt, to no honest ends.

"So, tell me everything about this Evet and what you think he might be planning," Cu-bér asked as he helped Brody back into the saddle for the third time since they had left the camp fire. Brody's experience on Indian ponies on rough ground was obviously not sufficiently comparable to the candyfloss donkey type of riding he had done all those years ago for about two weeks. Breaking wild fillies and bucking bronco-style colts, etc, might have been a slight exaggeration.

On this occasion his exaggeration and over-confidence had let him down somewhat and he ached severely as a result. Eventually, he became accustomed to the very good-natured pony that didn't even flinch each time he slipped out of the saddle to reacquaint himself with the path below.

By the time Brody had managed to get used to staying on the pony's back and had explained all that had gone on with Evet, the Vikings, Baylok and all the other stuff from the past eighteen months or more, they were already approaching Langgnād's bleak outskirts.

Much of what he told, was confirmed – Cu-bér having seen much of it from his distant vantage points. The main issue they discussed towards the end of the dusty journey and one both were still very concerned about, was the lack of protection against Evet's mental strengths now that the children were no longer there to help.

Physically, he was an easy target and two versus one was surely a given victory, they thought, but how they could overcome his mind control was still a worry. Equally, would Brody fall foul of Charlotte again, of course, if she was even alive herself? A feeling of trepidation shivered its way up Brody's spine as they kicked on down the winding path towards the centre of the silent town. All the memories of Charlotte's sexual exploitation of him and the bloodletting sessions came flooding back. He shuddered and steeled himself to the task at hand.

'No time for wimps now,' he thought. All was completely still and quiet. The only things interrupting the silence were the regular *ca-caw* noises from the circling birds overhead and the occasional waft of the eye-watering stench of death emanating from the bodies that lay rotting all over the place.

'Welcome to Langgnād, population nil,' Brody mused. He started humming a tune that seemed fitting for the occasion and quietly broke into song.

"All the clubs are being closed down… This tow-wn is coming up a gh–" Cu-bér shot him a glance that would have killed a bull elephant at twenty paces; he was obviously a music lover. As Brody cut short his rendition and watched the whirling crows and ravens, other more vulture-like feathered creatures joined them and also began to circle. The flighted reapers were growing in confidence and where corpses lay they started landing, pecking at eyes and tongues, niggling at each other for feeding rites. Brody couldn't help himself for bringing a sedentary image of Tippi Hedren and other similarly frightening birds to mind. Silence enshrouded the last short trot into Langgnãd as their mutual destinies awaited them.

They glanced down each alley and path as they led the horses through the main section of the town. Having decided to enter at the opposite side of the town from their last visit, and for the purpose of stealth, they moved slowly and took quite a while to relocate the street they were after.

"Bhylls Lane… Love Lane… Goldthorn Avenue… Acacia Avenue… Ahhh, here we are. If he *is* here, this is where he will be. I bet it's warm inside, the red light is still burning bright outside… open for business, eh?" Brody was mumbling but steeled himself for action.

"Well, Charlotte, my dear, and Evetzzirrah, we are coming in, ready or not." He spoke very calmly, but in pretend confidence. They tethered the horses and walked from the bottom of the avenue to their destination at number twenty two. No guards at the gate was unusually welcoming but felt ominous. They reached the entrance to the gloomy property.

'Lllllllleeet's get ready to ruumbleeeeeeeee!' Brody thought the famous line to himself in a very 'Buffer' sort of way as he cautiously pushed the outer ground floor door ajar.

As the door creaked, squeaked and swung open just like a classic horror film tension builder, Brody half expected some wig-wearing maniac to jump out, huge knife in hand, such was the foreboding atmosphere in the seemingly deserted house, but nothing happened. They cautiously decided to climb the stairs. Brody went first with Cu-bér following on a semi-reverse angle, facing down the stairs and stepping backwards in a covering pattern. Brody briefly thought to himself that, to an outsider of his own phase, it might have looked quite like either of the two popular cop shows he used to watch as a child. The main characters were partners and every week they would run dramatically up or down similar stairwells calling to each other for encouragement and confidence.

"Cover me." He whispered the line to himself but tried to concentrate on what they might soon need to take cover from. As they rounded the first floor landing and Cu-bér took the lead, it bizarrely seemed to Brody as if he should have done a forward roll. He mentally kicked himself for not concentrating on the job in hand. Considering the seriousness of the task he surprised himself with his subconscious frivolity and internally chastised himself again. Bizarrely, a picture on the landing wall which seemed as if it shouldn't even be there stared down at him, he tried to concentrate on the job in hand.

Unbeknown to Brody, Cu-bér was also having misguided thoughts as they climbed the stairs, but his were based on a different set of criteria. As he rounded the landing, he had unholstered his knife and flipped it into an attack position with the serrated edge facing forward and the extremely sharp tip pointing down. He accordingly dropped his centre of gravity, crouching as if stealthily approaching a stray shoat hog grazing, ready to pounce, ready for the kill. He did not actually see the animal, but his mind was stalking it as his body was, with Brody doing something far more important. Neither realised that their momentary lapses were derived of more sinister stuff.

The dark areas in the house hid many things and Evet was secretly attempting to make them lose themselves in those shadows and, as if searching for their own open graves, they drifted to another plane.

As they both reached the second floor landing, Brody was by now expecting to meet Cash for a beer and a TV dinner and Cu-bér was about to jump on the non-existent hog to kill it for his supper. Brody slipped back from fantasy to reality and silently motioned with his index finger to Cu-bér to go left and meet him on the other side of the balcony. The rendezvous point was just outside Charlotte's office; he painfully remembered it, having had more than one uncomfortable visit there before.

Cu-bér was also momentarily lucid. He took the instruction, crept round to the left and was immediately back stalking his invisible quarry. As they rounded the balcony and came back into visual contact of each other, Brody smiled seeing his old friend standing in front of him. He had arms open in a welcoming gesture, holding a take-out curry in one hand and two bottles of beer in the other.

He relaxed his shoulders, opened his arms wide pre-man-hug and took a quick step forward. Cu-bér saw the overly large hog turn, square up like an angry bull and start to run at him. He was surprised, such a beast was normally quiet and wary of any human contact, usually running away if disturbed, but this huge specimen was charging at *him*.

He side-stepped, dived forward, rolled over his shoulder in what Brody, if he had seen it, would have described as a very Bodie and Doyle way. As he landed and rolled, he thrust up hard and left with his serrated blade, catching the hog square between the ribs and tearing a six-inch gash in its side. Cash dropped the beer and food and disappeared in a cloud of dust as Brody hit the floor, blood spurting from the deep wound that Cu-bér had savagely but unintentionally inflicted upon him in his hunting daze. Brody screamed in agony and writhed on the floor grasping his side, just outside the office door.

Right on cue the door opened and Charlotte stepped out provocatively, partially dressed as ever. Before Cu-bér could realise what had occurred or even notice what she was wearing, she flipped one leg up to near head height and kicked him with the other in a Mr Miyagi-style crane technique, catching him square in the face with her stiletto heel.

'It's like being stabbed but with a stone,' Cu-bér vaguely thought as he reeled backwards and fell down the second flight of stairs towards the first floor… He landed hard, hitting the back of his head against the dry plastered wall where the picture that Brody had seen used to be and was knocked out cold.

Brody was still squirming on the second floor landing, but Charlotte's compassion had not improved since they last met. She spun around, knelt over his face and smothered his screams with her already moist nether regions, then leant forward over him, pressing herself further onto his face. She was forcing him to stimulate her by his gagging attempts to breathe. Leaning further forward, she tried to drink from his open wound and he started to convulse. Such was the blood flow from him that she was sent into a feeding frenzy not dissimilar to an orgasmic state as she jolted up and down on his now discoloured, purple, gagging face. He was shaking violently in an attempt to breathe and escape. She was similarly active in trying to bury her teeth into his severely split side. As she jolted her hips back and forth, it forced his face further into her and aroused her even more.

Had this continued for any greater length of time it would have certainly killed Brody just by suffocation if nothing else. Evet stepped out of the office from behind Charlotte and pushed her roughly off him with his foot.

Back on the first floor landing, Cu-bér started to come around and started to drag himself upright. Hearing the commotion above he picked up his knife and noticed the blood on the blade.

Recovering from Evet's shove, Charlotte sprang to her feet like a cat on hot coals and knelt animalistic, ready to launch another attack on Brody's now nearly motionless body. Blood was still pumping from his side but a lot slower now and his breathing was shallow. Her face, neck and hair were plastered in his blood and she licked her lips and hissed like a cobra about to strike.

"You were killing him, stupid bitch! That was not the plan!" Evet shouted angrily.

"No, please, no," Cu-bér muttered under his breath. As he heard the words from above him, the feeling of something very bad hit him at the pit of his stomach.

Scrambling to his feet he feared the worst. He knew, but he didn't know *what* he knew or how he knew it, but he knew it was bad. He sprinted to the top of the stairs and saw Brody prone, expiring from blood loss and now beginning to twitch. His native battle-hardened breeding took over and, without thought for his own safety, he sprang into action.

He swiftly holstered his knife and swinging powerfully, struck Charlotte on the side of the head with the back of his right fist, her head snapped sideways, lolled back and then forward as she instantly collapsed to the floor, face down lying in an ever-increasing pool of Brody's blood. Without even looking to see the results of the first blow, Cu-bér lunged at Evet with both hands and grabbed him around the neck in a choke hold. The power of his leap took Evet down and Cu-bér pinned him with both knees whilst still throttling him.

Evet let out a guttural scream as Cu-bér's left knee pressed into his chest and his shirt suddenly changed colour as his own wound, inflicted by Brody's previous knife-throwing activities, now burst open.

"GET OFF!" Evet powerfully screamed verbally whilst simultaneously sending his thought patterns straight into Cu-bér's head. Cu-bér capitulated ears and mind ringing from the power of the command, allowing Evet to crawl back and hoist himself up against the wall by the office door.

"This is *not* helping anyone... For us to get home and leave this place undamaged both Brody and I MUST survive and use the *Necronomicon* at triclipse," Evet now pleaded with hands up in a very defensive and apologetic manner in a bid to avert a secondary attack.

"So, why try to get me to kill him then? You bloody liar!" replied a furious Cu-bér ready to re-grip the throat of his intended victim if no good explanation was forthcoming.

"It was not my intention. I did not realise you were armed and had only thought to try to capture you both by subterfuge. I am sorry... Really, truthfully sorry."

"So, save him then, you bloody evil *bastard*."

"Yes, I will... I must."

"*You* made me kill my own brother and I vow to you on his sacred life that *I will* avenge him and eventually kill you. That is my solemn promise to you, but if you do not save Brody *right now,* I won't wait. I will certainly kill you here and now. **NOW MOVE!**"

Evet rose, clutching his bleeding chest wound and motioned to Charlotte with a twisted wave and click of the fingers. She instantly awoke from her knock-out slumber, got up, wobbled, flinched, shook herself and looked completely lost as if just awoken from a coma.

"Where... what? Arrrghh, my head hurts." She suddenly felt the bruising on her temple and instantly realised she was covered in blood before noticing Brody's body and realising it wasn't her own.

"Help him, then me," Evet curtly instructed.

"You're going to trust that monstrous bitch not to suck him dry," Cu-bér argued vehemently.

"Have no fear, she is re-transformed now, back to her own reality. She was not the prostitute that the others had surmised but was originally a nurse trying desperately to stem the tide of the disease that broke out in this town – the very disease I deliberately created." This new revelation did not surprise Cu-bér much but did explain a lot of the other aspects of life in sleepy Langgnãd.

"I subverted and twisted her to her vampiric ways by using my powers channelled through the others without them even knowing I had done it." Evet's explanation sounded disgustingly boastful and full of pride.

"Now she is back as she was; she is of no danger to anyone and with your help can save us both. You are a medicine man, right? Then help her to help Brody and then help me. No tricks or I will switch her back in a flash and you know she will rip your throat out just as your beloved Selene did to Corvin." Cu-bér had to bite his lip and tense himself to avoid a very brutal attack, as Evet goaded him with painful memories of his faithful pets that still burned in his subconscious.

Gradually, the newly revived Charlotte regained her perception of herself and listened to instructions from Evet. Cu-bér lifted Brody's limp, blood-soaked body and carried him to the office table.

"Run now to the dispensary in Hospital Lane, get bandages and any medicines you think you can use," suggested Evet. Cu-bér barred Charlotte's way with an outstretched arm.

"Fetch towels, girl, and tear them into strips. I have medicine in my bag that will help. It is in the rear satchel on the big horse in the square. As soon as you are back with the towels you can take my place and put your weight on his wound to stem the bleeding and try to keep him awake whilst I fetch the medicine."

"OK, but how?" The blonde, blood-soaked young nurse looked dazed and still not fully herself from the sudden re-transformation from her vampiric alter ego. She seemed to be in a typical dumb blonde state.

"Talk to him, if nothing else. He is in love with you after all; it will help."

"What… really… how?" she blushed sweetly, something she hadn't experienced for months.

"Just do it, girl – anything. Get the towels now, then hold him, comfort him – keep pressure on that wound; understand? I will try to explain the rest later." Cu-bér waited for her to get to and from the bathroom in the other annexe and then as soon as she put pressure on Brody's wound, he jumped up, ran out through the doorway, leapt down the two flights of stairs, barged the outer door and sprinted up the avenue back to the horses. His bag was still hanging around the stallion's hindquarters and he quickly grabbed it, leapt onto the big steed's back and dug his heels in.

Somewhere deep within Brody's unconscious mind, a tiny corridor flooded with blood and as he watched, it flushed over him like a tidal wave.

The massive animal bolted into action and reacted perfectly to his heel dig, slap on the neck and pull of the mane – no reins were required and it took him straight back to the avenue where he had just come from. He jumped off his faithful companion before it had even fully stopped, forward rolled into the yard of Charlotte's abode, sprang through the open door and sprinted back up the two flights to bring his kit to Brody's aid.

For Brody, the repeating REM dreams were growing in intensity. As his body twitched, more images of the same empty corridor erupted, one after another, each with a lava-type flow in slow motion. Like multiple blood tsunamis, they always ended up engulfing him to the point of drowning before disappearing and starting all over again.

Charlotte was sitting by his side holding his hand, her other hand keeping pressure on the towel-covered wound. She had obviously been crying as her skimpy top was soaking wet and had become very see-through now from the combination of blood and tears. She glanced down at herself and could not comprehend what had happened and why she was dressed in this way. The only thing she knew for certain was that there was a dying man in front of her with blood everywhere and she was covered in that very same blood. She felt dirty, degraded, not herself and worst of all, was nagged with a strange feeling of guilt that she did not understand.

Cu-bér pushed her aside and took over, administering a few drops of a knockout strength version of his 'Evet controlling brew' before applying a more gel-like substance direct to his gaping wound. It was touch and go for the next two or three days as Brody had lost so much blood, but with the help of Cu-bér's marijuana-based balms and other medicines found in the town's deserted dispensary, he started to pull through. Feverish nightmares haunted his recovery. Charlotte did everything she could to help, including some tidy stitching of the huge wound in his stomach and much passive cuddling up to him for body warmth at night to try to aid his recovery.

Periodically he slept, but the same horrific imagery of being completely engulfed in a tidal wave of blood returned to stab at his slumber and wake him prematurely to relive the recent horrors once more. Each time he saw it, it got bigger and each time bolder and more horrific; often when waking he would need to shower as his cold sweat had swamped his bed clothes and smelt to him of his own fear.

His regenerative powers were strong enough and over the next week he started to improve, as did Evet. Cu-bér, for now at least, temporarily preoccupied with Brody's recovery, had magnanimously helped him as well.

Days ago Evet had suggested to them to seek alternate clothing as they were all variously blood-stained and, by then, smelling quite acrid. Finding clothes was quite easy as nearly all the residents of Langgnãd were either dead, dying in the streets or in hiding. Even most of the burly henchmen that Evet had supplied Charlotte with when she was trance-induced had mostly run away, so clothes were plentiful.

CHAPTER 18

Destinies Entwine.

They found many empty properties and got cleaned up and dressed more appropriately which, for Cu-bér, was simply a pair of tight jean-like trousers. Cu-bér found similar trousers and a casual-looking t-shirt for Brody to use but Charlotte chose for herself, a prim blue dress, open backed but high fronted – very demure.

She started to feel more like herself and over the next week, conversations with Cu-bér out of earshot of the recuperating Brody and Evet, revealed to her what had happened and how she had been forced to help Evet to keep Brody captive. She cried a lot and wanted to run away but Cu-bér would not allow it, assuring and supporting her with descriptions of Brody's true feelings towards her which he heavily embellished to gain an effective response.

"He loves you as if you were another from his own phase and you might be the only thing he has to survive for, especially if he can't see the other again by getting home." She broke a smile at this thought but was also saddened that if he *did* recover and managed to return home, she might lose him forever. She desperately wanted to apologise and make up for her previous terrible but involuntary treatment of him.

Evet was nearly fully recovered and Brody was up and about; his horrific and unexplained nightmares now equally oddly forgotten.

"You'll have an amazing scar to show off," Cu-bér noted, as Brody, still un-shirted on one particular morning walked passed his open bedroom door. Later, as Brody walked past the other way, Cu-bér beckoned him in, asking,

"Tell me more about these markings on your back."

"That is a very long story, my friend, one I doubt you will fully understand," Brody replied.

"We seem to have plenty of time," countered his now further intrigued friend.

"Well, the thing is…" Brody then proceeded without any further encouragement to lay out the various ins and outs of every single tattoo on his body. He explained the full deep and meaningful relevance to various topics, mostly music and film-related. He even tried to explain the relevance of the differences between the various colours used and how he had specifically designed it all himself that way to show his interpretation of stories he had dreamt up, which *he* felt were the true meanings behind his favourite band's song lyrics – amongst many other convoluted things. The concept of music and songs were apparently another universal constant and Cu-bér totally got it all, but unlike many who had asked in the past he was genuinely interested. However, when asked why he had no similar or tribal markings, he merely scoffed, "I carry many scars and mental references in the same way that *you* do." As he spoke he smiled, tapping his temple.

"I do not choose to give them life." Under the current circumstances, Brody, glancing down at his stitches, found this very intriguing and thought long and hard about the full meaning of his friend's enigmatic statement.

Another week passed. Brody and Charlotte had started to form a very strong bond, learning more about each other. There was still an edginess between them that Brody struggled to surmount and

Charlotte felt that he was still unsure of her.

Brody loved and was missing his Charley with all his heart, but this other girl reminded him so much of her and was so physically nearly identical, that he couldn't help himself but to start to feel similarly about her. To that end he knew that if he ended up stranded or estranged from his true desire and allowed himself to fall for her that, as easy as it might be, the substitution would not be right and could never truly work. The thought of never seeing Charley again was so tough for him to accept. Charlotte's striking physical resemblance to her was just making it worse. Although he knew it was probably only a side issue left over from Evet's deliberate manipulation, it held his attention. He started to get feelings of guilt about looking at her at all, but secretly found it difficult not to.

Charlotte herself, just as Charley had done, didn't seem remotely interested in the age gap. She saw Brody as her saviour even though she was unsure if he fully forgave her previous horrific indiscretions. He had totally but also feared that her vampiric remission could be at some point reversed.

The subconscious damage she had caused him was far greater than any lasting physical injury. Although it was not always openly visible, he did now tend to flinch when her hand neared any part of his body other than when she was tending to his stomach wound. She felt that he *feared* her, but knew it was more of a mental scarring than physical fear. As days passed the eventuality of having the 'what happens next' discussion, loomed.

Brody and Cu-bér discussed how to handle Evet who had been surprisingly quiet since Brody's recovery. It was decided to just get it all out in the open and try to find the best solution. As Brody getting back home seemed to be dependent on them both, the previous suggestion to just kill Evet was, for the moment at least, a non-starter.

Cu-bér played negotiator and set up a meeting in what used to be Charlotte's office. The four met in the early evening of the next day. As they entered they all sat uncomfortably staring inwards at each other. Four strangers, four stools. Four destinies entwined in whatever might come from this meeting. Cu-bér got the ball rolling.

"What are your true intentions, Evet? Remember, I don't trust a word you say so please try not to antagonise me. If you do, and I get *my* way, the only place you'll be going is six feet under." He spoke like he was bordering on anger but tried to keep it curt. It could have seemed an aggressive opener but he wanted a response and tried to create an early advantage for Brody to exploit if negotiations were to be weighted. The irony of good cop, bad cop missed Cu-bér completely but not Brody. He had to stifle a laugh and coughed dramatically into his hand whilst glancing at Evet as he did so to gauge his reaction.

"We have very little time left and I need Brody's help," Evet announced.

"You have hidden in the shadows of others for far too long, but I am standing ready to lead you straight to the grave if you mess us around any more. You have been running in too many yesterdays and have been saved for far too many tomorrows," Brody randomly interjected, very mystically, then looked away in disgust.

"Agreed," Evet concurred and Brody was slightly annoyed that his deliberately confrontational comments had not hit the nerve they had been aimed at.

"Even though you keep looking through the lies, you may need to pray for the next daylight – saving you is definitely not my choice," Cu-bér added, starting round two.

"After seeing my brother and the seven children all face their killer with a smile, I am unlikely to be swayed by more of your deception. Remember, dead men can tell no tales, so you can no longer peddle your lies or buy and sell your murders… You are the jailbird now and this may be the very cell where you die… Think carefully before making any rash statements or big ultimatums." Cu-bér's calmly delivered threat reverberated and the room fell silent.

Charlotte fidgeted uncomfortably in her seat not fully sure if anything she might say would even have any relevance, let alone help in any way. Brody, who was staring out of the window, feigning quiet contemplation, broke the silence with another sudden, but more questioning interjection.

"Why kill your own?" Evet looked sheepishly at the floor then glanced up at Brody.

"I have lied so much I sometimes believe myself; it has become a life's work to keep the truth from people. Like Cu-bér said, my face is constantly pressed to the window trying to look in on the truth that only I believe, but I am like a mirror reflecting others' fears as they tremble right down to the bone." His reply seemed to hold feelings of apologetic resignation but as usual was cryptic enough to be considered trivial.

"What is that even supposed to mean?" Brody asked with an air of dismissiveness.

"How long can you hide and twist things? How long until someone comes along who truly has your measure? Is that today, by chance? Just tell us WHY! Have you **NO** remorse?" Brody's battery of questions was rising in tone and volume.

Suddenly he felt a severe pain in his mid to upper back which was strange and confusing to him – he had expected that any excitement could make his slowly healing scar twinge, but this was more like a cramp across his shoulders. He flinched, gritted his teeth and jumped back on the offensive.

"WHY?.. Damn you, Evet!" Evet sat a moment and calmly replied, "I am like a rat in a trap, but I must survive. You don't fully understand but, without you and I, Brody, none of this will exist. *We* created it – accidentally, perhaps – but it was us and we have to admit that to ourselves… Once, when I was free for that while, I was glad. The air in different worlds tasted good and these new phases and alternate places were like new friends to me, but it seems to have corrupted my mind… And then came the day when these hard times began."

"Shut up, now you're just waffling and wasting time. Get to the point," Cu-bér piped up.

"So, now you want to travel alone again. How long do you think we can let you travel, or even let you live for that matter?" Brody asked rhetorically.

"I think right here in Langgnãd this particular jailbird may die today." Cu-bér dived in again and sneered as he attempted to verbally frighten the truth from Evet. A more earthly criminal may have been pressured into capitulation by this badgering interrogation but that description was not apt here and Evet acted according to type.

"Your threats are useless; I am already dead in every way but physically… Put your knife through my throat right here, right now and all you will do is add another body to the pile. Fulfil your promised contract; come on, give me a smile, you know you are itching to do it." Evet goaded Cu-bér, questioning his resolve, knowing it would not waiver, but also knowing that Brody had to find more answers before allowing anyone to resort to further violence.

"You would murder me for vengeance; at least I murdered others for gain. Death is the same whether in here, in jail or out on the streets," Evet lamented smugly, knowing Brody would not allow Cu-bér's revenge to intervene at this point.

Brody spoke up again.

"We want to hear less of this amateur psychology and your fake attempts to wriggle out of answering the questions. You sound like a $50 whore screwing an American politician, Once and for all, give me the truth – why did you kill the children of others?" He pushed again for one solitary truthful statement from the accomplished liar.

"The truth… you can't handle the truth." Brody smiled broadly at this, knowing that Evet had certainly not consciously meant to play his game and make an appropriate film quote, but the smile dropped from his lips as he continued the statement.

"They killed themselves!" The room fell deathly silent.

"They knew that all their powers I had managed to syphon off and into me could not be allowed to remain with me permanently after their deaths. They resigned themselves to the fact that, although they could not let me go, neither could they take me back. The longer they survived the stronger I became, so they just stopped trying." Brody sat down, disheartened at learning of such a meaningful sacrifice but such a meaningless waste of life.

His previously open wound had healed well but this revelation felt open and raw like a fresh incision. Evet continued to pour the salt into it.

"Ironically, it was their best tactic ever and I had no defence against it. I was trying desperately to kill them. When they merely stopped trying it drained us all, leaving them dead and me reduced to no more than a parlour magician. I think they had overcome their own egos and realised I was too strong." His statement was so matter-of-fact it turned Brody's stomach and he briefly thought to resort to Cu-bér's plan, but held his emotions and allowed Evet to continue.

"I could have retained everything if I killed them but because they chose their destiny, the powers flowed back to them. My only remaining powers are fading now and without you, the

Necronomicon and a large slice of luck, we are all completely doomed to live out the rest of our days here in this manufactured nightmare." Evet, for once, actually looked and sounded sincere. Brody believed the reality that he was still stuck in, but could not trust Evet's version of events. He was just not trustworthy and it was all too convenient.

Everyone sat in stunned silence for what seemed like days. Charlotte was the first to break the ice.

"So, if you have lost all your powers, am I safe now? You can't make me do any more horrible things to Brody or anyone else for that matter, right?" she asked hopefully.

Cu-bér was sitting listening intently, cleaning his serrated knife in a menacing way, no doubt for effect.

"My dear girl, you and this knife-wielding maniac..." He paused, casually motioned towards Cu-bér, but was still staring directly at Brody as he continued:

"You don't even exist in mine and Brody's other phases, so fear not, I have no desire or great ability to harm anyone in that way now, especially Brody or you – I just want to get home." Cu-bér flinched as if to react physically to the insult but tempered himself and raised an eyebrow before speaking,

"How will this reality fare if you two can manage to use the *Necronomicon* to return to your homes?" His question was delivered calmly.

"I believe it will not fare at all. I am afraid our accidental creation will cease to exist. I know you won't believe me, Cu-bér... I am actually sorry." Brody suddenly had another surge of pain in his back and lurched forward as if to outrun the feeling. He arched away from what felt like an elephant kicking him in the shoulders.

"Damn, I thought it hurt when my inky put these tattoos in, but this is bloody ridiculous! It feels like they are all trying to peel themselves off me and run away." Grimacing, he briefly and ironically thought back to all the hours of agony he had endured. All the complex multiple story-telling tattoos he had designed. All the ink. All the pain. The images now permanently inked into his skin. Images put there by his friend and award-winning tattooist, Giles. Unbeknown to him, they were all glaring clues. The irony of him not being able to see them without the aid of a mirror was never more pertinent than now as he saw nothing of relevance in his own recollections. Nothing other than the current pain that he compared them to. The tattoos were not too deep in his skin compared to the pain in his body but the clues were hiding far deeper in his memory.

Too deep to register just yet...

The memory felt more like enjoyment and nothing in comparison to this unknown internal kicking he was experiencing. He tried to shrug the pain away and get back to the interrogation.

"Even if we believe you about the children and your current willingness to rehabilitate yourself, it doesn't explain why you were on the run in the first place. Why were they pursuing you so indefinitely?" Cu-bér asked forcefully.

"Because I am guilty as charged of everything that they have told you." Another cold silence gripped the air and lasted for nearly a full minute as the reality of this statement started to sink in for all involved.

"So, how are we possibly to believe anything you say, then? Even about this or the reality of your power loss," Brody asked very logically, trying to trip a mistake from him.

"Would I still be here?" was his curt retort; undeniably it was a good question.

"Well, maybe, you just need me as you said, after all I am here too." Over the next hour or so more argumentative banter passed back and forth, but eventually the only fact that seemed unquestionable was that Evet, was, as he said, still there.

He might now be virtually powerless or possibly just biding his time. Cu-bér wanted to kill him on the spot anyway regardless, but Brody fully believed that Evet was the key to getting back to his own phase. Although he cared deeply for the new friend he had made and was also very slowly falling for Charley's double, he knew that home was where his heart was and where he wanted to be. After hours of unproductive bickering, Brody, fed up, just asked bluntly:

"What next then?" This time Evet was quick to respond.

"I understand your scepticism as my track record is not impeccable, but you have to trust me now. The volume called *Necronomicon Ex-Mortis* holds the answers." He was now starting to sound sincere.

"I believe that if you… that is to say… YOU, Brody, recount the phrase at the very moment of triclipse twin corona when the maximum energy is released. A rift will open as predicted in the earlier passages." Evet glanced up at the ceiling as if looking through it towards the darkening sky.

"This rift will only remain open for moments but if you or anyone else for that matter steps through it, their individual DNA patterns and memory engrams will be drawn back to their own original phase," he delivered with a wry smile.

"It is like an eddy in water, but this is in time, space and reality. Knowing your true and full original name the term 'Eddy' is so apt yet so insultingly coincidental. On another day I would have taunted you with it." Brody was unimpressed, but unsure how Evet could possibly have known his full name *or* his frustrations at it ever being used, let alone the hang-up he had as a boy over its incorrect spelling when used in its shortened form.

Evet pressed on, his knowledge held power. How honestly he distributed that knowledge held even more.

"So, it won't matter who goes through first, they should automatically return to the correct place."

"There *is* no proof of this; however, the book is centuries old and has diagrammatical and pictorial evidence of it having been done as a routine, many eons gone by."

"Why me especially?" Evet paused a second and then looked him straight in the eye.

"*Because,* Brody, you effectively created and traversed a rift to get here, creating and locking us all in this paradoxical place and only *you* can open and close it on the way back." Initially dumbstruck, a feeling of guilt washed over him. He wondered if he could really be the one responsible for all of this. He spent the next few minutes contemplating the real possibility of Evet having changed his leopard's spots but thought,

'Could he now be telling the truth?' The thought was made without consideration of Evet's ability to read it. Evet was pleased that Brody still had, or was developing doubts. Doubts help the unscrupulous and he knew it. Any lever is a good lever.

"So, if I opened the rift with my experimentation, how does that explain *you*, Evet?" Evet paused again before answering, for a long enough time that Brody felt it would have even flattered the judges in any beyond its sell-by date talent show. However, when he finally spoke, he released upon them the revelatory fire bolt of all non-proven hypotheses ever made, which virtually tore Brody's universe apart as he heard the words leave Evet's mouth.

"*We* have done it before..." Another trimester of a pause heightened the tension.

"**Explain!**" Brody shouted. He gagged and was nearly completely lost for words in the attempt to hold back the urge to vomit.

"I... th...ought you have no proof." As he forced the question out, it tasted like the voluntary puke wretched up after a self-inflicted hangover. Instinctively spitting was his next reflex. Evet glanced at the muculent spot on the floor with distain.

"I said 'there *is* no proof;' only a subtle difference but by now you should have at least learned that the best lies are ninety percent truth. I *know* the *Necronomicon* works because my ancestors wrote it. Its cover is made of my great-great-grandfather's skin. I have sought it for centuries and then, just as I finally found it again, it was whisked away from me once more." He pulled an anguished face and continued:

"I was seeking what you unknowingly possessed. I suppose it was inevitable that we would eventually find each other. We have always been there but neither aware of the other." Clanging bullet casings bounced on the wooden floor of Brody's imagination and he searched for the name of the shooter and the weapon, but it wouldn't come to him – he re-focused on Evet who still seemed to be speaking in riddles.

"*Your* damn meddling in *your* science in *your* phase created this whole mess." Brody was stunned and remained silent, listening intently to the continuation of Evet's elusive confessional, spill out. Was it just more lies, or were they actually quite damning, home truths? Evet continued...

"Whether that was a complete fluke or just fate, I genuinely don't know but it is completely irrelevant now. We *are* both here, I have sought to get *Necronomicon* back after it was lost from my family's possession more than once down the years and now I have it back again. It can return us all but this time only with YOU recanting the lines. In this accidentally manufactured phase, *you* are the god, the teacher and *I* am merely the infidel, the pupil."

The silence that followed was once again palpably loud. Cu-bér,

Brody and Charlotte stared at each other in disbelief and then they all stared back at Evet for more.

"What about *your* powers?" Cu-bér asked bluntly.

"In this phase only, the children had control of the power, I merely leached it from them slowly until they were not strong enough to stop me. In truth it was futile as in *my* phase their abilities were insignificant in comparison to my natural power. Here I am now naked after their last-ditch ploy – virtually human. Back in my phase I was a deity, feared and worshipped."

"What about in theirs?" Brody pressed, realising now what the implications of this statement were.

"In their phase I was hated and vilified but I would have triumphed and destroyed them all for their insolence," he crowed scornfully, full of controlled rage and anger. This accidental admission that his original phase was not the children's point of origin explained almost everything the children had suspected about his lineage.

"You have travelled from phase to phase destroying and controlling, using this accursed piece of shit of a scripture and then, by accident, you end up here!" shouted Brody, pointing to the shelf in the corner of the office where the *Necronomicon* lay.

"You want me to help you continue with such a damnation of a journey?"

"What choice do you have, as far as you can prove with your pathetic sciences, this phase doesn't even really exist – it is only a whisper in time. It has no real long-term substance, yet STILL WE ARE HERE despite all your desires, expectations and fears. You know deep down… you MUST help me!" Evet was on a roll and Brody found most of what he was saying virtually undeniable.

"You can certainly die here as can I, but long-term, neither of us can actually *live* here. You and I would just be living a lie and punishing others. Those that you love who are left behind mourning you in your own phase, for example."

The saying that the truth hurts really did hurt and Brody winced as he thought of Cash and Charley once again. On cue, his back pulsated and agreed with the painful sentiment.

"Help me and help yourself, we may never see each other again and lessons will have been learned." Evet's proposition seemed inescapable, but Brody's own wounds were real and what about Cu-bér, Charlotte and, for that matter, all of the many others, that the accidental tampering in science may have created, affected or even killed. Furthermore, what of any whom he had not even met yet?

'I am not completely powerless, but you will have to choose; either sacrifice these here to save yourself and all you ever knew, or...' His pause for effect was excruciating.

'Sacrifice yourself and all that you now know to save those here. Either way, I am still here... or there!' Evet had mentally transferred this last ultimatum in an attempt to keep the suggestion from the other two and Brody was relieved he had done so.

Cu-bér though, since first being acquainted with the children of others had got used to the reception of mentally transmitted information. Unfortunately, he had never found time to learn how to use it himself so was unable to reply. He grimaced to himself; Brody's eyes both glazed and a tear escaped the corner of one as he realised the desperate futility of the situation. Charlotte's temporary ability to send or receive thoughts had been given and taken away by Evet himself so she remained unaware of this latest revelation. The looming question of what to do next hung over Brody like a noose....

What had he done by meddling with his theories and big ideals back home? Was it all, entirely his own fault? And would things that no one could have ever imagined now be released upon them if he made the wrong decisions? Or was it just more of Evet's lies? Was this phase real and possibly his new and final destination? Many rocks and hard places fled around his tortured mind in an avalanche of conscience and he was stuck between them all.

If this alternate scenario was reality, the case for his ever-growing feelings of love towards Charlotte and his friendship with Cu-bér could not be ignored as insignificant minutiae. This thought reminded him of the minute data returns he had not fully heeded in his haste to get his work done and through to Mr. Harris.

That could have been the cause of the phase cross-over. This time he must not make the same mistakes… If any were actually made, nothing was beyond the bounds of possibilities now!

'Every detail must be weighed and considered;' he realised Evet would have experienced all these thoughts. His head felt as if an explosion was imminent and his back once again agreed.

'What if you are lying and the opposite is true? I might kill everyone trying to save them; I don't know how you expect me to make such a decision,' he transmitted back to Evet who sat smiling a Cheshire cat's worth of a conceited smile.

'You must decide that for yourself and soon. Triclipse is coming in the next few days.' Evet's cerebral reply was calm now…

However, it threatened much…

EPILOGUE

The pause that followed this horrendous no-win scenario ultimatum could have swallowed the earth and Brody hoped he would be consumed along with it. If he chose one way he must trust Evet and risk everything; the other option was no different and equally as stark.

He started to invent alternate scenarios that could possibly weigh things in his favour, but nothing seemed to make sense enough to be worth verbalising. Within the brief lull of horrific revelation he envisaged Evet's death in many forms, from the dreamt up children of others' version of fire and brimstone to a simple bullet through the head, but none that flashed through his mind left any different outcome. Evet's or his own death seemed not to be the solution but, on the contrary, their mutual survival was now almost imperative.

He needed confirmation, clarification or just a simple sign from the gods that he had always denounced would do. At this point his desperation to not make the wrong choice was mind-bending…

He sucked in his gut, puffed out his chest and summoned all his courage for what might be his biggest blag ever. Blowing out his breath he readied himself to try again.

AFTERWORD

As with quite a few sections of this book, to complete it satisfactorily I have had to do quite a bit of research. I really wanted to keep to an older traditional style as, in my humble opinion, the reading of a book should be a fun and enjoyable thing, not a task or 'chore'. Not just the story itself but the whole feel of the book should make you want to read every word, no matter how innocuous. Things that many will skip past such as the acknowledgements, dedications, epigraph, preface and these very afterword pages should invite you in and add to the overall enjoyment of the reading experience.

I wanted to provide the potential reader with something they would really enjoy. To that end and much to the printer's and editor's frustration, I continually pushed and insisted on having pictures to try to give life to some of my descriptions and to create a deeper feeling to the things the characters were seeing, doing and experiencing. As you have seen, none made it past the final edit, but if this is successfully received, a more pictorially re-edited version will be made available as soon as possible if I get my way.

The afterword pages were a section I had never seen in any book that I had ever read and, as such, they sounded so antiquated and unlikely to be read by anyone that I just had to have them in my first attempt – then I could, hand on heart, call it a traditional, old-fashioned BOOK.

Through my delving around the Internet, I have found that the afterword page or pages are traditionally the place where the author discusses how the book came about, but I felt I have covered that sufficiently in the preface. A bit more research revealed another angle which I have chosen to use. The matching of the afterword to the content of the foreword is apparently an acceptable practice, similarly as tradition suggests that if there is a prologue so there should be an epilogue.

With that in mind, I hope that some of the hidden detailing that Nick eluded to in his so eloquently written foreword has been a bit of fun for you to find and added to the overall enjoyment of the read. The more minutiae-observant of you might even have had to do the odd Google or Wikipedia session to see if they had spotted yet another subtle reference to another innocuous, something else or other. The plagiarising nature of mentioning various other works through the characters, in itself, plagiarises the very way I often obtusely see things in the real world.

I think most will know them all too well, but Brody's favourite band, who were so influential in the plot but so conspicuous by their absence from the story itself are, for various reasons, never transparently named.

So, I must add a footnote here that each and every chapter of this and the forthcoming next two parts of the story are, even if you had not spotted all the hidden clues, quite deliberately meant in their own right to be individual mini homages to all the tracks from various albums of that particular band. They were – after all is said and done – the true awakening; the very place where all the original dreams that I experienced, originated from. And not only for the book but also for the final tattoo, which incidentally *I* wear with pride.

I would really like to thank the anonymous members of that very particular band for unknowingly and unintentionally inspiring many parts of the story you have just taken the time to start reading. Hopefully you will continue.

To those ends, I would also like to take this opportunity to thank my good friend Nick Hancock for agreeing to be my test subject on the rough draft of this, my first attempt at writing anything more than a shopping list.

I have known Nick for many years and consider him one of the most down-to-earth people within what I would call, 'show business', 'stardom' or 'celebrity status', that you could ever wish to meet. His patience, insight and constructive input has been invaluable to me, helping to just add that little edge to a few parts here and there that otherwise might have been glossed over.

I really did appreciate him agreeing to read the first draft of the trilogy as well as writing the foreword for part one, but he also then took time out to spend hours with me discussing how this sentence or that could be arranged slightly differently for a desired effect. Thanks, Nick.

So, here we are right at the end of the first instalment of the story, but for the characters the journey is still ongoing. I started well over twelve years ago with that first horrific dream that, in hindsight, was an ironic reflection of one of the greatest albums the world will ever hear, along with probably, if my dear old mom and dad were to be believed, too much pickle in my late-night cheese sandwiches.

I sincerely hope you decide to progress on to parts two and three to find out how things will pan out for our intrepid hero as he battles to put the Universe and reality to rights. Whether he survives the current situation and finally gets home to Charley is unsure. You might be surprised at the final solution to the story as it was not how I would have envisaged writing it had I already been an accomplished author. It merely happened that way in my dream world, one night in 2006 and repetitively on and off up to now. I still see the various episodes that became chapters in full colour on an irregular basis.

Well, there it is, you have had a quick peek inside my head. I hope you were intrigued, scared, entertained, amused and above anything else, pleased that you took the time to look.

Thank you so much for reading my first attempt, I hope you enjoyed it. If you did, all I would ask is…

TELL A FEW OTHERS and check out part two…

E.C. Johnson

ABOUT THE AUTHOR

Edward Charles Johnson was born in Wolverhampton, England, to Marjorie Phyllis and Henry Sylvester Johnson on 17/11/1965. He was one of five children but was the only boy as they had tragically lost their first son, Ward, many years before. As such, Edward was something of a surprise and came to his parents relatively late in their lives, his mother being forty-three and his father fifty-five at the time of his birth.

This age disparity was the cause of some teasing when he was at school and led to a few fights but Edward, although relatively small as a youth, was never one to run from trouble and came home with a few bruises and missing teeth on more than one occasion.

Edward did, and still does to this day, suggest that it was not the difference in his parents' ages but the difference in age of his parents in comparison to most of his peers' parents which was what set him apart and caused him some early confusion in life.

The actuality that his parents were born in a completely different era and were much older than his friends' parents was a huge factor. In most cases, *his* parents were old enough to be his friends' *grand*parents. When the other dads played football down the park at age thirty to thirty-five his father was invariably at the golf club aged sixty-five. He soon came to realise that, beyond the teasing and an occasional fight, it really didn't matter but gave him a unique perspective on life that only a few of his *real* friends could understand.

Growing up in a rapidly developing technological age but with all the old-fashioned and early twentieth century war era values shaped Edward's outlook on life.

He has had many jobs in his chequered career and currently still works as a domestic appliance service engineer by day and goalkeeper coach in the evenings whilst tapping away into the early hours of most mornings attempting to develop a meaningful career as a writer.

Who knows what the future might bring? The truth is quite often stranger than fiction. If you want to contact Edward (Eddie as he prefers to be called) he is happy to receive your feedback.

Contact can be made via e-mail on:
info@edjpublishing.com

Printed in Great Britain
by Amazon